MW00784242

José Silva's

Ultramind ESP

System

Think Your Way to Success

By
Ed Bernd Jr.

New Page Books
A division of The Career Press, Inc.
Franklin Lakes, NJ

JOSÉ SILVA'S ULTRAMIND ESP SYSTEM
Cover design by Cheryl Finbow
Printed in the U.S.A. by Book-mart Press

To order this title, please call toll-free 1-800-CAREER-1 (NJ and Canada:
201-848-0310) to order using VISA or MasterCard, or for further
information on books from Career Press.

The Career Press, Inc., 3 Tice Road, PO Box 687, Franklin Lakes, NJ 07417

www.newpagebooks.com
www.careerpress.com

Library of Congress Cataloging-in-Publication Data

Bernd, Ed
    Jose Silva's ultramind ESP system : think your way to success / by Ed Bernd.
        p.   cm.
    Includes index.
    ISBN 1-56414-451-8 (pbk.)
    1. Silva, Jose, 1914-   2. Silva Mind Control.   I. Title.

BF1127.S54 B27   2000
158.1—dc21
                                                                    00-022353

DEDICATION

We gratefully dedicate this book to authors Philip Miele and Robert B. Stone. Their wonderful talent for expression, along with their skill, effort, and sense of caring, has opened the door to the alpha level and the spiritual dimension to millions of people around the world.

Bob Stone expressed the way many of us feel: "When I see a shining light that is not being properly disseminated, I am compelled to try to give it the greater exposure that it merits. My additional goal in life is to be a public-relations man to Jose Silva via my writings and tapes. If in so doing, I am also doing public relations for our Creator, so much the better."

We miss you, Bob. We miss you, Phil. Although you have moved on to new assignments, we are grateful that you are still with us through your writings. Thank you for doing such an outstanding job of fulfilling your mission during your time here on earth.

ACKNOWLEDGMENTS

On behalf of Jose Silva, I want to express our heartfelt appreciation and gratitude for the many people who have helped with this project.

The contributing authors have done far more than share their experiences so freely. Every one of them has been there to help us when we've needed it.

It has been said that the biggest problems are given to the best problem-solvers, and we have had some big challenges in the last couple of years. Every contributing author in this book has answered the call. Most have helped without waiting to be called. Jose Silva said that the finest human beings are those who correct problems without any expectation of compensation, and all of our authors measure up to that standard many times over.

If you have an opportunity to meet any of these authors or take a course with them, by all means do so——and treasure the experience. You will be in the presence of one of the finest human beings on the planet.

We also want to thank Ron Fry and the entire staff at Career Press, especially Stacey Farkas, Jodi Brandon, Karen Wolf, and Michael Lewis, who have been so patient and so generous with their help on this project. It has been fun working with you again. We truly appreciate your patience, support, encouragement, dedication to excellence, and great talent.

Ron Fry must have a special talent for selecting outstanding editors. From the time Jodi Brandon first read the manuscript, she understood and appreciated the vision we had for this project, and put in extra effort to make that vision a reality. These last few weeks that we have worked together, Jodi has been more like a co-author than an editor. She went beyond the call of duty, tolerating my incessant attempts at humor and continually encouraging me. If you don't like the book, blame me—it was my idea to do it this way. On the other hand, if you find it an enjoyable, enriching experience getting to know Jose Silva through these pages, then send a big thank-you to Jodi, because her talent, energy, and creative insights made that vision a reality.

Jeff Herman, the world's best literary agent, has helped us spread our message throughout the United States and around the world. Thanks again, Jeff.

Regina McAloney has been a trusted friend and valued advisor on this project for the last four years. Thank you for believing in us, Regina, and for helping us.

We also want to thank Dr. Carlos Floresvega and the entire staff at the Laredo VA outpatient clinic. His care and compassion have meant as much to us as his medical competence. There are many young doctors who could learn a lot from him.

Ed Bernd Jr.
March 2000

CONTENTS

FOREWORD

Come and meet the most extraordinary man I've ever known: Jose Silva.

I was privileged to work *for* him and *with* him for the last 17 years of his life. Let's join him in his office at Silva world headquarters in Laredo, Texas. It is July, the weather is hot, instructor-training has just started, and our annual International Convention is a little over a week away.

I expect this to be a routine visit; I am in for a big surprise.

Even before I enter his office, I can see inside; he installed windows in all of the offices so he can see what's going on.

His office is modest in size. In the left-hand corner is a nice wooden desk, angled to face toward the door. In the right-hand corner, directly inside the door, is a round table piled high with magazines, books, and audiotapes.

To our left, under the windows that face the hallway, is a small sofa. Jose sits behind his desk in a comfortable high-backed chair. In front of his desk are two padded straight chairs waiting for visitors.

On the front edge of his desk sits a row of books dominated by his most important books—his dictionaries. He uses them to be sure he understands the exact meaning of words and exactly how each word affects the person who hears it. This is extremely important to the programming we do in the Silva training.

On the desk, to his right, is a tape-player, connected to a small "guitar" amplifier, which makes it easier for him to listen to audiotapes. There are several neatly stacked piles of papers on his desk, so he can quickly get to work on the project of his choice. A couple of notepads are in front of him, with pencils beside them ready for action.

On the walls behind him are various pictures, plaques, and certificates.

➤ There is a large picture of Christ standing next to a child, to remind Jose to continue to strive to improve conditions so that when we move on, we will have left behind a better world for those who follow.

➤ There is a diploma from a hypnosis course that he took long after he had taught himself hypnosis, in order to learn how the human mind works. He took the course and got the diploma so he would have credentials to show those who sought them.

➤ There are pictures of classes, plaques from grateful graduates, and a small, very beautiful, handmade inspirational poster from Sister Charlotte Bruck, who had arranged for an entire issue of *Counselling and Values* magazine to be devoted to the Silva System at a time when it meant a lot to the Silva organization.

➤ On a credenza, against the wall towards our right, sits a bronze Buddha, a gift from an instructor halfway around the world. Other mementos surround it.

It is an office that belongs to a man who has worked every day since he was 6 years old.

I am here to get his reaction to a script I left for his review. The script is for the opening show of our annual convention. We are celebrating the fact that psychic ability has finally become mainstream, that it is now accepted as reality by people from all walks of life who would have denied it and blasted us as charlatans a couple of decades ago.

He doesn't suggest any changes to the script, which is a bit unusual. It turns out he has something much more important on his mind. "Just remember," he says, "that the reason we were given psychic ability is so that we can use it to get information from high intelligence to find out what we are supposed to do, and how to do it."

Kaboom! I sense instinctively that I have just heard something incredibly important and valuable. But I have no time to think about it, much less analyze it and incorporate it into the show. So I file it away in a corner of my mind, with a big note attached to remind myself to check it out after the convention.

I came back to his statement as I began work on this book. The more I thought about it, and the more research I did into the relevant literature, the more I realized just how profound and valuable that one statement was. *Imagine using your intuition to get guidance from high intelligence!*

I concluded that it is the most important thing Jose Silva ever said.

It makes Napoleon Hill's observations a reality for the average person. Hill, who conducted more than 20 years of research on the wealthiest and most successful people in the world, wrote the following in his book, *You Can Work Your Own Miracles* (Fawcett Gold Medal Books, 1971): "I began to make inquiries of the hundreds of successful men who collaborated with me in the organization of the Science of Success, and discovered that *each of them had received guidance from unknown sources*, although many of them were reluctant to admit this discovery."

Jose's statement fulfills the promise made in 1977 in the first sentence of the first paragraph of his first book, coauthored with Philip Miele:

"Imagine coming into direct, working contact with an all-pervading higher intelligence and learning in a moment of numinous joy that it is on your side. Imagine too that you made this contact in such simple ways that for the rest of your life you need never again feel helplessly out of touch with something you always suspected was there but could never quite reach—a helpful wisdom, a flash of insight when you need it, the feeling of a loving, powerful presence."

I studied literature going back thousands of years to learn what people had said about obtaining guidance from a higher power.

➢ Cicero said, several decades before the birth of Christ, "No man was ever great without divine inspiration."

➢ In the 18th century America's first president, George Washington, said, "Providence has at all times been my only dependence, for all other resources seem to have failed us."

➢ And, of course, there were the observations of Napoleon Hill and Jose Silva in the 20th century.

The promise has been with us for a long time. But nobody—not Cicero, George Washington, Napoleon Hill, nor any of the countless others who had claimed this guidance from a higher power—could teach us how to connect with high intelligence and obtain guidance for ourselves. Not until Jose Silva developed the UltraMind System.

As we move through our journey, we meet people who have used Jose Silva's techniques to achieve things they never dreamed possible. We see how he built upon their experiences to develop new techniques to help even more people.

In Chapter 14 you will learn techniques that this father of 10 children, 28 grandchildren, and six great-grandchildren has developed for you to teach your own children so that they can use all of their mental faculties the way the most successful people use theirs, so that they will not need to attend a Silva seminar.

When they learn it before the age of 14, they are far ahead of those of us who had to learn as adults.

In Chapters 18 through 25 you will hear from businesspeople who have used Jose Silva's techniques to help them learn to detect more information to use to solve problems. When they do this, they gain greater control over events in their lives, and thereby reduce the level of stress that they experience.

In Chapter 27 you'll read about a technique, which Jose Silva never taught publicly, that he shared when we asked him for something that would help athletes during training as well as in the heat of battle.

You are beginning a journey through time and space. You will experience these revelations the way that Jose Silva found them. You will be up-to-date on the most current research and understanding of this new science.

This is literally the ultimate Silva book, bringing together in one place the wisdom and insight, and the sheer genius, of the man who created a whole new science: psychorientology, the study of how to use your mind to achieve the success that you were made for and sent here for.

Thank you for joining us on this journey.

Ed Bernd Jr.
April, 2000

INTRODUCTION

Imagine if you could actually connect with a higher power that could guide you to make the correct decisions in your life.

Imagine having a guide who *actually knows* what lies ahead, who can guide you to success, happiness, and fulfillment.

Everyone is entitled to success, happiness, and fulfillment. We were sent here, to planet earth, with a job to do and with the resources to succeed at that job.

So why do so many people fail to achieve success, happiness, and fulfillment? The answer is simple: The wrong goals and the wrong methods will get you the wrong results.

People fail to achieve success, happiness, and fulfillment because they are not aware of—and do not use—the help that is available to them.

> Many people set the wrong goals. They try to do what they *think* they should do, instead of what they were sent here to do.

> They try to go it alone, instead of taking advantage of the help from a higher power, and they do not reap the rewards that come with a mission's success.

> Even if they achieve the success they thought that they wanted, many people still wonder if their hard work has produced anything worthwhile. Were all the "toys" they gained really worth the sacrifices? They often wind up frustrated, confused, stressed, and dissatisfied.

There *is* a better way.

Help from high intelligence

Jose Silva conducted 22 years of research to learn what makes some people more successful than others. And he developed a system that everyone can use to achieve success in life.

He learned that we function in two dimensions: the *physical* world, at the faster *beta* brain wave frequencies, and the *spiritual* world, at the lower *alpha* brain wave frequencies.

He developed dozens of formulas that you can use at the alpha level, in the spiritual (or mental) dimension to correct problems. They have been taught in the Silva Method Basic Lecture Series (BLS) since 1966. The BLS is currently being taught in more than 100 countries and in 29 different languages.

Jose Silva thought of this as his mission in life—learning how to use the subconscious consciously, thereby converting the subconscious to an inner-conscious dimension.

Now this idea is mainstream. His trailblazing research has spawned a whole new industry of people who promise to teach you how to use more of your mind to get what you want in your life. Millions of people around the globe have benefited from Jose Silva's years of research.

The real value of psychic ability

Imagine what a gigantic step forward it was to develop a system to teach us all how to detect information that is not available to our physical senses.

Jose Silva's research revealed that the people who are the most successful are people with good intuition—the natural psychics. They have access to information that 90 percent of humanity doesn't.

Now, thanks to Jose Silva, we can *all* use our intuition.

Still, some people are much more successful than others. Why? High intelligence finally revealed the answer to Jose Silva.

"The reason we were given psychic ability," he said one day, "is so that we can use it to get information from high intelligence."

With that simple statement, he began the mission that he was *really* sent here to do: to teach people how to connect to a higher power and obtain the guidance they need to be successful, happy, and fulfilled.

That's what this book is about: to teach *you* how to connect to a higher power and obtain the guidance you need to be successful, happy, and fulfilled.

What you must do to succeed

You can learn how in three simple steps:

1. Learn to function at the correct dimension, the alpha level. If you have taken any of the Silva courses, you already know how to do this. If not, we'll teach you. All you need to do is relax. We'll tell you exactly how.

2. Have the correct attitude. You will learn exactly what to do with the guidance you receive. We'll show you how to discover exactly what your mission is, so that you can carry it out.

3. Communicate with high intelligence in the correct manner—using mental images (visualization and imagination) rather than words. We'll show you exactly how. It is easier than you think, and everybody can do it.

You need to invest a few minutes each day to learn how to do this. You need to use your spiritual communications tools in order to get the guidance you need.

If you will use the techniques that you learn in this book—in the correct manner with the proper attitude—then you will enjoy the kind of success that countless others have enjoyed.

You will learn the most fundamental laws of the universe. This is not just theory. It is based on what actually works. It works for the 10 percent of people who are natural alpha thinkers, and it works for the millions of people who have learned the Silva Method during the last 33 years.

Belief in psychic ability is now universal

Psychic ability belongs to everyone. It is something that you can learn to use and can benefit from.

Leading scientists, along with leaders in every field of human endeavor, are speaking out about the value of intuition and psychic ability:

➢   John Mihalasky conducted 10 years of scientific research with thousands of business executives and found that those who are the most successful have the best precognitive abilities. Details of his research are discussed in Chapter 18.

➢   Doctors in California demonstrated that prayer groups actually help heart patients. Their research persuaded Dr. William Nolan, who has written a book trying to debunk faith healing, to say: "It sounds like this study will stand up to scrutiny....Maybe we doctors ought to be writing on our order sheets, 'Pray three times a day.' If it works, it works." Details of this work and much more were published in the book *Healing Words* by Larry Dossey (Harper San Francisco, 1995).

➤ Researcher Cleve Backster has demonstrated thousands of times that plants—and even your white blood cells—detect and respond to your thoughts! His research is highlighted in Chapter 9 and is also covered in detail in *The Secret Life of Your Cells* by Robert B. Stone (Whitford Press, 1989).

This knowledge is not limited to the scientific community. It has become mainstream:

➤ Country-music superstar Billy Ray Cyrus believes that his life has been guided by God. "I had learned as a kid that I always had this little voice inside that would tell me different things. When I would listen, it was always right. When I wouldn't listen to the little voice I would always find out why I should have listened because it was always right," he said. When he follows his left brain logic, he fails; when he listens to the spiritual voice within, he succeeds.

➤ Dr. Drew, a board-certified physician and co-host of the popular MTV show *Loveline,* recognizes the reality of intuition. "You can't explain," he said, "but one day we'll understand more about how humans communicate through air and through impulses and through some sort of telepathic ways. I mean, there's something to all that." Dr. Drew, we have news for you: The mechanism is now known. We know now what it is, why it works, and how to use it.

Jose Silva's genius is acknowledged

Jose Silva's genius has been acknowledged in scores of books and articles over the past three decades:

➤ Dr. Wayne Dwyer, motivational speaker, author, and a very popular self-improvement "gurus," said in his best-selling book *Real Magic* (Harper Mass Market Paperbacks, 1993), "I've used the Silva Method for many years. It has helped me overcome illnesses...I urge you to attend Mr. Silva's training sessions that are presented around the world." He demonstrated an understanding of Jose Silva's UltraMind concept when he said on a recent television program that you can learn to influence the coincidences in your life.

➤ Shakti Gawain, author of numerous books, including *Creative Visualization* (Bantam Books, 1983) and *Living in the Light* (Bantam Books, 1993), wrote: "One of the earliest workshops I took was the Silva Mind Control course....The most important technique I learned in that course was the basic technique of creative visualization....Our rational mind is like a computer....The intuitive mind, on the other hand, seems to give access to an infinite supply of information. It appears to be able to tap into a deep storehouse of knowledge and wisdom...."

➤ Author Richard Bach said, "Creative visualization is what the Silva Method is all about." In Chapter 30 you'll read how the Silva techniques helped him complete his best-selling book *Jonathan Livingston Seagull* (Buccaneer Books, 1991).

Stories about the success of Silva graduates have appeared in virtually every major magazine and newspaper in the United States, and scores more around the world, including *Success*, *Life*, *Playboy*, *Mademoiselle*, and countless others.

What can you expect?

Here are some real-life examples from typical Silva graduates in the areas of health, relationships, and business:

➤ A medical doctor has a dream about a 75-year-old friend of his who has just had open-heart surgery. The next morning he hurries to advise his friend's physician and family not to let his friend get up too soon.

➤ A woman whose sister has been diagnosed with cancer in one lung mentally detects that her sister also has cancer in the other lung. Doctors confirm it during surgery.

➤ A woman who lives in an atmosphere of racial bigotry is devastated when her daughter marries a man of a different race and becomes pregnant with his child. When problems develop and the child is born prematurely, the new grandmother uses her psychic ability to help correct the problems. The experience is so profound that her relationships with her daughter and her son-in-law improve dramatically. The spiritual connection that she experienced at her psychic level changes the way she feels about people who have superficial differences from her.

> ➤ A karate instructor is kicked in the groin by one of his brown-belt students. It is a wakeup call. He uses his psychic level to find out what he is doing wrong. He follows the guidance from higher intelligence and builds a spectacularly successful direct-marketing business that earns him far more money—and serves far more people—than ever before.

How this book is organized

In Section I you will learn a simple system that you can use to find the correct dimension, the relaxing alpha level, and how to function there—that is, how to activate your mind while remaining at the alpha level. Then you will learn exactly how to connect with a higher power—how to actually communicate with high intelligence from this level.

In Section II you will learn a series of specific self-management techniques so that you can get rid of any impediments to your success and be better able to carry out your life's mission.

Section III provides specialized step-by-step guidance in many different fields, with chapters written by people who are recognized authorities and who have used the Silva techniques for many years in their field. You can use their guidance to help you develop a specific plan to help you carry out the instructions you receive from high intelligence.

Today not tomorrow

If you want to enjoy more success—on your terms—you can begin today. In fact, today is the only time you can begin, because if you wait until tomorrow, then tomorrow becomes today!

The way to put power into your decisions is to use **TNT**—to take action today, not tomorrow!

NOW is the time. There is **no** other **way** to get anything done. Sooner or later you begin. You can do it now, or you can postpone now until later.

It is as easy as turning the page and doing the simple exercise in Chapter 1. Please let us know of your successes, and what we can do to serve you better.

Now it is time to turn the page and get started.

SECTION I:
INTRODUCTION TO
SILVA TECHNIQUES

Please read these chapters in sequence in order to establish a good foundation about how to use the alpha level to help you obtain guidance and achieve success in your life's mission.

If you are new to Jose Silva's mind-training systems—that is, if you have not already learned to enter the alpha level in a Silva seminar or from a Silva home-study course—then we have a special 40-day program you can use to find your level. You can read this book from beginning to end, just like you would any other book, but before you try to use the techniques, make sure you know how to enter your level by practicing the exercises in the first four chapters if necessary. Practice the exercises in Chapter 1 for 10 days. Then practice the exercises in Chapter 2 for 10 days, then Chapter 3, and finally Chapter 4. Once you've taken the 40 days to establish a good foundation at the alpha level, you will be ready to use all of the techniques in this book.

CHAPTER 1
HELP FROM A
HIGHER POWER

Is it really possible to get help from a higher power who will guide you and direct you to success?

Throughout history, many people have claimed such guidance. For example, in the 17th century, playwright William Shakespeare said, "There's a divinity that shapes our ends, Rough-hew them how we will."

Filmmaker Cecil B. De Mille urged, "Let the Divine Mind flow through your own mind, and you will be happier. I have found the greatest power in the world in the power of prayer. There is no shadow of doubt of that. I speak from my own experience."

So from ancient times when Cicero said, "There is, I know not how, in the minds of men, a certain presage, at it were, of a future existence, and this takes the deepest root, and is most discoverable in the greatest geniuses and most exalted souls," people who have achieved great things claimed divine guidance.

Science learns how to contact a higher power

Aside from the claims that these people make, though, is there any kind of scientific evidence that this is really true? Religion says we must take it on faith. That was all we had until Jose Silva, while seeking ways to help his children learn to use more of their minds so they would do better in school, found a way to apply scientific method to the study of the mind and human potential.

"Science depends on the repeatable experiment," Jose explained. "If you can replicate your experience—if you can do it again with predictable results—then you have scientific evidence that you are on to something."

This was revealed to Jose, along with a great many other things, during his initial 22 years of research.

Let me give you one example, taken from Jose Silva's autobiography. In this instance, Jose won a substantial prize in the Mexican lottery.

A series of coincidences

In 1949, after Jose had been conducting research for about five years, he became so frustrated with his study of psychology that he decided to quit.

But something—or someone—wouldn't let him. As he recalled:

"Freud, Adler, Jung—these intelligent, educated men—they cannot even agree with each other. How could I, a simple, uneducated man, ever hope to understand? If these bigwigs don't agree with each other, who am I to straighten them out? I am just an amateur!

"At this time, I was working a very busy schedule. I closed my radio repair shop at 9 p.m. to go home to have dinner with my family.

"Late one night I sat in the living room reading a psychology book while my wife, Paula, and the children slept. But I'd had enough.

"I've learned enough to help my family, I thought. My church thinks I'm wrong to delve into these areas. People in the town, religious people, are beginning to shun me. I'm taking time and money that I could use for my family and spending it on this research. Why should I continue?

"I threw the book across the room. Paula heard it hit the wall after it slid under the sofa. Apparently someone on the other side did, too.

A message from high intelligence

"I went to sleep right after that, but two hours later a bright light inside my head woke me up. It was a light like the midday sun when you look up into space on a cloudless day. Hanging in space were two sets of numbers, one on top of the other. The first set was 3-4-3; the second set,

under the first set, was 3-7-3. Right after that, an impression of Christ and One Solitary Life *given to me at the army reception center came to me.* Why Christ? *I wondered.* Why me? What does this have to do with the numbers?

"I opened my eyes and it was dark. I glanced at the clock on the nightstand. It was 4:30 a.m. I said to myself, Maybe it was a telepathic message. *I had become aware of parapsychology by this time, and had read that such things could happen. I figured maybe this was the way it was done.*

"Fascinated, I tried some experiments with myself and the light. I closed my eyes and tried to keep the bright light from disappearing, because it was fading gradually. I tried breathing slowly, but that did not help. I tried changing positions, but that did not help. I tried to slow down my heart, but whatever I did was not enough. The light faded until it disappeared.

"I stayed awake the rest of the night, trying to analyze what had happened. I thought of Paula and how she used to tell me that people who read too much go crazy! I was not about to tell her about the light in my head because I knew her answer would be, I told you so! *In fact, I might have agreed with her, as I started thinking,* Maybe this is how people start going crazy, by seeing lights in their heads. *But one thing I kept thinking was that, for whatever reason this happened, it must be all right because of the impression of Christ and* One Solitary Life *that came to me with the experience.*

Searching for answers

"The first explanation I thought of was that maybe I was supposed to call someone who has that phone number. (At this time in Nuevo Laredo, Mexico, phone numbers had six digits.) I searched the telephone book from cover to cover but did not find any listing for the numbers.

"My next idea was that maybe I should go to someone's home who had these numbers as part of their address, because maybe they would have a message for me. But when I studied a city map, I found that the home addresses in Laredo, Texas, did not use those numbers.

"It was about 4:00 the next afternoon when I came up with another idea: checking automobile and truck license plate numbers. I did

this for the rest of the day, ready to ask for my message from the driver of any vehicle that had those numbers, but I did not find a match for my mysterious numbers.

"It was 15 minutes before 9:00 when I started to close my shop. My wife came in from our house next door and said to me, 'If you go across the river into Nuevo Laredo, Mexico, for a service call, please get me a bottle of alcohol.' (We use Mexican alcohol for medicinal purposes because it is pure and costs less than alcohol in Laredo.) I said to Paula, 'Honey, I don't have service calls from across the border, but I will go and get you a bottle anyway.'

A friend has another idea

"At that very moment, an old friend of mine came in to invite me to go for some coffee. I said, 'Help me to close my place and we'll go right now.' I asked him if he was in a hurry or if we could take a ride to Mexico for Paula's alcohol.

"Since my friend had been studying psychology with me for a year, I told him about my experience the night before. I felt sure he was not going to think I was crazy. I had not told anyone all day, and I needed to tell someone, so I told him. While crossing the bridge into Mexico, my friend suggested, 'Now that we are coming into Mexico, and Mexico operates a national lottery, maybe there is such a number.' I hadn't thought of that, and I had nothing to lose—the lottery agency was just a block and a half further up the same street where we were going.

"We stopped right in front of the lottery agency. It closed at 9:00, and we had just missed it. 'Finding it closed means for me to forget it. It is not supposed to be here,' I told my friend. We then went to the liquor store to get Paula's alcohol. While I waited for the clerk to put some camphor into the liquor (this way it would be unfit for drinking, so we wouldn't have to pay liquor tax to take the alcohol into the United States), my friend went to a back room where he found some lottery tickets.

Success at last

"'What numbers are you looking for?' my friend called from the adjoining room. I told him, and he called back, '3-4-3 is here.' I said,

'You are kidding me, are you not?' My friend then answered, 'Come and see.'

"Sure enough, there were five segments of an active series numbered 3-4-3. A complete series contained 20 segments. Someone had already purchased the other 15 segments. My friend asked what I was going to do. 'Buy these, of course!' I told him. So I bought them. I had never ever thought of buying lottery tickets, but I bought five segments and would find out in two days if the number 3-4-3 would win anything.

"I found out that the ticket with the numbers 3-7-3 had been sold in Mexico City. It could not have been found anywhere else because 3-7-3 was assigned to be sold in Mexico City only. If I had purchased that ticket, I would have cleared, after paying the Mexican income tax, about $1,000.

"On the other hand, 3-4-3 was assigned to be sold by the liquor store in Nuevo Laredo, and nobody else in the whole Republic of Mexico could have had it. The 3-4-3 had a prize also, and after paying the Mexican income tax and exchanging the Mexican pesos into U.S. dollars, I cleared a little more than $10,000 with just my five segments on the ticket. I came home dazed, with $10,000 in my pocket—and in 1949, that was a lot of money!

Why did this happen?

"In trying to figure out who had put that number in my head and why, I went back over my experience step by step, and found many coincidences. For example, my wife wanted a bottle of alcohol from Mexico. I could have told her I'd get it the next time I made a service call. Or I could have asked her to send someone else. Instead I went that night. Paula did not know about my experience, much less know that she was sending me to the one place in the entire Republic of Mexico where the ticket was sold.

"And what timing! If my friend had come only 10 minutes later, I would have left already. If my friend had not gone with me, I would not have thought of buying a lottery ticket, let alone walked into the other room and seen the tickets. And even if I had thought about the lottery, I would not have continued to look for the tickets after finding the lottery agency closed.

"After backtracking and after going over every detail of the experience, I found myself faced with many coincidences. I felt that those coincidences were trying to tell me something, or that somebody was trying to tell me something through those coincidences. I then felt that I must seek and find out what it was that I was supposed to do, or not do.

"I started going back prior to having the experience, hour by hour, step by step, seeking a clue. The only thing I saw that could have had a connection and could have brought on the series of coincidences was the decision I made to stop studying psychology.

"With that realization, I pulled the psychology book out from under the couch, dusted it off, and continued studying.

"This chain of coincidences—not just one coincidence but five coincidences on the same subject—is what I consider divine intervention.

Verification and confirmation

"Scientists always look for verification. Having all of those coincidences happen the way they did provided me with the verification that it was divine guidance.

"I believe that a spontaneous event with detrimental end results is an accident, and that a spontaneous event with beneficial end results is a coincidence that could be divine guidance.

"A series of beneficial coincidences is surely divine intervention.

"Many people in Laredo would have thought about the lottery immediately, just as my friend did. If I had thought about it, I would have checked the lottery agency immediately, which means that I wouldn't have found the ticket.

"High intelligence guided me, through the series of coincidences, to the right place, so that I would find the lottery ticket, and would understand that it was not just luck or coincidence, but divine guidance.

"My many coincidences with the lottery-ticket experience was a means of getting back on track.

"From then on I started experimenting, trying to put together a method that would help to enhance what I used to call 'the guessing faculty.' What I called 'the guessing faculty' turned out to be the psi— or intuitive—factor."

Able to overcome opposition

Jose was attacked from every angle. The Catholic Church considered excommunicating him for what they *thought* he was doing. When they saw he was helping people, and not causing any harm, they backed off.

The state district attorney called him in and said that people had complained about how he was defrauding the public. "How have I defrauded anybody when I have never accepted any money, not even reimbursement for my expense?" Jose asked. The D.A. complimented him on his foresight and sent him on his way.

People he thought were his friends shunned him. Some even went out of their way to avoid him. "Many people wouldn't look me in the eye," he said, "because I was practicing hypnosis. They were afraid I might use it to take advantage of them!"

Other times he saw people cross the street to avoid coming too close to him. The local newspaper refused to accept advertising from Jose for his radio repair business!

All that has changed now, of course. People fear what they don't understand, and in the early days, many people feared the messenger, Jose Silva.

"Even my wife was against me," Jose recalled. "She was afraid I was practicing witchcraft. But when she finally saw how much this was helping our children, she started supporting me. She even learned how to condition the children and helped me with that."

"In fact," he added, "by the time I had managed to convince her, I was well-prepared for my other critics. Maybe that was how high intelligence prepared me for the big job that lay ahead of me, when I had to convince scientists and others of the value of our work."

Everyone can do this

By the time he had conducted 22 years of research, Jose knew that everyone could learn to use their psychic ability, and if they could achieve a deep level of mind with conscious awareness and maintain that deep level once they activated their mind, then they could seek and receive guidance from high intelligence.

He developed a system that required just 48 hours to teach people to do this. The Silva course has now been shortened to one-third of that time, now that humanity has evolved in its understanding of this field.

Of course, you need to practice and develop your expertise at using the Silva techniques just as you must practice anything else.

But for those who persisted, they could learn to remember dreams and use them to get guidance when they didn't know what to do next.

In fact, once you develop your psychic ability sufficiently, you can simply "enter your level"—a meditative level that we will explain shortly—analyze your problem, and get the guidance you need.

This has been the case with many Silva graduates. Here is an example from Rev. Teresa F. Finkley of Sacramento, California:

"I was an unhappy little girl who wondered if her parents loved her. My mother had left me with my grandparents, and my father only came to see me once. Mother remarried and didn't want a stepfather over me. I couldn't understand that!"

When she was grown, Teresa got married and had two children, but her son died after just fifteen days. *"Because I couldn't see that I was being divinely guided, I became ill and had a brush with death. But I was given another chance. I had a spiritual experience that was the beginning of a new way of living. In the hospital bathroom mirror I saw a Spirit Being that extended an invitation for me to 'come.' I cried out loud, 'No, I have to live for my daughter!' It backed away and I sank to the floor and became wet from head to foot. The next morning I was better.*

"Later a very spiritual woman explained to me that I had been given a second chance, and that there was special work for me to do. I had no idea what that work was to be."

Then one day, several years later, Teresa saw an ad for the Silva Method and took the course. *"This again had to be divine guidance. Learning the basic program helped me to see that I was on the right path. I learned to appreciate my oneness with the universe, with all of nature."*

Through Silva, she met Rev. Helene Mellas, who became her teacher and mentor. Teresa was finally persuaded that she was to become an ordained minister, teacher, and healer.

"It wasn't easy to accept the fact that I had been chosen to do this work. The Silva Method played a great part in helping me to get on the right track. I discovered that I needed balance. I had the professional, the social, and was making giant strides in the emotional, but I was lacking the spiritual. The spiritual gave me balance. We all must seek this balance if we hope to have true happiness.

"I hope that my life experiences, challenges, and joys can serve as a glimmer of encouragement to others. It took all these things to bring me to the gateway of

universal awareness and happiness. I am happy because my work is truly what I love to do. I do it well because God works and speaks through me. I don't fool myself into thinking that the power is mine alone.

"I am a diamond in the rough. The 'Master Jeweler' is still putting on the finishing touches to make me into a highly polished and breathtakingly beautiful diamond."

The next step

After more than 30 years of experience with the Silva Method, a new system was revealed to Jose.

At the age of 82, he was not interested in developing a new course. But when several members of his family began to pressure him to change the original course, he decided it was easier to switch than fight with them.

So he began working on a new course.

Over the next two years, it evolved into something much more than just a course. He called it a *system*.

The Silva UltraMind ESP System is the course he would have liked to have taught in 1966, but people were not ready for a course that promised to train them to be psychics. They were primarily interested in helping themselves.

The original Silva Method moved many people from a "me-centered" approach to a "we-centered" attitude. One of the first beneficial statements was this: "My increasing mental faculties are for serving humanity better."

Other statements were primarily me-centered. "Positive thoughts bring me benefits and advantages I desire," and "every day in every way I am getting better, better, and better" are good examples.

The statements in the new UltraMind System are all we-centered:

➤ Do unto others only what you would have others do unto you.
➤ The solution must help to make this planet a better place to live.
➤ The solution must be the best for everybody concerned.
➤ The solution must help at least two or more persons.

Thanks to Jose Silva and the Silva Method, humanity has experienced a shift in consciousness. People now understand that they are not just physical beings, but are physical *and* spiritual. People now understand that the tools of their

spiritual nature are visualization, imagination, and psychic ability. They understand that we are all connected to one another, and we must all work together.

Today people are eager to develop their psychic abilities so that they can
connect spiritually with other people and project mentally to correct problems.

In the remainder of this chapter and in the next three chapters, Jose Silva
will provide step-by-step guidance for you to learn to enter a deeper level of mind
so that you can develop and use your psychic abilities.

In Section II, there is information on self-management techniques that
you can use to remove any impediments to your success.

Section III provides specialized guidance from authorities in several fields,
who have used the Silva techniques for many years and who will share their knowledge and experience with you.

Now let's get started by explaining the alpha brain wave level, and giving
you your first alpha experience.

What is alpha?

Your "bio-computer" brain operates on a small amount of electricity, just
like a personal computer does. It can process and store information, retrieve that
information, and then use that information to make decisions and solve problems.

Unlike other computers, the electricity that the brain generates and functions
with does not remain at a fixed frequency. Sometimes this electric current vibrates
rapidly—20 times or more per second. Other times it vibrates very slowly—one
time or less per second. Scientists call these vibrations cycles (or hertz) and have
divided the brain frequency spectrum into four different segments, based on the
number of cycles per second (cps).

- ➤ Beta is above 14 cps, typically 20 cps when your body and mind are
  active and you focus your eyes.
- ➤ Alpha, from seven to 14 cps, is associated with light sleep and
  dreaming.
- ➤ Theta, from four to seven cps, is associated with deeper sleep, and
  with the use of hypnosis for such things as painless surgery.
- ➤ Delta, less than four cps, is associated with deepest sleep. In the next
  chapter, we'll talk more about the delta level and how you can use it
  for two-way communication with high intelligence.

Developing the alpha level

During his research in the 1950s, Jose reasoned that the best range to use for mental activity would be the range that has the least impedance and the most energy. Not only did most scientists disagree, but they doubted that it was even possible for people to learn to remain at the lower alpha brain frequencies once they activated their mind.

Jose proved them all wrong.

The alpha frequency is the strongest (as far as currency) and the most rhythmic of the four. That's why it was the first to be discovered by scientists with their primitive sensing equipment; it was named "alpha" for the first letter in the Greek alphabet.

Until now, delta has been a big mystery to researchers. People lose awareness when the brain frequency lowers to delta. Now, for the first time, we have a technique to allow us to use the delta level purposefully.

How people use their minds

It seemed logical to Jose that the alpha level would be the ideal level to do your thinking, if you could learn to actually activate your mind while at alpha.

➢ You could think more clearly, because it provides more energy.
➢ You could maintain your concentration better.
➢ You could access more information, more easily, because it is in the absolute center of the brain's normal operating range.

But here's the catch: Research revealed that most people do their thinking at the beta frequency!

Most people, when their brain frequency slows to alpha, enter the "subconscious" area and then fall asleep.

Most people are using the weakest, the least stable frequency to do their thinking: the beta level.

But the super successful people stay awake at the alpha level and do their thinking there.

Your first alpha experience

Will you invest 15 minutes a day for 40 days to learn to enter the alpha level with conscious awareness? If you will do this, and then will learn to apply the techniques of the Silva System, then you will succeed. We'll provide step-by-step guidance, so you will know exactly what to do.

It is easier to do it than to explain it, so let's get right to your first mental training exercise, also known as a conditioning cycle. For that, read the instructions in Jose Silva's words:

In the two-day Silva training program, attendees learn how to function consciously at alpha in just a few hours, because they have the help of a trained lecturer who guides them step by step and answers all of their questions. Since you are going to be learning by reading this book, it will take longer. It will take you approximately 40 days.

I will give you a simple way to relax, and you will do better and better at this as you practice.

I will also give you a simple statement to affirm to yourself.

This is how you train your mind. You relax, lower your brain frequency to the alpha level, and practice using imagination and visualization.

Because you cannot read this book and relax simultaneously, it is necessary that you read the instructions first, so that you can put the book down, close your eyes, and follow them.

Here they are:

1. *Sit comfortably in a chair and close your eyes. Any position that is comfortable is a good position.*
2. *Take a deep breath and as you exhale, relax your body.*
3. *Count backward slowly from 50 to one.*
4. *Daydream about some peaceful place you know.*
5. *Say to yourself mentally, "Every day, in every way, I am getting better, better, and better."*
6. *Remind yourself mentally that when you open your eyes at the count of five, you will feel wide awake, better than before. When you reach the count of three, repeat this, and when you open your eyes, affirm it again ("I am wide awake, feeling better than before").*

You already know steps one and two. You do them daily when you get home in the evening. Add a countdown, a peaceful scene, and an affirmation to help you become better and better, and you are ready for a final count-out.

Read the instructions once more. Then put the book down and do it.

The magic of thinking at alpha

Thanks to Jose Silva, you have just experienced "programming."

Your ability to program improves with practice. With practice, you relax more quickly and reach deeper, healthier levels of mind; you visualize more realistically; and your levels of expectation and belief heighten, yielding bigger and better results.

Programming in this manner at the alpha level produces far better results than programming at beta.

You can repeat affirmations a thousands times at the outer level and not have as much effect as you can with just one repetition at the alpha level.

That is why some people are able to visualize their goals and then reach them, while most people get very little result.

Jose Silva's research found that only about one person in 10 naturally thinks at the alpha brain wave level and acts at the beta level.

Now you will be one of the one-in-10. Remember, the only way to get superior results is to learn how to function at the alpha level with conscious awareness, the way the 10-percenters do.

Using the alpha level consciously

When you attend the Silva UltraMind ESP Systems live training programs, you learn to enter the alpha level and function there with just one day of training.

With a Silva home-study program, you can use the audiotapes to learn to enter the alpha level within a few days.

If you have already learned to enter the alpha level by one of those methods, you can skip the following instructions for practicing countdown-deepening exercises for the next 40 days.

If not, then follow these instructions from Jose Silva:

When you enter sleep, you enter alpha. But you quickly go right through alpha to the deeper levels of theta and delta.

Throughout the night your brain moves back and forth through alpha, theta, and delta, like the ebb and flow of the tide. These cycles last about 90 minutes.

In the morning, as you exit sleep, you come out through alpha, back into the faster beta frequencies that are associated with the outer- conscious levels.

Some authors advise that as you go to sleep at night, you think about your goals. That way, you get a little bit of alpha time for programming. The only trouble is, you have a tendency to fall asleep.

For now, I just want you to practice a simple exercise that will help you learn to enter and stay at the alpha level. Then in 40 days, you will be ready to begin your programming.

In the meantime, I will give you some additional tasks that you can perform at the beta level, that will help you prepare yourself so that you will be able to program more effectively at the alpha level when you are ready at the completion of the 40 days.

Your first assignment

Here is your alpha exercise.

Practice this exercise in the morning when you first wake up. Since your brain is starting to shift from alpha to beta when you first wake up, you will not have a tendency to fall asleep when you enter alpha.

Here are the steps to take:

1. *When you awake tomorrow morning, go to the bathroom if you have to, then go back to bed. Set your alarm clock to ring in 15 minutes, just in case you do fall asleep again.*
2. *Close your eyes and turn them slightly upward toward your eyebrows (about 20 degrees). Research shows that this produces more alpha.*

3. *Count backward slowly from 100 to one. Do this silently; that is, do it mentally to yourself. Wait about one second between numbers.*

4. *When you reach the count of one, hold a mental picture of yourself as a success. An easy way to do this is to recall the most recent time when you were 100 percent successful. Recall the setting, where you were and what the scene looked like; recall what you did; and recall what you felt like.*

5. *Repeat mentally, "Every day in every way I am getting better, better, and better."*

6. *Then say to yourself, "I am going to count from one to five; when I reach the count of five, I will open my eyes, feeling fine and in perfect health, feeling better than before."*

7. *Begin to count. When you reach three, repeat, "When I reach the count of five, I will open my eyes, feeling fine and in perfect health, feeling better than before."*

8. *Continue your count to four and five. At the count of five, open your eyes and affirm mentally, "I am wide awake, feeling fine and in perfect health, feeling better than before. And this is so."*

These 8 steps are really only 3

Go over each of these eight steps so that you understand the purpose while at the same time become more familiar with the sequence.

1. *The mind cannot relax deeply if the body is not relaxed. It is better to go to the bathroom and permit your body to enjoy full comfort. Also, when you first awake, you may not be fully awake. Going to the bathroom ensures your being fully awake. But, in case you are still not awake enough to stay awake, set your alarm clock to ring in 15 minutes so you do not risk being late on your daily schedule. Sit in a comfortable position.*

2. *Research has shown that when a person turns the eyes up about 20 degrees, it triggers more alpha rhythm in the brain and also causes more right-brain activity. Later when we do our mental picturing, it will be with your eyes turned upward at this angle.*

Meanwhile, it is a simple way to encourage alpha. You might want to think of the way you look up at the screen in a movie theater, a comfortable upward angle.

3. *Counting backward is relaxing. Counting forward is activating. One-two-three is like "get ready, get set, go!" Three-two-one is pacifying. You are going nowhere except deeper within yourself.*

4. *Imagining yourself the way you want to be—while relaxed— creates the picture. Failures who relax and imagine themselves making mistakes and losing frequently create a mental picture that brings about failure. You will do the opposite. Your mental picture is one of success, and it will create what you desire: success.*

5. *Words repeated mentally—while relaxed—create the concepts they stand for. Pictures and words program the mind to make it so.*

6–8. *These last three steps are simply counting to five to end your session. Counting upward activates you, but it's still good to give yourself "orders" to become activated at the count of five. Do this before you begin to count; do it again along the way; again as you open your eyes.*

Once you wake up tomorrow morning and prepare yourself for this exercise, it all works down to three steps:

1. *Count backward from 100 to one.*
2. *Mentally picture yourself successful and affirm your continuing success.*
3. *Count yourself out one to five, affirming good health and wide awakeness.*

40 days that can change your life—for the better

You know what to do tomorrow morning, but what about after that?

Here is your training program:

➢ Count backward from 100 to one for 10 mornings.
➢ Count backward from 50 to one for 10 mornings.

➢ Count backward from 25 to one for 10 mornings.
➢ Count backward from 10 to one for 10 mornings.

After these 40 mornings of countdown relaxation practice, count backward only from five to one and begin to use your alpha level.

People have a tendency to be impatient, to want to move faster. Please resist this temptation and follow the instructions as written.

You must develop and acquire the ability to function consciously at alpha before the mental techniques will work properly for you. You must master the fundamentals first. We've been researching this field since 1944, longer than anyone else, and the techniques we have developed have helped millions of people worldwide to enjoy greater success and happiness, so please follow these simple instructions.

CHAPTER 2
THE CORRECT
DEPTH

People tend to follow those who demonstrates that they are guided by a higher power to make the correct decisions and achieve great success in their endeavors. Religious leaders gain followers. Businesspeople build great business empires.

Many successful people listen to the "little voice inside" and reach lofty goals.

People have long recognized the value of having this ability, even if they have to fake it. There have been instances of people who do not actually have this ability but who pretend to have it, like the evangelists who use slight of hand to make it appear that they can actually heal people on the spot in order to gain followers and the monetary contributions they bring.

The problem is, while some people have had this ability, they have not been able to leave behind them a method that the ordinary person could use to gain this same kind of ability, to learn to do this too.

They don't know what it is about themselves that is different, that gives them the ability to do this. They know how they function, and assume that everybody else functions the same way. Why would they think differently? They have only their own experience to draw on.

The followers have been so busy following the leaders that, even if they somehow pick up some clues and develop this ability themselves, they do not learn enough to be able to pass on this knowledge to anyone else.

The naturals who have this ability are usually not even able to pass it on to their own children.

The law of success

At the beginning of the 20th century, a newspaper reporter named Napoleon Hill met one of these geniuses who had been guided to achieve success. Andrew Carnegie, a steel magnate, had become the wealthiest person in the world.

Carnegie advised Hill that there was something different about the super-successful people. He knew a lot of super-successful people personally, as well as a lot of ordinary people, and he knew that they were different.

So he made a proposal to Hill: If Napoleon Hill was willing to make a study of these people and determine what the differences were, Carnegie would secure appointments for Hill with these super-successful individuals.

During the next 20 years, Hill identified several characteristics that the super- successful people had. By far the most important, Hill discovered, was their ability to sense information with their minds, an ability the average person did not possess.

"If you can find a way to stimulate your mind to go beyond this average stopping point," Hill said in his *Reading Course on the Law of Success* (published in 1925) "fame and fortune will be yours." Hill understood that psychic ability was the foundation of everything, especially if you could also connect with a higher power for guidance.

Although Hill apparently developed these abilities himself, he never found a way to teach them to others. He was never able to unlock the secret; he never found the key to train people to do this.

The key to unlock the secret of success

In the middle of the 20th century, from 1944 to 1966, Jose Silva conducted research to learn why some people were so much more successful than the average, such as he had been, so that he could teach this to his own children.

Early in his research, Jose looked to religion to see what it said on the subject. He was born into a Catholic family in a Catholic community, so his first investigation was into Catholicism. He wanted to be sure that the techniques he was experimenting with did not violate any of the teachings of his religion.

He found that they did not conflict. The teachings of Jesus both supported what he was doing and gave him ideas for additional experiments. "It has always seemed to me that Jesus was guiding me to the discoveries that I made," Jose said.

While this offered some assurance, it was not enough for Jose. He realized that if he had been born into some other religion, he would have looked to that religion for clues to success. So he took time to study all religions. "I studied the origin of each religion," he said, "when it was founded and who founded it. I wanted to know what their beliefs were, their philosophies. I wanted to know what their goals were."

What he discovered was pretty amazing. "I saw that all religions were trying to accomplish the same thing," he said. "It reminds me of what somebody once said, that all paths lead to the same God."

Many paths to the same destination

In fact, religious leaders throughout history have said much the same thing. Here are some examples:

➢   In the fifth century B.C., Lao-tze said, "The broad-minded see the truth in different religions; the narrow-minded see only their differences."

➢   More than 300 years before Christ lived, Aristotle said, "God has many names though he is only one being."

➢   The New Testament of the Bible seems to agree: "There is neither Jew nor Greek, there is neither bond nor free, there is neither male nor female: for ye are all one in Christ Jesus" (Galatians 3:28).

➢   The Koran offers an explanation as to why people see things differently, even if all religions are trying to achieve the same thing: "Every child is born into the religion of nature; its parents make it a Jew, a Christian, or a Magian."

So it was the founder of the Christian religion, a Jewish rabbi named Jesus, who, through the writings in the Bible, provided some of the most important clues in Jose's search for the "secret of success."

Now it is all available to you. No matter what your religion, no matter what you believe, this will work for you. The Silva System does not violate any religion's belief, nor does it violate any scientific principle.

The Silva System holds the unique position of being consistent both with religious philosophy and scientific method. Jose Silva, a simple man from a small town deep in southern Texas, without any formal education, achieved what no one else has: He has brought science and religion together.

Finding the correct dimension

You have already started the mental exercises necessary to find the correct dimension for applying the self-management techniques that you will find in Section II of this book and for developing your psychic ability.

If you have graduated from one of the Silva seminars or completed a Silva home-study program, then you have already learned to enter your level, and you do not need to use these countdown exercises for this purpose.

However, it is still valuable to practice the countdown-deepening exercises in order to insure that you maintain your level. Learn to activate your mind while maintaining this level in order to use the self-management techniques and your psychic ability.

Exploring a whole new dimension

Until now, the delta level has been a mystery.

We all function at beta whenever we focus our eyesight.

More than 30 years ago, Jose authored a system that everyone can use to learn to function at the alpha level with conscious awareness.

He also provided his students with a couple of techniques to use to reach the theta level. While you cannot activate your mind while at theta, you can be aware of information. As soon as you begin to analyze the information, your brain speeds up to alpha.

But delta remained a mystery. Even with our training, people could not deepen themselves into delta.

The only way to achieve delta is through sleep. The deepest part of the normal sleep and dream cycle is spent in delta. Yet even when sleep and dream researchers awaken their subjects while the subjects are in delta, there is no recall of anything while at that level.

Now the mystery has been solved. The purpose of delta has been revealed.

Although we still cannot use it consciously, we can make use of it while we sleep to communicate with high intelligence. (You'll read more about that and the specific technique that you can use in Chapter 4.)

For now, let us mention that it is also important to learn to function at alpha so that you can correct problems that could prevent you from using the Mental Video Technique effectively.

What could prevent you from using this technique effectively?

Sleeping pills, for one thing. When you use sleeping pills to go to sleep, then the drugs try to take control of your central nervous system. The drugs prevent you from going through the normal 90-minute cycles associated with sleep and dreams.

And to the extent that the drugs prevent you from entering the delta level, you are precluded from using the Mental Video Technique effectively.

Drugs always have side effects. If you are taking medication for migraines, for instance, or for other kinds of pain, those drugs will have side effects. They often interfere with the normal functioning of your central nervous system.

Habits such as smoking or drinking also have undesirable side effects.

At deep levels of mind, you can gain control over these and other problems.

I will now turn the rest of the chapter over to Jose Silva to teach you how to do that.

Physical and mental relaxation lead to alpha

"Once you feel that you are able to maintain your concentration during your daily countdowns, you're ready to learn to relax with the Long Relaxation Exercise.

"To do this, I want you to use your mind to relax your body. And then I want you to relax your mind. When you do this, your brain will relax into the alpha level.

"Here is how to proceed with the first part, using your mind to relax your body:

"Find a comfortable position. Let your body do what it wants to do in order to be comfortable. However, I do not want you to fall asleep; if you fall asleep during this exercise, then make yourself a little less comfortable and do it again.

"When you have found a comfortable position, then close your eyes.

"Why do I ask you to close your eyes? Several reasons:

"Whenever you attempt to focus your eyesight, your brain automatically goes to 20 cps beta frequency. You can use all of your other senses while you are at alpha, but not your eyesight. So I do not want you to focus your eyes or try to 'see' anything while you are at alpha.

"Now I want you to mentally repeat and visualize the number three several times. To make this easy to do, get a piece of paper before you

begin, write the number three on it; then just recall what it looks like. We will associate the number three with physical relaxation.

"The next thing that I want you to do is to imagine your body relaxing from the top of your head to the soles of your feet. Here is how to proceed:

"First, concentrate your attention on your scalp, the skin that covers your head.

"You will sense a fine vibration, a feeling of warmth caused by circulation. Use your imagination for this. Do not just wait for it to happen by itself; imagine what it would feel like. Imagine that you can actually feel it.

"Now release and relax all tensions and ligament pressures from this part of your head completely, and place it in a deep state of relaxation that will continue to grow deeper and deeper as we continue.

"What will your scalp feel like if it is completely relaxed? Will it feel like a warm dishcloth lying over your skull? Will the roots of your hair be gently washed in the warm flow of blood in your scalp?

"Use your imagination to sense your scalp relaxing. Then do the same thing with the rest of your body.

"Your forehead, the skin that covers your forehead—concentrate your attention on your forehead; you will detect a fine vibration, a tingling sensation, a feeling of warmth caused by circulation. Then release and relax all tensions and ligament pressures from this part of your head completely, and place it in a deep state of relaxation that will grow deeper as we continue.

"Your eyelids, and the tissue surrounding your eyes. We have great control of the eyelids, so allow them to relax. It is important to realize that you do not 'force' yourself to relax; you 'allow' yourself to relax.

"Your face, the skin covering your cheeks.

"Your throat, the skin covering your throat area.

"Within the throat area.

"Your shoulders. To help you concentrate on your shoulders, concentrate on and 'feel' the clothing in contact with your shoulders.

"Your chest. Again, feel your clothing in contact with your chest.

"Within the chest area—relax all organs, relax all glands, relax all tissues including the cells themselves, and cause them to function in a

*rhythmic, healthy manner. How do you do this? You use your mind—
your imagination—the same as you do for the skeletal muscles.*

"*The abdominal area.*

"*Within the abdominal area.*

"*Your thighs.*

"*At this time, I want you to do something extra. Sense the vibration
at the bones within the thighs; by now these vibrations should be easily
detectable. Go ahead and sense them.*

"*Your knees.*

"*Your calves.*

"*The toes of your feet.*

"*The soles of your feet.*

"*The heels of your feet.*

"*Now you have gone from head to feet, using your mind to direct
your motor nerves to relax your muscles, and even your internal organs.*

"*Now I want you to relax your sensory nervous system as well. I
want you to be so relaxed that you are not even aware of your body, not
aware of sensory information coming through your sensory nerves.*

"*Here is how:*

"*Cause your feet to feel as though they do not belong to your body.*

"*Cause your feet, ankles, calves, and knees to feel as though they
do not belong to your body.*

"*Cause your feet, ankles, calves, knees, thighs, waist, shoulders,
arms, and hands to feel as though they do not belong to your body.*

"*This is your physical relaxation level three.*

"*Now I would like for you to mentally repeat and visualize the number three several times, to associate this feeling of relaxation with the
number three. In the future, whenever you desire to relax physically, as
relaxed as you are now, just mentally repeat and visualize the number
three several times, and you will relax physically as you are now, and
even more so.*

Mental relaxation

"*Next, mentally repeat and visualize the number two several times. The number two is for mental relaxation, where noises will not distract you. In fact, noises will help you to relax mentally more and more. You may be aware of noises and distractions, but your desire will cause you to disregard them and relax mentally more and more.*

"*Mental relaxation is very simple: To relax mentally, simply recall tranquil and passive scenes.*

"*Any scene that makes you tranquil and passive will help you to relax mentally.*

"*You may find that you are very relaxed after strenuous physical activity, such as a fast game of tennis or some such similar activity. But this is not what we want here.*

"*I want you to recall something where you are passive, relaxed, and not moving around very much. Just enjoying yourself. Maybe it's a day at the beach or a day out fishing.*

"*A tranquil and passive scene for you might be a walk through the woods on a beautiful summer day, when the breeze is just right, where there are tall shade trees, beautiful flowers, a very blue sky, an occasional white cloud, birds singing in the distance, even squirrels playing on the tree limbs. Hear birds singing in the distance.*

"*Remember to associate this level with the number two.*

Enter the alpha level

"*After you are completely relaxed both physically and mentally, repeat and visualize the number one several times, and take it for granted that you are now at level one, the alpha level, a level that you can use for a purpose, for any purpose you desire.*

"*If you have graduated from one of the Silva seminars or have used the recordings in the Silva home-study program, then you can do this immediately.*

"*If you are brand new to the Silva System and are learning by practicing the countdown exercises every morning, then your first goal is to learn to maintain your concentration during the countdowns. If this is difficult for you, practice until you get the hang of it.*

"Then you can begin to use the Long Relaxation Exercise.

"I recommend that you practice the Long Relaxation Exercise once a week for the next three months.

"Of course, you can practice more than that if you wish. Many Silva graduates continue to practice the Long Relaxation Exercise for many years, to insure that they maintain a deep, healthy level of mind.

"They do this because it helps the body to maintain vibrant good health, and it is necessary in order to use the self-management techniques in Section II of this book. It is also the level that is required for psychic functioning.

"For the next 10 days, I want you to practice your countdown exercises every morning, counting from 50 to one."

Chapter 3
The correct attitude

In order to obtain guidance and help from high intelligence, it is important that you have the correct motive for doing so.

What is the correct motive?

Is high intelligence going to help you in order for you to have a wonderful life, to get everything you want, to enjoy yourself?

Will high intelligence help you to gain at somebody else's loss? Will high intelligence help you to take prizes and deprive your opponents of winning them?

We do not think so, and the evidence supports us.

We believe that the correct reason for seeking help is so that you can use the help and guidance that you receive to do the job you were sent here to do.

And what is that job? To correct problems, and by so doing, to perfect the creation and convert planet earth into a paradise.

Common sense guides us

If we want a higher power to help us, then we have an obligation to do what the higher power wants us to do.

Several years ago, a beer company advertisement theorized that "you only go around once, so grab all the gusto you can." But that attitude doesn't make much sense.

There is an obvious parallel in our lives: If you work for someone and that person pays you to do a job, then you have to do the job, or else they will fire you and stop paying you.

Well, that's a good theory, but is there any evidence to support it?

And more importantly, is there a way that we can actually determine what our job is? Is there a way to find out what task high intelligence has assigned to us?

Fortunately, the answer to all three questions is: Yes! Yes! Yes!

Jose Silva learned very early in his life that the more you give, the more you get back. His research and study of successful people confirmed that over and over.

Jose Silva learns how to get more money

After his father died and his mother remarried and moved away, 6-year-old Jose found himself the oldest male in the family, and he felt an obligation to earn enough money to support his sister and younger brother. He asked his uncle for guidance, and he helped Jose set up a shoeshine business.

Jose learned that men would pay him to shine their shoes. The more shoes he shined, the more money he made. The better job he did, the more repeat business he got.

Then one day he asked his uncle, who was helping him, why so many men were looking at those big sheets of paper. His uncle explained that they were reading the newspaper to learn what was going on in town. So Jose found out where to get newspapers and offered them for sale to his customers.

And he made more money by doing that.

When he overheard some men talking about how difficult it was to find an honest, reliable person to clean their offices at night, young Jose offered to do it. He was so enthusiastic about it that they decided to give him a chance.

They tested him by leaving a watch and some money out. Jose put the items away, and the next day came and showed the men where he had put them. They knew that they could trust him, and they saw that he would do a good job, and Jose made more money.

It's just logical: The more people you serve, the more service you provide, the more problems you solve, the more rewards you will receive.

The attitude that made the Silva Method possible

There's no better proof of that than the Silva Method itself.

The more people Jose Silva helped with what he was learning in his research, the more he learned.

It is as though the other side was giving him more information as they confirmed that he was using it not for selfish purposes, but to correct problems.

He never accepted any money for what he did; he was happy to do it.

And he was rewarded. The other side found a way to get $10,000 to him once in the early 1950s, to let him know that he should continue his research, by way of a lottery ticket. He told that story in Chapter 1.

Unfortunately, some people think that the Silva Method is just about getting things for yourself. We have had instructors who have tried to market the course that way. But in the course, you learn that Jose had something else in mind.

Underlying principle of the Silva Method

The first Beneficial Statement used in the Silva Standard Conditioning Cycle is this: "My increasing mental faculties are for serving humanity better."

You are advised that your mental faculties are increasing, and at the same time you are advised of what your obligations are.

How could a person not want to help someone who is hurting? How can anyone just walk away when he or she sees somebody in need?

If you were not taught this when you were young, or if you have outgrown those natural instincts to help and to do constructive and creative things, then start working on getting to deep levels of mind. Get back to a level—brain-wise—before you were contaminated, before fear and insecurity distorted your natural instincts and judgment.

That's what the Silva Mental Exercise does for us: It takes us back on the scale of brain evolution to an earlier age—when we were young and the brain functioned predominately at alpha—and reprograms us with these statements. It is almost like going back and changing your past. If you were not taught properly, now you can go back and do it right!

What makes successful people different?

Jose Silva conducted more research on success than anyone else in history. He was the first person ever to use the electroencephalograph (EEG) to actually look inside the heads of people and determine what separates the super-successful from the ordinary.

What he found is that super successful people do their thinking—get information and make decisions—at the alpha brain level. He used to ask people questions while he had them connected to the EEG and noticed that most people would remain in beta when they answered questions. But a few—about 10 percent—would dip into alpha; then they would come back to beta and answer the questions.

After this happened a number of times, he realized that the people whose brains dipped into alpha—apparently to obtain and analyze information there—tended to be more successful than those whose brains remained at beta. Evidently there was more information available at alpha than at beta.

A new attitude

Jose's research went way beyond that. He discovered that the people who experience the most success in *all* areas of life—not just financial, but health, relationships, happiness, sense of satisfaction, and so on—had a different attitude than the average person.

He continued to research and observe people, and this research—along with his own experience and the experiences of people who followed his guidance—convinced him that there is a certain attitude that is necessary.

His advice was always to program to provide service, and keep in mind what your needs are, plus a little bit more. He said that we should be helping to convert the planet into a paradise.

When we develop these wonderful mental tools that we have, we should be using them to correct problems—without being concerned about whether we are compensated for this work or not.

We are beneficiaries of other people's efforts

If Jose had not worked for 22 years without ever accepting a penny for his efforts, we would not have the Silva System today.

Based on his research and his experience for more than half a century, Jose felt that if we are only trying to help ourselves—or if this is our main focus—then we are on our own, we are not going to get any help from high intelligence.

But if we are working to correct the problems of humanity—because that is the right thing to do, because this is what we were sent here to do—then we will qualify for help from high intelligence.

Do it because it is right, not for what you will get

We know people who will do anything to help anyone as long as there is something in it for them. But that's not sufficient.

Anything that you program for should benefit at least two people, according to Jose. That's the minimum; the more the better.

The more problems you are solving—the more people you are helping—the more you qualify for help from high intelligence.

If you are just working for yourself, and doing things for yourself only, then you are not likely to get help from higher intelligence. You are on your own. The techniques will still work for you, but it is much easier when you have help from other graduates and from high intelligence.

Worry about obtaining money—or "the love of money" as a preacher would say—causes much suffering. John D. Rockefeller Sr. was probably the wealthiest man in the world, but he worried so much about gaining even more money that it destroyed his health. His doctor told him that his money was going to kill him. That's when the senior Rockefeller became a philanthropist.

John D. Rockefeller Jr. later observed, "Giving is the secret of a healthy life. Not necessarily money, but whatever a man has of encouragement and sympathy and understanding." In an address at Fisk University he said, "I believe that every right implies a responsibility; every opportunity, an obligation; every possession, a duty."

The Koran agrees that it is our duty—our duty—to help those who need our assistance, with more than our prayers: "Woe be unto those who pray, and who are negligent at their prayer."

You do not have to be wealthy to help others. "Even the beggar who lives on alms should himself bestow alms," the Babylonian Talmud suggests.

You can see an example of how all of us can help others in the story of Marge Wolcott a little later in this chapter. She could not sit up by herself—she had to have a brace on her neck to hold her head up—and still she spent much of the day helping others.

You have probably heard the saying that if you give a person a fish, he will satisfy his hunger for a day; but if you *teach* him to fish, he can feed himself from now on.

The Talmud agrees: "The noblest charity is to prevent a man from accepting charity; and the best alms are to show and to enable a man to dispense with alms."

Not an easy challenge, but one that Jose Silva accepted. The Silva Method gives you the tools, the guidance, and the direction that you need to take care of yourself, and to help others also.

Many graduates start by working on themselves—on their own problems. This is quite natural. They get rid of tension and migraines, overcome insomnia, get rid of bad habits, heal the "wounded inner child," and so on. A lot of graduates have great success doing this.

Then they turn their attention to earning more money, getting a raise, improving their position, attracting the ideal mate, and things like these.

All of these things involve other people. If you want to improve your position within humanity, then you need to work just as hard to correct the problems of humanity as you would work to correct your own personal problems. The truth is, the problems of humanity are your problems.

When you lift up humanity, you are also lifting up yourself, because you are a part of humanity.

A correct attitude leads to success

What Jose Silva realized, as he studied both unsuccessful and successful people—as he studied the ancient writings and at the same time worked with thousands of people—was that *a correct sense of values* is an important factor in success.

In fact, this was very important to Jose in his very important work as a holistic faith healer. Here is what he wrote about the necessity for a correct sense of values in his autobiography (Vol. 1, page 245):

"I would ask the patient some questions, such as, 'Do you really want to be healed?' and I would add, 'because my time is very valuable and I do not intend to waste it.'

"Of course the answer was, 'Yes, I want to be healed.' Some even felt insulted by my asking such a question.

"My next question was, 'Why do you want to be healed?'

"If the answer was, 'To be a better wife (or husband, or son, or daughter) and help by being a perfect human being who will help solve the problems of my neighborhood, my city, state, or nation,' there was no more to say. I would go to work and help the patient.

"But if the answer centered on how the patient needed to live it up, enjoy life, not helping anything or anybody, then I would try to straighten out the patient's way of thinking before starting the healing."

We realize that not everybody is ready to accept all of these ideas. That's fine. Feel free to study them, and take as long as you need. As we say in the Silva Standard Conditioning Cycle, "You may accept or reject anything I say, any time, at any level of mind."

Once you learn to analyze information while at the alpha level, these ideas will make more sense to you.

How a chicken ruined two families

Jose Silva believed that it is very important that we understand what's really important in life.

Two of his neighbors in Laredo, years ago, got into a silly argument about chickens that had tragic consequences.

One neighbor had a small garden in the backyard. The other neighbor had some chickens. One day, one of the chickens jumped the fence and damaged some of the plants in the neighbor's garden.

The two women got into an argument about the damage. Should there have been a better fence? Was the homeowner responsible for the actions of the chicken?

When their husbands got home at dinnertime, both wives were upset and wanted their respective husbands to take some kind of action. The two men got into an argument, which led to one man shooting and killing the other.

What a tragedy! One husband dead, the other in prison, two women raising their children alone, children deprived of their fathers, the loss of two wage-earners—the tragic consequences go on and on.

We *must* learn to put things into perspective and focus on what's really important in our lives.

What is important?

It is important that we fulfill our mission in life. And we submit for your consideration that your mission seems to be to correct problems and help make our world a better place to live.

Why do we feel that way? Two reasons:

1. Our observations of successful people.
2. People who follow this path experience success.

We know people who put themselves at the center of their world. We know people who work 20 hours a day, who stay focused on their goal and let nothing dissuade them, people willing to win at any cost. We've seen them make a lot of money, but the money still didn't really make them happy.

We're not saying that money keeps you from being happy. We know people who are constantly doing for others, sacrificing, and giving—and these people never have enough for themselves, and they aren't very happy either. They feel like they have been shortchanged. And in a sense, they have.

We must always have a balance. There is a relationship between what we give and what we get.

Jose's formula for prosperity and abundance is simple: Program to correct problems and make the world a better place to live, and keep in mind what your needs are, plus a little bit more.

Do you "prey" or do you "pray"?

Let's take a practical example: Suppose you want to sell or buy a house. You contact a few real estate agents. The first agent who comes to see you is desperate for money and will do anything to make that commission, even if it is not in your best interest.

The second agent is determined to make the best deal for all concerned, even if it takes a little longer and even if it means a slightly lower commission.

Which one do you want to deal with? Which one has your best interest at heart? Which one are you going to refer to your friends? Who is going to end up with the most customers? The selfish one or the selfless one? You know the answer.

Sometimes, from a beta (left-brain) perspective, it may seem as though we should be trying to get everything we can for ourselves. But from an alpha (right-brain, or spiritual) perspective, we see otherwise.

According to Jose, we prey *on* each other at the beta level, but we pray *for* each other at alpha.

Keep in mind that you must have a balance—you give, and you also receive.

If you do not permit the people to whom you give to compensate you, then you are cheating them of the wonderful opportunity to gain all of the benefits of giving. Be unselfish—keep a balance in your life between giving and receiving.

You can determine the value of your work based on the compensation that you receive.

Compensation comes in many ways

There is not always a direct relationship between giving and receiving: When you do $5 worth of work for somebody, you may not receive $5 compensation from that person. But overall, you will be compensated.

Read Jose's story about a time when he healed a man in Mexico:

"I crossed the Rio Grande River three times a day, every day, for a month, to perform the 'laying on of hands' to correct a health problem that the man had.

"At the end of the 30 days, the illness was gone.

"One of my friends, who had doubts about helping somebody without requiring them to pay for the help, told me, 'I'll bet he didn't even offer to reimburse you for the bridge tolls, did he? How much did it cost you to go over and treat him almost 100 times?'

"I figured out that it cost me approximately $500, but added that it did not matter, that my needs were being taken care of.

"That night, I did not have any appointments, so my wife, Paula, asked me to go to the church recreation hall with her to the bingo game.

"Although I was not interested in playing bingo, I knew that I should spend some time with my wife, so I accompanied her there. Naturally, I participated in the game.

"Guess who won the big jackpot that night?

"I did!

"Guess how much the jackpot was?

"It was $500.

"The next day, I called my friend and told him about winning the $500. 'Maybe that is the way high intelligence sees to it that we are compensated,' I told him.

"'Oh, you and your strange ideas!' my friend said. He just didn't understand."

How to win friends

Would you want to do business with somebody who was only interested in how much he can get for himself?

Would you want to marry a person who only wanted to get all they could from you?

If you are dedicated to helping humanity—without expecting to be directly compensated for it—then everyone will want to be associated with you, to do business with you, to be your friend.

You don't need to spend any money to find people who need help and to program for them.

When you help other people, especially for people who are hurting badly, then you will have many successes.

You will be improving your skills a great deal. This is like anything else—the more you practice, the better you get.

But Jose always pointed out that we should not practice just for what we will get out of it; we should correct problems because that's what we're sent here to do.

If you give to get something, you're not giving—you're trading. Your motives are second in importance only to your actions.

This makes sense at the spiritual dimension

At deep levels of mind, people seem to understand this without any problem. So if this seems like too strange a concept to you, then practice deepening your level until you get back to the level before you were contaminated, to a time when things were more pure, clean, and positive.

In meditating on these ideas, Jose found a Bible verse that the spiritual dimension seems to emulate: "Seek ye first the kingdom of heaven, and function within God's righteousness, and all else will be added unto you" (Matthew 6:33).

In our model, the Kingdom of Heaven represents alpha. God's righteousness represents doing what God wants. All else represents everything you need, plus a little bit more.

If you need a million dollars, Jose said, it's easy to get. Just give $10 million worth of service to humanity, and if you *need* a million dollars, you'll get it.

Praying for others helps overcome incurable illness

People who understand the principle that we are all connected here on planet earth, and that whatever affects one human being affects all of humanity, are the people who achieve miraculous success.

Marge Wolcott attended the Silva Method Basic Lecture Series in Laredo in February 1982. She was a very religious person, who was accustomed to praying for other people's health. Here is her story, in her own words:

"I had multiple sclerosis (MS) for 15 years. When I came to the Silva Mind Control lectures, I was wearing a body brace and a neck brace. I had to bring in a special chair to sit in.

"When I came to Silva Mind Control, I had strong faith, but it was doubled after I finished the Basic Lecture Series.

"Two months after graduating, I took the neck brace off. Two months after that, the body brace broke, across the back and shoulder area. My daughter, who had taken the Mind Control course with me, suggested I quit wearing it. She knew I had been tempted to take it off.

"I tried it, and have not worn it since. In fact, later, a doctor from Dallas who had a crippling illness and had to close his practice, came to visit me. I didn't know it then, but he knew a lot about MS, and said later he could not detect any signs that I'd ever had it!

"He took Mind Control, recovered, and reopened his practice, I heard.

"After I recovered from the MS, I saw my doctor again. His only comment was that he'd heard of this kind of thing happening, but this was the first time he had ever seen it. He had felt there was no hope of my recovering. I had worn the brace about seven or eight years.

"Here's what I did, using the Silva Mind Control Method:

"I programmed three times a day. Many people were calling me, asking me to help them, so I would go to level three times a day to program for them.

"Since I was programming for them, I'd also program for myself after I had finished programming for them.

"I knew the doctors felt there was no hope for me, so I had little hope myself. I had desire, of course, and I would not have bothered programming if I had not had some expectancy that it could help. But I was not concerned about it. If I got better, that would be great. If not, I could accept that.

"The Bible says that whatever you do for others comes back to you tenfold. Apparently, when I programmed for the other people, I was helping myself, too. The thoughts of healing seemed to have influenced my own brain to make corrections in my own body.

"It has been 12 years since I graduated from Silva Mind Control, and I have had no trouble since then with the MS.

"One of the challenges I had at that time was severe pain in my face muscles. When I heard about the Headache Control Technique, it felt like someone placed a hand on my shoulder. The pain in my face stopped and has not been back since.

"Also, ever since I graduated, I have used the 'better and better' phrase. I use it all the time and feel sure that it has been a big help to me in my programming and my success with the Silva Method.

Formula for success

Jose Silva gave us a formula that covers this. It is in a paragraph that is found at the very end of the Silva Standard Conditioning Cycle.

It is the formula for prosperity and abundance, for self-confidence and self-esteem, for happiness and contentment. It reads like this:

> **You will continue to strive to take part in constructive and creative activities to make this a better world to live in, so that when we move on we shall have left behind a better world for those who follow. You will consider the whole of humanity, depending on their ages, as fathers or mothers, brothers or sisters, sons or daughters. You are a superior human being; you have greater understanding, compassion, and patience with others.**

Let's take a detailed look at this paragraph.

An intention to correct problems

You will continue to strive...

Some people question the use of the word "strive." They think that it is like the word "try" and that "try" is a negative word.

Well, it can be negative or positive, depending on how you use it.

What's really important is the mental picture that you are creating. Suppose you are very busy, and you have other priorities ahead of this particular thing that you would like to do. You can say, "Okay, I'll do it!" But that can put a lot of pressure on you and make you feel bad if you don't manage to get it done. Perhaps that works for some people.

Or you can say, "I doubt if I'll have time to get to it." What kind of mental picture does that create?

Maybe a better way is to leave the door open by saying, "I've got a lot of things to do, but I'll certainly try to get this done, too."

What mental picture does that create? The idea of doing it stays in the back of your mind, and perhaps your mind, subconsciously, guides your actions so that you are now able to accomplish the task.

How to know the difference between right and wrong

...to take part in constructive and creative activities to make this a better world to live in...

A lot of good people today seem to be confused about the concepts of right and wrong. Jose tried to make this plain and simple by talking about doing constructive and creative work.

Figure out what your purpose in life is. To help figure it out, ask yourself this: When you were a young child, what kind of things did you do that made you feel good about yourself? Enter your level and think about it. What can you do that needs to be done?

President John F. Kennedy said that happiness comes from doing worthwhile work that you are good at and that you enjoy doing.

Sometime when you have a few minutes, do what Jose used to do: Get out a dictionary and look up some words. Look up the words that he uses, words like constructive, creative, good, honest, pure, clean, and positive. Meditate on them.

The highest—Godly—motive

Back to Jose's instructions.

...take part in constructive and creative activities to make this a better world to live in so that when we move on, we shall have left behind a better world for those who follow.

That seems like a strange instruction, doesn't it?

When asked if that was a statement of unselfishness, Jose answered simply, "If it had not been for that attitude, we would not have the Silva System today."

He never accepted payment of any kind for his efforts to help people during the entire 22 years of his research. He would not even allow people to reimburse him for expenses, such as gasoline and bridge tolls. Interestingly enough, Napoleon Hill conducted research of successful people for more than 20 years without receiving any money, even for expenses, before he put together his Law of Success Course. It has been said that you have to give before you receive.

A blueprint for correct service

The next idea touches on the popular idea that we are all brothers and sisters here on planet earth.

You will consider the whole of humanity, depending on their ages, as fathers or mothers, brothers or sisters, sons or daughters...

For many years, there have been people who promoted the concept of "the brotherhood of man." By the 1960s, amidst the struggles for equal rights for all people—including women—people began to recognize that we are all "brothers and sisters." Jose was even ahead even back then. He was already emphasizing that our relationships go beyond treating everyone as a peer.

People who are old enough to be your parents, do you accord them the same respect and patience that you would give to your own parents? Do you turn away from an old person who needs help because you are busy, or do you do what you would do if this was your own father or mother?

Do you respond in the same way to your peers as you would your own brothers and sisters? Brothers and sisters may fight with each other, but they still love each other. Can you do that with other people as well?

What about young people? In a business situation, would you take advantage of someone who is young and inexperienced? Or would you help that person, nurture and teach him or her, the same as you would your own son or daughter?

We are caretakers

You are a superior human being. You have greater understanding, compassion, and patience with others.

As humans, we are the highest life form on this planet. According to Jose, we are like gods on this planet; we can do the same things on this planet that God can do throughout the universe.

If we do a good job while we are on this planet, we will be promoted and will be given larger responsibilities and opportunities when we move on.

Think of those words: understanding, compassion, and patience. Look them up in the dictionary. Meditate on them at your level. And program yourself to let them guide you.

A specific assignment on our journey

When we move on. Now there's an interesting phrase. We don't just put in a few decades of work, and then everything comes to an end. Our responsibilities continue as we move on to whatever comes next for us.

Do not let the fear of failure stop you from trying.

Please don't think that we are saints. We're ordinary folks who make our best efforts, and sometimes we come up short. Like the old saying goes, it's not how many times you fall down, it's how many times you get back up.

There was a young gymnast in the 1996 Summer Olympics who made two terrible mistakes. Her team was going for the gold, and she had asked the coach to let her anchor the team. She said she was strong enough to go last, so she could see what was needed to win, and then go get it. Her coach agreed.

The athlete who competed before her, her training partner, fell on both of her vault attempts.

After watching that, Kerry Struggs made her first attempt and fell exactly the same way as her training partner had done. That's "Mental Housecleaning" in action—she manifested the picture that she had in her mind.

Kerry had one attempt left, and only needed an average score to beat the second-place Russians. But she had made the one mistake that an athlete simply cannot afford to make: She had injured herself, spraining her ankle on her first vault. She couldn't even walk on the ankle, much less run fast enough to gain enough speed to complete her vault.

But the coach told her to shake it off. "I couldn't shake it off," she said later. But she made the attempt anyway, and somehow managed to keep her form through all the pain, and "nailed" the landing—winning the gold medal for the U.S. women's Olympic team for the first time in decades.

Kerry Struggs was an instant hero, the most famous athlete to emerge from the 1996 Olympic Games.

But think about this: If she had simply done her first vault correctly and gotten the necessary points to win the gold, we wouldn't even remember her name today. She'd just be one member of the team. She didn't score any perfect 10's, she didn't do anything to distinguish herself—until she made that terrible mistake and injured herself, when she was the last hope for her team to win the gold.

If she hadn't made the mistake, she wouldn't have been the hero.

Heroes are not people who always do great things. Heroes are people who persevere, who hang in there, who are not afraid to try—to strive—and to make mistakes—and to fail—and then to come back and try, try again.

Your next assignment

In the next chapter, Jose will teach you the new Mental Video Technique, which you will use when you go to sleep at night. Prior to going to sleep, you need to review your Mental Videos at the alpha level, so continue your practice of counting yourself into your level.

Your Mental Videos will be delivered to high intelligence while you sleep, so that your helpers in the spiritual dimension can guide you and help you to achieve your goals.

Before we get to that, here are two assignments for you:

1. Meditate on what we have written in this chapter. Think about your attitude, your motivation, and your purpose in life. We live our lives on the choices we make. Be sure to make the best choices possible.
2. Continue to practice your countdowns for another 10 days. This time, count down from 25 to one each morning.

CHAPTER 4
COMMUNICATING
CORRECTLY

The Mental Video Technique is a way for you to communicate with a higher power—what we refer to as *high intelligence*—to find out what your purpose in life is, and how to go about fulfilling your mission.

Anyone can use this technique. You do not need to be a graduate of the Silva UltraMind ESP System or the Silva BLS, although it helps if you are.

Why is it better to be a Silva graduate? Two reasons:

1. The better able you are to use your inborn psychic ability, the easier it will be to send and receive messages to your helpers in the spiritual dimension.

2. Your ability to do your thinking at the alpha brain-wave level—the ideal level for thinking—will help you to better interpret and understand the information that you receive from the other side.

The Mental Video Technique provides you with a method to give a report of your activities to high intelligence every night. You let your tutors on the other side know what the problems are, and what you are doing to correct them.

Then your tutors send you guidance to help you make the best decisions and proceed in the most efficient and effective manner. They want to help you to be a big success and will send you all the help you need.

In order to understand the concept, Jose used an analogy about our relationship with high intelligence:

Your mission

"If you're like me, you have probably wondered about the big questions of life, questions like, **Where did I come from? Who sent me here? Why did they send me? What is my purpose? What am I supposed to do while I am here?**

"Throughout the years, my research has involved those questions. And I have come up with some answers that stand up to the scrutiny of scientific method. That is, when my findings are applied by myself and by other people, the results are predictable, reliable, and repeatable.

"I believe that we were sent here from another dimension, by somebody who had the power to send us here without our consent if they so desired, because I don't remember anybody asking me if I wanted to come.

"As for why I was sent here, and what I am supposed to do, my research confirms again and again that we were sent here to correct problems and to convert the earth into a paradise.

"Why do I believe this? Because the people who correct the most problems are the people who are the most successful.

"What do I mean when I say they are successful?

"I am not talking about just making money. To be truly successful, you have to be successful in all areas: health, family and relationships, and a sense of satisfaction, as well as financial success.

"Some of the most successful people have enough money for their needs, but little extra. Look at someone like Ghandi or Mother Theresa; neither had many physical possessions, but they lived long, productive lives and received more satisfaction out of their work than most people can even imagine.

Communication with headquarters

"In order to know what to do to fulfill our mission, we need guidance from high intelligence.

"All of those who work on the other side—from the highest level of intelligence down to those who are assigned to help us individually—to tutor us—are all spiritual beings, in a spiritual dimension. They don't have physical senses.

"Since they don't have physical senses, they cannot detect directly what is taking place in the physical dimension, where we live.

"I believe that we were created to function in a physical dimension, to send them information about this dimension, and to carry out the work they want done.

"It is like the astronauts who are sent to the moon, or maybe to Mars before long. The astronauts have certain assignments. They know that they are supposed to collect samples.

"The reason the scientists need samples is because their knowledge of the moon is limited. So the astronauts call back to headquarters and say, We found three different kinds of rocks. We will describe them to you and you tell us what you want us to bring back, how many samples of each.

"The astronauts have been trained to fly to the moon and land successfully, and to gather samples, but they do not know the details of what the scientists need or what they will do with the samples. So it is up to the scientists back at NASA headquarters to tell them.

"The scientists are not going to get samples unless the astronauts bring them. If the astronauts ignore their mission and decide to do what they please, the scientists will not get the samples they need. And if the astronauts are not able to get information from the scientists about what to collect, their mission might be only partially successful, or not at all.

"The scientists back at NASA headquarters cannot see what the astronauts see, because the scientists are not in that environment. The astronauts are.

Getting the guidance we need

"This parallels our situation.

"We are in a physical environment. We report back to high intelligence, to headquarters.

"Headquarters then determines what they need, and lets us carry it out, just like the scientists at NASA headquarters determine what they need in order to conduct their research, and then convey the information to the astronauts on the moon so that the astronauts can carry out the instructions and complete their mission successfully.

"It is up to the astronauts to determine how to move around, where to go to avoid obstacles and move towards their goal. The scientists are too far away to tell them every detail, like stepping around this boulder and picking up that rock.

How to best do our job

"In the same way, the details of how to carry out our assignment are up to us. It is our choice whether to accept our assignment or not, and how to carry it out.

"The better you are at detecting information psychically with your mental senses, as well as detecting information physically with your physical senses, and then analyzing at the alpha level, the greater your chances of achieving complete success.

"It takes a cooperative effort to have a successful mission. If the astronauts just go up there and do nothing but hit golf balls, and do not bring back the samples that the scientists at headquarters need, the mission will be a failure. They can have a little fun hitting a couple of balls, as long as they carry out the mission that has been assigned to them.

"If the astronauts do not receive the proper instructions and guidance from the scientists at headquarters, and if they are not given all of the tools and training that they need to do the job that's been assigned to them, the mission will be a failure.

"So the scientists and engineers at headquarters provide the spacecraft and the appropriate tools for this particular mission, and they train the astronauts so that they have the knowledge and skills that are required, and then they send them into space, into another environment, fully equipped to succeed at the mission that the scientists have established for them.

"If the astronauts try to change their mission's objectives, their mission will be a failure.

"If they do not maintain communication to get the guidance they need, their mission will fail.

"If they do not use their own judgment—as the people who are actually on the scene—to overcome obstacles, their mission will fail.

"They have free will to do what is necessary to complete their mission successfully, based on the guidance from headquarters.

"They also have the free will to disregard the instructions and fail if they so choose.

You are fully equipped for success

"We have been equipped with bodies suitable for the physical dimension and have been sent here to accomplish certain objectives.

"I believe that each one of us has been given all of the tools, talent, and training that we need to accomplish the mission we were sent here to do.

"People who select their own goals, and then fail, disregard the mission that was given to them. If they had used their given abilities for the mission that was assigned to them, they would have succeeded.

"Some people say that we have been given everything we need to succeed at anything we want to do. My research indicates otherwise: that we have been given everything we need to succeed at the mission that has been assigned to us, the mission that we were sent here to do."

Communication with high intelligence

Now let's take a look at the practical side of things, the specific ways that we can establish and maintain contact with "headquarters" in the spiritual dimension.

The Mental Video Technique is an outstanding way to send reports of what you are doing and what you intend to do back to headquarters in the spiritual dimension.

Another system is required for receiving information back from them. Let's talk about that for a moment.

The second best way to receive guidance from high intelligence is through thoughts—dreams, inspiration, and ideas you get while at alpha, and so forth.

The problem is that sometimes we want things so badly that we think that our own thoughts—our own fantasies—are actually messages from God.

And sometimes we just plain misunderstand the ideas and instructions that are sent to us mentally.

The more practice you have detecting information psychically and analyzing information at the alpha level, the better you will be at interpreting correctly.

Praying for help

There is a story about the time that it rained so much that a river overflowed its banks. To make sure that everyone knew there was danger and they should evacuate, the sheriff's department sent a deputy around to warn residents.

When they got to Farmer Brown's house, he told the deputy that he had faith in the Lord, and that he would pray and would be okay.

The deputy did not have time to stay and argue, for there were many other people who needed to be warned.

Sure enough, the waters rose, and soon Farmer Brown had fled to the second floor of his house. He looked out the window and saw a boat from the Marine Patrol. The officer called to him to get into the boat, but Farmer Brown, his strong faith undaunted, declined the offer, syaing, "I'll trust in God to take care of me."

When the waters had risen so high that Farmer Brown had been forced to climb to the very top of his roof, he heard a loud clattering and looked up to see a helicopter from the Air National Guard. "Grab the rope" they yelled down, "and we'll lift you to safety."

Again Farmer Brown declined the offer.

A little while later, as Farmer Brown appeared at the gates of Heaven, St. Peter greeted him. "You have been such a devoted and faithful servant," St. Peter said, "would you like to meet the Lord?"

After he was ushered in, God asked Farmer Brown if he had any questions.

"Well, I do have one," Farmer Brown answered. "I always believed that you would protect me and take care of me. Why did you let me drown, instead of keeping me safe?"

"What do you mean?" God answered. "I sent a car to get you out. When I checked back and saw that you were still there, I sent the Marine Patrol by with a boat. When I saw that you had missed the boat, I even arranged for a helicopter to come get you and take you to safety!"

Recognize help when it comes

If Farmer Brown had known how to use the alpha level to analyze the situation, he might have figured out what was happening. Good intuition—the ability to detect information—certainly would have been valuable to him.

High intelligence is spiritual, in a spiritual dimension. Spiritual beings do not have vocal cords to talk to us. They communicate with us through mental projection and through coincidence.

In order to insure that you do not confuse your own fantasies and desires with the guidance and instructions from your tutors in the spiritual dimension, you need to have a way to test the information and verify it.

How do you verify it? How do you determine that it was mental projection from your tutors and not your own fantasies?

By acting on the information and ideas and observing the results.

If you pray for help, and help arrives, take it! Farmer Brown would have been much better off if he had understood this.

Action speaks louder than words

It is always better to evaluate people by what they do, not what they say.

We live in a physical world; tangible results are what count.

Jose adopted this philosophy in his studies and research. He read so many books that made so many claims—often conflicting—that he had to develop a system to evaluate the ideas and information from those authors.

To test the value of the ideas in the books, he put them into action by trying them out. If they corrected problems, he considered them to be real.

He said it this way: "The truthful truth, and the real reality, is that which—when applied—corrects problems."

The same thing works for evaluating the guidance you think you are getting from high intelligence.

Try it out. Use it. Apply it. And then notice what happens within the next two or three days. If, after you act on the information, something positive happens—something that moves you toward your goals—this is an indication that you could be on the right track.

If, on the other hand, you encounter new obstacles after you apply the information you receive, this is an indication that you could be headed in the wrong direction.

A formula for evaluating ideas

Jose explained it this way:

"As you work on your project, you will usually encounter obstacles. Notice how long it takes you to overcome the first obstacle. Then when you encounter a second obstacle, notice how long it takes you to overcome this second obstacle.

"If it takes twice as long to overcome the second obstacle as it did the first, then this might indicate that you are moving in the wrong direction. But we are not yet sure. We do not want to give up too soon.

"So you continue. When you encounter a third obstacle, notice how long it takes to overcome the third obstacle.

"If it takes twice as long to overcome the third obstacle as it did to overcome the second, and it took twice as long to overcome the second obstacle as it did the first, then you can be pretty sure that you are going in the wrong direction.

"However, if it only takes half as long to overcome the second obstacle as it did to overcome the first, and just half as long to overcome the third as it took for the second, then you can be pretty confident that you are moving in the correct direction. Keep going, full speed ahead.

"Remember, we do not batter down doors. If a door doesn't open for you, and you have made a good effort to open it, then back up and take another look. There might be another door that will open right up for you. That is the door to take."

And as former Silva instructor Marie Burleson pointed out, "When you stop struggling and back up to survey the situation, you might find that the door you were pushing on actually opens toward you!"

A wrong interpretation is corrected

After Jose had been conducting research for about a decade, he began to feel that maybe he had done enough, that it was time to bring his research to an end.

There were several reasons he felt this way:

1. He had used hypnosis to learn more about how the brain and mind work in order to help his children make better grades.

2. His research had even helped him to develop specific techniques to correct additional problems. What more could he need?
3. He had been neglecting his radio- and television-repair business. He was spending his own money on his research instead of on his family.
4. He was traveling quite a bit and was spending a lot of time away from his family and his business.
5. And, one of the most troubling things to him personally, he was receiving a lot of criticism. Friends thought he was a witch doctor because of his holistic faith-healing research; he was an excellent holistic faith-healer. Even his church was critical because they didn't know what he was delving into and they feared for his "soul."

So one rainy Saturday morning, it all came to a head. He decided to end his research. He put his psychology books into boxes and climbed up to the attic to store them away. Jose recalled the story this way:

A decision to quit

"I had written to Dr. J.B. Rhine to tell him that I had trained my daughter Isabel to be a psychic. But Dr. Rhine, a leading parapsychology researcher, wrote and told me that ESP could not be taught, and that my daughter was probably a 'natural' psychic. He pointed out that I had not 'pretested' her to make sure she was not already a psychic.

"I figured the number-one man in parapsychology was saying it so it must be right. But the thought of starting all over again with a new subject that I must pretest first was just too much for me. It had taken three years to get where I was, and that turned out to be a big zero, according to Dr. Rhine.

"It was with these bleak thoughts on a dismal, cloudy Saturday morning that I decided to quit this nonsense. So I put my books in the attic and sat on the sofa in my living room, thinking.

"My mind reached back into the memories, the feelings associated with the research I had done to that point, the research that now had come to a dead end."

Although Jose was disappointed, he had learned to pay attention to the "coincidences" that high intelligence sends to us to let us know how to proceed.

Although he didn't realize it, he was about to be told that he had misinterpreted the situation.

An unexpected messenger

"Suddenly Ricardo, my second son, who was almost ten years old, came bursting through the front door and interrupted my thoughts.

"It had been raining and was still drizzling outside. Ricardo was soaked, but the roll of heavy paper he dropped on the table was dry!

"When I unrolled that paper, I got the surprise of my life:

"Christ was staring at me!

"It was a picture of Christ's face, as large as life, looking at me with dark piercing eyes, not judging, but full of love and compassion and I felt as though He was asking, 'Why did you stop studying? Did I not tell you to study psychology?'

"Tears came to my eyes and a feeling as though I had been a bad boy for not obeying.

"I swore then that I would continue with this work, and not ever again stop for the rest of my life, even if it meant giving up on my very successful electronics business."

Many coincidences

It was a prior "coincidence" that triggered so much emotion in Jose. The first time he ever encountered the field of psychology was when he was interviewed by two psychiatrists when he was inducted into the army in 1944. During that same induction process, he was given a picture of Christ, something familiar to him in that strange environment farther from his home than he had ever been before. As a result, he always associated his study of psychology with Christ.

True to his word, he never stopped his research after getting that message via the picture of Christ. The picture still hangs inside the entrance to Silva International Headquarters in Laredo, Texas, along with a photograph of Jose looking at the original, a full-length painting of Jesus with a child standing by His side, painted by Carl Heinrich Bloch and now hanging in a church in Denmark.

Let's review and see just what happened: Jose has always had a strong connection with high intelligence, as evidenced by his success his entire life. Relaxing on the sofa on a Saturday morning while a gentle rain fell outside is a perfect prescription for this natural alpha thinker to be at alpha, a condition where communication with high intelligence is very easy.

Evidently, his tutor observed that Jose had interpreted the criticism of him and his work as a sign to end his research.

But, as Jose came to understand later, much more formidable criticism lay ahead from skeptical scientists that he would have to contend with if he hoped to have his work accepted. The criticism of his nonscientific friends and neighbors strengthened him, and it showed him how to deal with resistance and opposition.

So how did high intelligence get this message to Jose?

By using a symbol that Jose could understand.

They got Jose's attention through the strange circumstances surrounding the picture—the papers were dry.

And what did Jesus represent to Jose? Someone who endured criticism and suffering in order to help humanity.

Jose got the message. His emotions were so overwhelming that he went into the bathroom, locked the door, and had a good cry.

Here's how to proceed

The Mental Video Technique is the first technique that uses the delta brain wave level. Until now, nobody knew how to use the delta level, since the only way that most people can get to the delta level is in the deepest part of their sleep cycle.

Here are the steps for guidance from high intelligence:

1. Follow the instructions for creating the Mental Videos at beta and at alpha.
2. When you go to sleep at night, use the technique to deliver your Mental Videos to your tutor in order to give a full report to high intelligence while you are in delta sleep.
3. Let "coincidence" and the results of your efforts guide you to correct problems and reach your goals.

Specific examples

If you have not yet found your purpose in life, your first step is to analyze and find out what your tendencies are.

What made you happy when you were young? What were your dreams? Why were they important to you?

What has brought you the most satisfaction in your life? What do you seem to be good at? What do your friends think you are good at? What do they think you are well suited for?

Questions like these can help you find a starting point.

Then, use the Mental Video Technique, and get into action.

Start working towards what you think your purpose in life might be. Notice how it goes: Do you encounter many obstacles, and each one takes longer to overcome than the previous one? You might be on the wrong path. Try again.

If each obstacle seems less difficult to overcome than the previous one, and if coincidences are making it easy for you to move toward your goals, you are probably on the right path. Keep going!

Whenever you need to make decisions, use your level—the alpha level—to help you make the best decision you can. Deliver your Mental Video while in delta sleep, and the next day notice the results of your action. This will let you know whether you actually made the correct decision or not.

As long as you continue to give reports to the director back at headquarters in the spiritual dimension, the director will arrange things to either help you or to redirect your efforts, whichever helps to accomplish what needs to be accomplished to conform to the plan of high intelligence for this physical dimension.

Remember, you are the eyes and ears for high intelligence. They need your reports, so be sure to report in every night.

Then, whenever you try something and it works, keep doing it. If it doesn't work, do something else. Don't give up too easily—make a good effort. Just remember that we do not batter down doors. We do whatever is the best, most efficient way to reach our goals. Or if we keep getting blocked, we change our goals.

It is such a simple system that it is easy to ignore it. Give regular reports. Then do what works, and avoid what doesn't work.

Mental Video Technique

Whenever you need to solve a problem with the Mental Video Technique, proceed as follows:

1. At beta, the outer-conscious level, analyze your problem. Make a good study of the problem. Imagine that you have a video camera

and that you are making a video recording of the problem. Make sure that your video explains the details of the problem.

2. Later, when you are in bed and ready to go to sleep, enter level one with the three-to-one method. (See page 15.)
3. Once you are at your level, review the Mental Video of the problem that you created at beta.
4. After you have reviewed the problem, mentally convert the problem into a project. Then create with imagination a Mental Video of the solution. The Mental Video of the solution should contain a step-by-step procedure of how you desire the project to be resolved, what you expect to happen.
5. After both of the Mental Videos have been completed, go to sleep with the intention of delivering the Mental Videos to your tutor while you sleep. Take for granted that delivery will be made.
6. During the next three days, look for indications that point to the solution. Every time you think of the project, think of the solution that you have created in the Mental Video in a past-tense sense.

Your videos should include everything that has life. We can only influence life. And we definitely *can* influence life: humans, animals, plants, and so forth. Researcher Cleve Backster has demonstrated that plants—and even your own white blood cells—can perceive our thoughts and emotions, even at great distances. You can read about this research in Chapter 9.

In your second video, include all of the people who will benefit. The more people who will benefit, the more help you will get from the other side. At least two or more people should benefit. The solution should improve conditions on planet earth.

The following laws are to be considered when programming:

1. Do to others *only* what you like others to do to you.
2. The solution must be within the possibility area.
3. The solution must help to make this planet a better place to live.
4. The solution must be the best for everybody concerned.
5. The solution must help at least two or more persons.

When you use the Mental Video Technique, do it with the expectation that while you are in delta sleep, the videos will be delivered into the proper hands—the correct intelligence, your tutor—on the other side, to help in the preparation of the solution.

The more that your tutors in the spiritual dimension know about conditions and what is being done to improve them, the better able they will be to arrange things so that we get the help that we need. That is why it is important that as many people as possible are using the Mental Video Technique every night.

Remember, after you review your Mental Videos, remain at alpha and go to sleep from there, with the intention of delivering them to the other side while you are in delta sleep.

Using delta purposefully

Why is this done at the delta level?

We have observed that delta is like a doorway to the other side. The first brain frequencies ever detected in the fetus are the slow delta frequencies. After birth, the child first develops the delta dimension, then theta, alpha, and beta by the time the person is fully mature.

When a person dies a natural death, the last frequencies detected are the delta frequencies. This "delta doorway" seems to bring us from another dimension into the physical dimension and then take us back to the spiritual dimension again.

The only way that most people can get to delta is by natural sleep. If you take sleeping pills, the pills interfere with your normal sleep rhythms, and often keep you out of delta.

Drugs always have side effects. It is much better to attend the Silva Method Basic Lecture Series and learn to use the Sleep Control Technique to get to sleep without drugs.

Many projects

You can the Mental Video Technique for several projects.

As always, let your results guide you as to how to proceed.

When you first begin, do just one project at a time. After this becomes successful for you, then you can try two projects at a time. You can continue adding projects as you feel necessary, always observing the results.

If your success rate declines, then go back to including fewer projects in your Mental Videos. If your success rate remains high, then continue on.

As always, do what works, and avoid what doesn't work.

One more set of countdowns

For the next 10 days, practice counting down from 10 to one each morning when you wake up.

Remember to practice the Long Relaxation Exercise from time to time.

After you have completed this set of countdowns over the next 10 days, you are ready to use the three-to-one method to enter your level.

When you desire to enter your level, find a comfortable position, close your eyes, take a deep breath, and while exhaling, mentally repeat and visualize the number three, three times. You have been associating the number three with physical relaxation, so this will help you to relax your body.

Take another deep breath, and while exhaling, mentally repeat and visualize the number two, three times. This will help you relax your mind.

Take another deep breath, and while exhaling, mentally repeat and visualize the number one, three times, and take it for granted that you are at the alpha level, a deeper level of mind that you can use for a purpose, any purpose you desire.

You can deepen this level by doing countdown deepening exercises, and also by relaxing your body. Maintain minimum mental activity in order to keep your brain frequency lowered to the alpha level.

As you continue to practice, over time you can learn to enter the alpha level by simply recalling your "points of reference," the special feeling of being at alpha. It is like an emotional or a mental feeling.

You can even learn to be in alpha with your eyes open, so long as you do not focus them on anything, but remain in a sort of "daydreaming" state. Any time you attempt to focus your eyes, your brain will adjust to beta. You can use all of your other senses at alpha, but not the sense of eyesight.

As always, your results will let you know how you are doing. If your results are not as good when you do not use the three-to-one method, then go back to using the three-to-one method. If your results are just as good when you have your eyes open and defocused, then by all means leave your eyes open and defocused whenever you need to function this way.

Whole-brain functioning

Eventually this will all become second nature to you. Your brain dips into the alpha level approximately 30 times every minute. Once you have learned to function at alpha with conscious awareness by practicing as Jose has directed you to, then those brief excursions into alpha will become very valuable to you.

Remember the way Jose was sitting on the sofa that rainy Saturday morning, reflecting on his decision to end his research, and his son Ricardo came running in with some rolled-up papers?

What was really going on?

Jose always had a strong connection with the other side, with his tutors. That is obvious from the high degree of success that he achieved. So sitting there, relaxed, the gentle sound of the falling rain, he was surely producing a lot of alpha.

And his tutors sensed what was going on. He had made an incorrect decision, so they quickly sent him a message. As a result, he resumed his research and never stopped again. Otherwise, we would not have the Silva UltraMind System today.

A characteristic of success

This is typical of the way that successful people function. They seldom realize that they are doing anything different from the average person. As Napoleon Hill found, most of them prefer to take the credit themselves.

If you pay attention to the stories, you can see what is really happening.

Rock-and-roll singer Jerry Lee Lewis is a good example. He was lamenting one time that guitar-players have an advantage over piano-players because they can move around, get in front of different members of the audience, and get them involved in the performance, while a piano-player is stuck in one spot.

One of the guitar-players asked him, "Do you have to play the piano sitting down?"

"I can play it standing on my head!" Lewis answered. The guitar-player suggested he try playing part of the performace standing up.

An "accident" pays big dividends

So that night, when he got to an appropriate place in the song, Lewis stood up and tried to slide the piano bench back with his foot, but the bench fell over.

When it did, the audience reacted.

Lewis had been seeking a way to get the audience more involved, and he realized that the "accident" had done just that.

So the next time, he deliberately kicked the bench over. Hard.

The audience loved it.

Today, Jerry Lee Lewis not only kicks the bench around, but he climbs on top of the piano and does come pretty close to paying it while standing on his head as he reaches down to the keyboard. He swings the microphone stand around and delivers an exciting, dynamic performance that audiences have loved for three decades.

Was it an accident that the bench tipped over? Or did he receive help from what Napoleon Hill called "unseen guides"?

Mind guides brain, brain guides body

Perhaps this is the way that his tutors were able to help him:

Jerry Lee Lewis came from a religious family and is a highly creative person himself. Creative people are spiritual people—they have strong connections to the spiritual dimension, especially when performing.

So perhaps he was so well-connected to the spiritual dimension that his tutors were able to alter his actions slightly when he tried to push the piano bench back.

Here's how it could happen:

Whenever you have a thought, that thought causes a reaction in your brain. That reaction can travel down neural pathways and cause certain muscles to contract or relax.

According to Dr. J.W. Hahn, the first scientist to support Jose and his research, this is called an ideomotor response—an idea-motor response. An idea causes a reaction in the brain, which causes a reaction in the sensory-motor nervous system, which causes muscles to respond.

Dr. Hahn should know: For many years he was director of the Mind Science Foundation, the country's leading parapsychology research organization.

The "secret" of paranormal devices

Dowsing rods work on the ideomotor response. So do pendulums, ouija boards, and most other "paranormal" devices.

It is actually the dowser's mind that detects the presence of water through mental projection. Then the mind causes a reaction in the brain, which sends a tiny signal to the muscles, and as a result, the dowsing rods—which are very difficult to keep straight anyway—move.

It is the ultimate biofeedback. It is a way to use your body to show you that your mind has detected something.

It is the person's mind that detects information through mental projection and then, through the mechanism we have mentioned, causes the pendulum to swing a certain way, or causes you to move towards a certain part of the ouija board. It all begins with mental projection.

So could it be that Jerry Lee Lewis was sent a message from his tutors, which caused his mind to guide his brain to send the signals that caused him to topple the piano bench and begin the process that launched him into superstar status so that he could showcase his magnificent talent?

Practice makes perfect—a perfect world

First you have to practice. You have to do it because you want to do it. Count yourself into your level and use the techniques. Use them as much as possible.

It will become second nature for you to use the Mental Video Technique every night, think about it during the day, and notice the coincidences that come your way. Act on them and evaluate the results. Once this has become a normal part of your life, you may find that you are getting more and more guidance even without going through the complete ritual.

This is the way that it should be. We should all be able to take a deep breath and relax when we are faced with an important decision, and then make the correct choice with a little help from our tutors in the spiritual dimension.

Can you imagine what the future will be like when everyone is doing this?

Encourage all of your friends to learn to do this, and do it yourself at every opportunity.

It can really help to make the world a wonderful place to live.

It can make Jose's dream come true: to convert the planet into a paradise.

SECTION II: EXPAND YOUR CAPABILITIES

What is the Silva program all about? No one is more qualified to answer that question than Nelda Sheets. Nelda was a student in Jose Silva's first commercial class in Amarillo, Texas, in 1966, and she was the first person besides Jose Silva to start teaching the course.

So 13 years ago when her grandson asked her to explain to him what Silva was all about, she was ready. "I explained that it was a method for learning how to use more of your mind, how to learn to focus for what you want," she recalled.

"After my 45-minute explanation, he said, 'Oh, I get it, Mimi: The Silva System is learning to talk to your brain to get what you want.'

"He said in one statement what I took 45 minutes explaining to him. And I remember thinking to myself, *I knew he was a genius!*"

The chapters in this section will teach *you* how to talk to *your* brain so that you will know how to get rid of impediments to your success, and be better able to carry out your life's mission.

As a reader of this book, you are very fortunate. The techniques in most success books work well for the authors of the books, but they work for only a few of the readers. That's because the authors are natural alpha thinkers but don't realize that most people cannot do their thinking at the alpha level. Only the natural alpha thinkers are able to use the techniques in *those* books successfully, and the authors point to them with pride, ignoring the 90 percent of their readers who gain little or no benefits from the books.

And you are doubly fortunate—because you have access to something that most other "success books" cannot offer: Silva instructors around the world ready to help you learn to function at alpha level and use the techniques in this book.

Chapter 5
Practicing

Now that you have completed your 40 days of countdowns to learn to enter the alpha level—or have completed a Silva seminar or home-study course—you are ready to use the alpha level to correct problems and achieve your goals.

In addition to learning to enter the alpha level, it is important to maintain that level. That means practice. Here is how we recommend that you practice.

How to establish a good foundation

Use the three-to-one method to enter your level.

Remain at your level for at least five minutes. Ten minutes is better, and 15 minutes is excellent.

What do you do during that time? You can practice deepening exercises, such as countdowns from 25 to one, 50 to one, or 100 to one. You can practice relaxing. You can project yourself mentally to your ideal place of relaxation, a place where you have been before and have been physically passive and relaxed. You want to bring back into your mind a very vivid memory of a time when you were passive and relaxed. This will trigger a "conditioned response"—that is, your brain will try to recreate in your body the conditions that existed at that time. This means that your body will relax.

You can also review the projects you are working on, imagine succeeding at them, and recall how you will feel when you do.

The best time to practice is in the morning when you wake up. Your brain is just coming out of alpha, so it will be easy to go back there. Since it is morning and time to get up, you will not be as likely to fall asleep as you will be at bedtime.

The second best time is at bedtime. Your brain is ready to go to alpha when you go to sleep, so it will be easy to get there.

The third best time is just after lunch. It is natural to feel relaxed and a little drowsy after eating. When you relax after a meal, it is easier for your body to digest food. It is also easy to enter alpha.

Be sure that you stay awake during the time you spend at alpha. If you fall asleep, you do not get the benefits of alpha-functioning. This may take some practice. Do whatever is necessary to learn to remain awake while at alpha. Make yourself less comfortable. Raise your hand; holding your arm up will help to keep you awake. If it starts to fall, you will become alert again.

At the same time, you do not want to become too active mentally. That could bring you out of your level. So from time to time, check yourself out and make sure that you are still physically and mentally relaxed. To be sure, use a deepening exercise: Count down from 10 to one, or relax your eyelids and let the feeling of relaxation flow slowly down throughout your body all the way down to your toes, or visualize tranquil and passive scenes.

Once you feel relaxed and comfortable, continue with your programming.

As you continue to practice and continue to notice your results, you will become very proficient at doing this and confident in your ability to know when you are at your level.

Advice from a natural alpha-thinker

While working on this book, we came across a book by a natural alpha-thinker who had a special gift when it came to explaining what he did. Anyone who can function at the alpha level can benefit from his writings. The author is Robert Collier, and many of his books are still available from his family.

We found a paragraph in Collier's book *Riches Within Your Reach: The Law of the Higher Potential,* published in 1947, just three years before his death, that answers a question that many Silva grads have asked over the years: "Why is it when I have a really strong desire for something, and I really *need* it, and it will benefit many people, and I program *really hard* for it, I still don't get results? I get great résults on little things that are not so important; why not this?"

Collier's guidance also expresses one of the main principles that Jose Silva incorporated into the UltraMind System: We do all that we can to fulfill the plan that higher intelligence has for us.

Here is the way Robert Collier said it:

"Look at the first chapter of the Scriptures. When God wanted light, did He strive and struggle, trying to make light? No, He said— '*Let* there be light.'

"When you want something very much, instead of trying to make it come your way, suppose you try asking for it and then *letting* it come. Suppose you just relax, and *let* God work through you instead of trying to *make* Him do something for you. Suppose you say to yourself—'I will do whatever is given me to do. I will follow every lead to the best of my ability, but for the rest, it is all up to the God in me. God in me knows what my right work is, where it is, and just what I should do to get it. I put myself and my affairs lovingly in His hands, secure that whatever is for my highest good, He will bring to me.'"

Jose Silva said we were sent here for a purpose, with a job to do. If we fulfill that purpose, then we will be happy, fulfilled, and prosperous. Now you know how to program to fulfill your mission successfully.

CHAPTER 6
GET YOUR BRAIN TO DO WHAT YOU WANT

At your level you can correct virtually anything, as long as it is within the possibility area. What do we mean by "within the possibility area"? We do not yet have the formulas for certain things, such as growing a new flesh-and-blood arm or leg if one is missing. However, if the arm or leg is still there but is damaged, then it is well within the possibility area to correct the damage.

The steps in using your level to correct problems are:

1. Recognize the problem. Many writers simply tell you to think about what you want. Jose Silva realized that you need two points of reference in order to establish a direction of travel: the starting point and the destination. So the first step is to recognize the problem. I have a headache. I feel insecure. I am drowsy and sleepy. I lose my temper too easily. I crave fattening foods. Whatever your problem, identify it.

2. Replace the problem with a positive thought. What do you want instead of the problem? I want to be wide awake, feeling fine, and in perfect health. I want to be confident. I want to control my temper. I want to consume foods that are healthy and beneficial for me.

3. Make a plan. Use some kind of a mechanism to move you from the problem to the solution. In a moment I am going to count from one to five. Whenever I bring together the tips of the thumb and first two fingers of either hand. Whenever I blink my eyes.

4. Work your plan. Count yourself out of your level. Bring together the tips of the first two fingers and thumb of either hand. Blink.

5. Claim your rewards. Take it for granted that you have *already* achieved what you have programmed for. Even if it hasn't happened yet, pretend that it has. Fake it 'til you make it.

Following are some of the formulas that Jose Silva developed.

Relieving tension and migraines

Enter your level and at level one, mentally tell yourself, "I have a headache. I feel a headache. I don't want to have a headache. I don't want to feel a headache.

"I am going to count from one to five, and at the count of five, I will open my eyes, be wide awake, feeling fine and in perfect health. I will then have no headache. I will then feel no headache."

You will then count slowly from one to two, then to three. At the count of three remind yourself mentally that, "At the count of five, I will open my eyes and be wide awake, feeling fine, and in perfect health. I will then have no discomfort in my head. I will then feel no discomfort in my head."

Notice that we have made a change at level three, from ache to discomfort. We left the ache behind.

Then count slowly to four, then to five, and at the count of five, and with your eyes open, say to yourself, "I am wide awake, feeling fine, and in perfect health. I have no discomfort in my head. I feel no discomfort in my head. And this is so."

You replace the headache with no headache. What would a "no headache" feel like? That's what you expect.

If you apply this formula, open your eyes, and check to see if the headache is there or not, what are you likely to find? The headache! Instead, open your eyes expecting to feel "no headache." Tell yourself there is "no headache" in your head. Even if you think you still feel a headache, tell yourself you don't. It will go away.

For migraines, apply the same formula three times, five minutes apart. The first application will reduce the discomfort by a certain amount. Wait five minutes and apply the second application. This will take care of a greater amount of the discomfort. Wait five minutes and apply the third application, and the rest of the discomfort will disappear.

When you enter your level yourself, and apply the program yourself, then your brain will do whatever is necessary to correct the cause of the problem. This will bring the problem to an end, without any substitute symptoms. You will no longer experience the tension that was causing the headaches.

Headache technique put to the test

Linda L. Folk of St. Albans, West Virginia, wrote to tell us of her experiences with migraines:

"I had had migraines for more than 16 years when my mother put me through the Silva Method.

"I was going to the doctor at least once a month. He tried various medications, some of which were very powerful, but he was unsuccessful in finding relief for my migraines.

"There were times when the migraines were so intense that I could only stand in a corner leaning against the wall praying for them to go away. Lying down or sitting only intensified the pain.

"Sometimes, after leaning in the corner for hours, I would collapse from exhaustion. It would be several days after the attack before I was back up to my full strength.

"After learning the Silva Method, it took me several months to gain complete control over the migraines. Using the Silva Method, I was able to shorten and ease them immediately.

"Meanwhile, my mother could stop them using her programming skills. If I had to leave a message on her answering machine asking for her help, I knew when she had returned and was at level because my migraine would leave.

"The answer finally came at level during a migraine: I was focusing on the pain and not 'feeling fine.' When I changed the focus to 'I feel fine. Let it go,' that migraine stopped.

"After that, when I felt a migraine coming on, I simply went to level, went to my ideal place of relaxation, and said, 'I feel fine. Let it go,' and the migraine could no longer come into being.

"Needless to say, I have been migraine-free for several years now.

"As an added bonus, the money saved in doctors' bills and medicines quickly paid my husband's way through the Silva course.

"Those who have never experienced a migraine cannot fully appreciate the excruciating agony that accompanies an occurrence and, consequently, these individuals may not consider migraine mastery a truly notable victory.

"As a former sufferer, however, I can state unquestionably that developing the ability to prevent such torment from entering my reality has emphasized the basic principle of the Silva Method by making my life better and better.

"I welcome the opportunity to discuss my technique and success with anyone who may be interested, realizing that by helping others I am also helping myself."

Editor's note: You may contact Linda through Silva instructor Rebekah Hickman via the Silva organization. See Appendix A for the address.

Establishing a trigger mechanism

You can use the Three Fingers Technique as a trigger mechanism. Bring together the tips of the thumb and first two fingers of either hand. When you bring the tips together, your thumb and fingers will form a circle. Not the flat part, where your "fingerprints" are—let the tip of your thumb touch the tips of your first two fingers. That way, energy will recirculate rather than being lost out of the ends of your fingers.

If you need to remember what somebody says, such as a lecture from a professor, you can use the Three Fingers Technique to help you.

Enter your level and tell yourself mentally that you are going to listen to a lecture, and mention the title and subject of the lecture and the lecturer's name. Tell yourself that you are going to use the Three Fingers Technique. Tell yourself that noises will not distract you but will help you to concentrate. Tell yourself you will have superior concentration and understanding.

Count yourself out of your level and use your Three Fingers Technique while listening to the lecture.

Be sure to pay attention and listen to what the lecturer says. Make mental pictures—mental movies—of the things the lecturer covers.

When you need this information, you can use the Three Fingers Technique to help you recall it. You will remember it as well as you did immediately after the lecture. The information that you have impressed on your brain will also make it easier to use your intuition to detect information psychically when necessary (see Chapter 7).

Find information when you need it

Have you ever had a problem and you know there is a great solution, but you cannot quite figure out what it is? Most of us have experienced that.

Jose Silva always maintained that there is no such thing as a problem without a solution; there are just problems for which we do not have enough information to know what the solution is.

> ➤ Your doctor has given you options, and you are not quite sure which one to take.

> ➤ You are having a problem dealing with another person and you are not yet clear on what has upset him or her so much.

> ➤ You have two wonderful business opportunities and haven't been able to decide which one to pursue.

And to top it all off, you just don't have enough time during the day to investigate as much as you would like to, to gather more information, and analyze it thoroughly so that you can be sure you are making the correct decision.

Why not put your mind to work on the problem, at night, while your body is getting the sleep that it needs?

Your mind doesn't need to sleep. It can seek out the information, wherever it is, and bring it to you. You might get the information in a dream, or in a flash of insight during the day, or by way of a coincidence that helps you make the correct choice. Your mind can detect information stored in your own brain, and can also detect information stored in other people's brains. It can also bring you information from higher intelligence.

Have you ever had a dream that contained information that helped you correct a problem? Many people have. Or a precognitive dream—that is, you dreamed about something and then the next day, or a few days later, it happened? Most people report that one of those two things has happened to them.

Dreams are a very natural part of our lives, so it is easy to learn to program to have a dream that will contain information that you can use to solve a problem.

First, you must learn to recall your dreams. Program yourself at your level, when you are in bed and ready to go to sleep, that, "I want to remember a dream, and I am going to remember a dream." Then go to sleep from your level. Have paper and pencil ready to write down your dream. Prove you are serious by having the paper and pencil ready and by writing down your dream. In the morning, enter your level and review what you wrote down. This will help you to recall more of the dream.

Keep a dream log, or dream diary, and eventually you will begin to understand what your dreams mean to you. Analyze them at the alpha level, since that is where you had them.

After you have achieved the first step and are remembering a dream every night, then proceed to the next step: Program yourself, at your level just before going to sleep, that, "I want to remember my dreams, and I am going to remember my dreams." Continue to write them down as soon as you awaken with a dream, and then analyze them at your level when you wake up in the morning.

After that, you can program yourself that, "I want to have a dream that will contain information to solve the problem I have in mind." State the problem, and add, "I will have such a dream, remember it, and understand it."

In Chapter 8, you can read how a medical doctor uses information from dreams to help his patients, and in Chapter 19, you can read about a multimillion-dollar idea that came in a dream.

Another technique that works great is the Glass of Water Technique. Do not use it on the same night that you are using Dream Control; choose one or the other.

At bedtime, fill a water glass with water. While drinking approximately half of the water, turn your eyes slightly upwards and mentally tell yourself, "This is all I need to do to find the solution to the problem I have in mind."

Then put away the remaining half glass of water, go to bed, and sleep.

In the morning upon wakening drink the remaining half glass of water, turning your eyes slightly upwards and mentally saying to yourself, "This is all I need to do to find the solution to the problem I have in mind."

With this programming you may awaken during the night or in the morning with a vivid recollection of a dream that contains information that you can use to solve the problem, or during the day you may have a flash of insight that contains information you can use to solve the problem.

You do not need to count yourself into level when using this technique. You will enter the alpha level automatically when you turn your eyes slightly upwards while drinking the water.

Also, you do not need to be totally passive while waiting for the answer. Sometimes you will find that during the day when you are working on the problem, you will realize how to proceed. It feels very natural sometimes; that's the way higher intelligence gets the information to you.

CHAPTER 7
PROGRAM WITH IMAGES

Before the development of alphabets and sophisticated languages of various kinds, people communicated with pictures. Those ancient cave-drawings can be understood by modern people just as easily as they could by primitive people long ago. No matter what language you speak, you can still recognize their pictures of animals, trees, rivers and streams, and even people. Those pictures often tell stories about what happened to the people of that era.

Good communicators use words to create mental images in their audience's minds. An avergae communicator, for example, might say, "It's time for young people to exercise some leadership." President John F. Kennedy, a great communicator, said, "The torch has been passed to a new generation of Americans."

Mental pictures—in the form of visualization and imagination—can be one of the most powerful tools you can use in your mental programming. Pictures are the universal language. Everybody, no matter where they live or what their background, will "get the picture." They understand. Writers spend hours trying to describe what something looks like. A picture makes it easy.

We need to send regular reports to higher intelligence to let our helpers in the spiritual dimension know what is happening in the physical dimension and what we are doing about it. Mental pictures have proven to be the best form of mental communication.

Understanding visualization and imagination

Some people have clear, vivid mental images. Many of us do just fine by thinking about what something looks like. It doesn't matter. What's important is that we think in terms of what things look like.

When you hear the phrase "the torch has been passed" what does that look like to you? What kind of torch would you imagine? If you were looking at the event, what would you see? Where is the person who is passing the torch—to your left, your right, facing you, with his or her back to you? Where is the person receiving the torch? Is it a man passing the torch or a woman? What about the person receiving the torch? An adult? A child? How is he or she dressed? Describe how you would you have them dressed if you were directing this scene in a film.

That's all that we need when we talk about mental pictures. If you can think about what something looks like, and can describe it, you are doing it correctly.

In order to help us understand this better, let's define some terms the way that we use then in the Silva programs:

- ➤ **See.** You see with your eyes.
- ➤ **Visualize.** When you recall what something looks like that you have seen before, you are visualizing. It is the memory of what something looks like. It is not the same as seeing; it is not nearly as vivid. Most people say that dreams are more vivid than visualization. You can visualize with your eyes open or closed, at beta or at alpha. Just relax and recall what something looks like.
- ➤ **Imagine.** Imagination is a creative process. When you imagine, you think about what something looks like that you have never seen or imagined before.

If you have seen someone pass a torch to another person and you recall what that looked like, that's visualization. If you do not recall something you have seen before but make up your own scene, that's imagination. Later, when you recall that scene that you created with your imagination, you are using visualization, because you are using memory to recall something you experienced previously.

Words can often help you to create better mental pictures. You might want to describe a scene to yourself to help you recall it or imagine it. For instance, think of a relative or friend that you know very well and think of what his or her face looks like. It might help you to recall what the color of the person's hair, skin, and eyes and what his or her forehead, nose, cheeks, and facial characteristics are.

If you are visualizing a project you are working on, it might help you to imagine that you are discussing the project and how to go about doing it, in order to help you create a detailed mental picture of it.

Just remember that your words are there to *support* your mental images, not to substitute for them.

Establishing a communications system

Jose Silva developed the concept of the Mental Screen to use as a communications tool. If you want to examine an existing situation to determine what the problem is, project an image of it onto your mental screen so that you can make a good study of it.

Then when you are ready to correct the problem, you project the solution image onto your mental screen.

To locate your mental screen, begin with your eyes closed, turned slightly upward from the horizontal place of sight, at an angle of approximately 20 degrees. The area that you perceive with your mind is your mental screen.

Without using your eyelids as screens, sense your mental screen to be out, away from your body.

Your eyes should be turned upwards to a comfortable position, but not so far as to be uncomfortable. Turning your eyes upwards in this manner increases the amount of alpha brain wave activity.

Using the Mental Screen is the easiest way to detect information, and it is also the easiest way to transmit information.

In the physical world, you receive information with your ears, and you transmit information with your voice. In the spiritual dimension, you receive information with visualization, and you transmit information with imagination.

The mental screen can be as large as you want it to be. It can surround you if you like, so that you can observe things from all angles. You are in control and can make it what you want it to be.

Obtaining information to solve problems

There is no such thing as a problem without a solution, Jose Silva said. There are only problems for which we don't yet have enough information to find solutions.

We teach young people how to use their minds to detect information that they need, so that when they grow up, they will be able to apply this skill to the problems they encounter in life. Part of our instruction is that we want to be proficient in both the physical and the mental dimensions–not just one. Here is how we advise students to proceed when taking a test.

First, read your test questions the way you always do, but do not stay too long on any of them. If you have a ready answer, put it down. If not, skip that question and move on to the next one.

Second, use the Three Fingers Technique, and do as in the first cycle but stay a little longer on the unanswered question. If an answer comes, put it down; if not, skip that question and move on to the next one.

Third, use the Three Fingers Technique, read the unanswered question, and if still no answer comes, close your eyes, turn them slightly upward, visualize or imagine your professor on your mental screen and ask for the answer. Then clear your mind, and start thinking again to figure out the answer. The answer that comes is your professor's. Write it down. Do not turn in a blank paper.

Here is what we mean by the instruction to "clear your mind": After you pose the question to your professor, think of another topic for a few moments. This "disconnects" you from the "transmit" mode. Then go back to the image of your professor on your mental screen, and imagine what the professor would tell you. You are now in the receiving mode.

You might have to make up the conversation yourself. This is fine. The answers that you "make up" are your professor's answers. This is what we mean by "figure out the answer."

Once students learn this procedure in school, they can then use it in all areas of their lives.

➢ If you are having problems in a personal or business relationship, then put the other person on your mental screen and ask him what he is experiencing; ask him to describe the problem from his point of view. Then clear your mind, and start thinking again to figure out the answer.

➢ If you are experiencing a business problem and don't know what decision to make, call on an expert. It might be a professor or a specialist in a certain field, such as marketing, advertising, production, or management. Ask this specialist for the answer, then clear your mind, and start thinking again to figure out the answer. The answer that comes is from the expert. Take action on it.

> ➤ If you are trying to develop an exercise program that will keep you healthy, and you are not sure of some of the elements to include, then call on an expert, someone you respect. At your level, ask your question, clear your mind, and start thinking again to figure out the answer.

Correcting problems when you know the solution

You can use the Mirror of the Mind Technique when you know the problem and also know what the solution is. If you do not know what the solution is, then you can use Dream Control Step 3 or the Glass of Water Technique to obtain information that will help you figure out the solution. You can also do some creative thinking at the alpha level. There is more information available at alpha than at beta. You can imagine asking experts for guidance, as just described.

You can also use the Mental Video Technique (seeChapter 4) to obtain guidance and direction from higher intelligence.

Here is how to use the Mirror of the Mind Technique:

Create and project a full-length mirror on your mental screen. This mirror will be known as the Mirror of the Mind.

This Mirror of the Mind can be mentally increased in size to encompass within its frame a thing or things, a person or persons, a small or a large scene.

The color of the frame of the Mirror of the Mind can be mentally changed from blue to white. The blue frame will denote the problem, or the existing situation; the white frame will denote the solution, or goal.

To solve a problem or to reach a goal, enter your level and project the image of the Mirror of the Mind with blue frame on your mental screen.

Create an image of the problem thing, person, or scene and project it on your blue-framed Mirror of the Mind, in order to make a good study of the problem.

After making a good study of the problem, erase the problem image, move the mirror to your left, change the mirror's frame to white, and create and project a solution image onto the white-framed mirror.

From then on, any time you happen to think of the project, visualize the solution image you have created, framed in white.

Some programming tips

When Jose Silva said to make a good study of the problem, he meant that we should observe the details.

When you move the mirror towards your left before creating the solution image, this takes into account the movement of time from a spiritual point of view. Research has revealed that from a spiritual point of view, the past is to your right, the present is in front of you, and the future is to your left.

The frame of the mirror can only be changed from blue to white. You never go back to the problem. Whenever you think of the problem—which we will call a *project* from now on—immediately erase it from your consciousness, and visualize the solution image you have created, framed in white.

When you program, watch for objective feedback to let you know what effect your programming is having. We recommend that you program in such a way that you would expect something to happen within the next few days.

If you notice an improvement in the project within two or three days, then you know to keep on programming the way you have been doing. If the situation gets worse in the next two or three days, then go to level and analyze what happened. You might realize that you should alter your programming.

When you are not getting positive results, then try anything that you can think of at your level to see if you can change things and start making progress. Sometimes you need to program more; sometimes you need to program less.

Sometimes the problem is what Robert Collier mentioned in Chapter 5: Sometimes we are trying so hard to *make* something happen the way we think it should happen that we block ourselves. Instead, try to *let* it happen. Release it, so that higher intelligence can do whatever is best for all concerned.

The more desire you have, the better. How many reasons do you have for wanting to achieve this goal or correct this problem? Perhaps there are five benefits that you can think of. Enter your level and think about it again; you might come up with five more benefits. Then you will have twice as much motivation.

"The bigger your project is," Jose Silva told us, "the more help you will get from higher intelligence. What I mean by bigger is how many people will benefit. If you are just programming something for yourself only, then you are on your own; you're not going to get any help. But if your programming will benefit many people, then you will get help. The more people who will benefit, the more help you will get."

The more you practice, the better. Begin by entering your level as you have learned to do, and apply the techniques exactly as Jose Silva has instructed you to.

In an emergency, do what you need to do and expect the best. That's what Hector Chacon did when he found himself losing a golf match.

In 1989 Hector Chacon attended the Silva course in hopes of finding a way to lift the basketball team he coached out of a slump. He taught his players how to enter the alpha level and program, and they won the district championship.

But the Silva techniques helped him ith his golf game.

He had only completed half of the Silva course, and when he came for the start of the second half, he asked, "Can you go to level while you are walking?"

"Why do you ask?"

"Well, I was playing golf. The first three holes, my partner and I either lost or halved. So when I got back in the golf cart I closed my eyes to go to level. But the others in the foursome all started teasing me."

"So what did you do?"

"I got out of the cart and told them to go on ahead and that I would walk. I lowered my head, tried not to focus my eyes but just sort of daydream and watch where I was going out of the corner of my eye. And I used the Mirror of the Mind to picture myself winning the next hole."

"And did you?"

"We won every hole."

"Is that normal, that you would win so many holes?"

"No, absolutely not!"

"Then it sounds like you were at your level."

"Do you think so?"

"There's one way to find out: Keep programming and see what happens."

He won so much during the next three months that his friends didn't want to continue playing with him. He recommended that if they wanted to have a chance to beat him again, they should take the course!

In the chapters that follow, you will hear from authorities in a number of fields, people who have accumulated vast experience in using the Silva techniques in their area of expertise. They will give you many ideas of ways that you can use the Silva techniques in your life. Many of their stories will inspire you and motivate you. They also offer guidance and instruction. You can begin with the topics that you are the most interested in. Later on you might develop interests in other topics and explore them at that time.

Your instructors will be waiting for you whenever you are ready for them.

SECTION III: SPECIALIZED GUIDANCE

In this section of the book, you have an unprecedented opportunity to learn from the masters in this business, people who have accumulated vast amounts of experience actually using the techniques that you have been reading about.

Teachers teach classes. These contributing authors are all authorities in their fields. There is no theoretical supposition here; they speak from their experience.

Together, the people who are sharing their experiences, knowledge, and wisdom with you have spent more than 400 years using the Silva techniques in their areas of expertise. That's an average of almost 20 years each.

You will learn some techniques and strategies, but more than that, you will experience, through these masters, the kind of future that you can expect when you use your psychic abilities to seek and use the guidance from higher intelligence that is available to you.

You do not need to read these chapters in order. Simply go to the topics that you are most interested in.

For information on how to contact these authors, please refer to Appendix A.

Chapter 8
Programmed dreams

by Prof. Clancy D. McKenzie, M.D.

Programmed dreams offer a breakthrough in medical and psychiatric diagnosis and treatment. I first learned the technique from the Silva training in September, 1969, and I have been using it ever since.

You may have heard about problems being solved or discoveries being made during sleep or during the dream-state. These are mostly sporadic events, in which people just happen to awaken with a bright idea.

The programmed dream is different. It gives us the ability to awaken with that bright idea or solution to a problem, any night, at will.

You do not have to be a yogi and meditate for 50 years in a cave to achieve enlightenment. You reach just as deep a level of consciousness when you fall asleep—but you are unaware of this state and how to use it.

Utilizing the Silva techniques, you will be able to spend one minute prior to going to bed to formulate a question, and one minute when you awaken to retrieve the answer.

There are two techniques I use, and more are taught in the Silva training program. The first is to decide to have a dream about a problem, and decide that the interpretation of the dream will reveal the answer. You must also decide to awaken at the very end of the dream, remember it, and write it down.

The second technique is to decide that the mind will work on a particular problem throughout sleep, and that when you awaken, your first thought will be the answer.

I will focus mainly on examples—so you will begin to grasp the magnitude of what programmed dreams enable us to do. Programmed dreams are very valuable and are well worth the effort to learn.

One of my hospitalized patients, for example, suddenly developed excruciating chest and abdominal pain. The internal medicine specialist thought it might be either a heart attack or a kidney infection. He suggested transferring her to a medical facility. After persuading him to wait until morning, I told the patient—who was a good dreamer—that she had better have a dream that would tell her exactly what it was, where it was, how she got it, why she got it, and exactly what to do.

She also programmed that I would be able to interpret the dream for her, and oddly enough, I immediately knew the interpretation—even though it was highly complex. It is possible that I understood because that is what she programmed.

In her dream, she and her husband were driving along a winding road where they should not have gone when it began to snow. The snow got deeper and deeper, the car veered off the road, and it was covered over with snow. Just beyond where the car went off the road, the road came to a dead end and went into another road at right angles, then into another road at right angles, and then into still another road at right angles. To me this was an anatomical roadmap of the intestinal tract, with an obstruction at the ileocecal junction. But I didn't tell her this. Instead I asked her to draw the roadmap for me. She did, and it even was in correct proportion! The winding road corresponded to the small intestine and the dead end to the cecum. The three right angles were the ascending, transverse, and descending colon.

As soon as the car was covered with snow, her husband said "I have to cut off the engine." The first thing one does for an intestinal obstruction is shut off the fuel supply, the food intake. Then eight or 10 people came from the city to dig them out. Eight or 10 in dreams represents the fingers on two hands, and I did not know if this meant laying on of hands or surgery. When they were dug out, she and her husband were all right, but their three teenage children were gone. They were the reason for the obstruction. She wanted more of her husband's attention for herself.

Intestinal obstruction is an acute surgical emergency, so I immediately transferred her to a surgical hospital. Before she left I warned her that she needed to have a dream to overcome the obstruction or she'd need surgery.

At the surgical hospital the diagnosis was confirmed, based on X-ray findings of fluid levels in the gut and blood electrolyte studies. Surgery was scheduled, and she took a nap to program another dream.

In this dream she saw a tall dark man, wearing a turban—as if from the Punjab section of northern India—and he was massaging her abdomen. When she awakened, the obstruction was gone!

To the nondream programmer, these two dreams must sound like something out of *Alice in Wonderland*. But I am only reporting data, and I draw no conclusions about the data.

I further learned that 20 years earlier a surgeon had performed an operation on this woman for intestinal obstruction. I called the surgeon and asked where in the intestinal tract was the obstruction. He answered that it was the distal portion of the ileum. The ileocecal junction is the distal-most part of the ileum.

Solving problems with programmed dreams

Programmed dreams can be used to solve any kind of problem, such as problems at work, with children, financial troubles, decisions about whether to get married and other momentous decisions, and so forth. I will stick primarily to medical examples in this brief chapter, and you can learn other applications during the Silva training.

Let me start with one of my own. One time I wrote a very strong letter to a patient who was taking too much Valium. Two nights later during sleep I became aware that she was so infuriated by my letter that she decided to not come back. Then, during sleep, I realized that both of us were at the most telepathic state of consciousness, so I pictured her coming in the next day. When she arrived she said to me, "When I got your letter yesterday I was so peeved that I decided I would never come back. But when I woke up this morning I changed my mind." Of course, she thought that she changed her mind, but really it was me who put the thought there.

When you program long enough for dreams, the mind becomes aware that you want to gather information during sleep, and it automatically does this for you. The information reaches beyond the dreamer, and beyond information that you would presume is contained in the mind.

One time a dear friend complained about a heart condition that kept recurring. He had balloon dilation of the coronary arteries and also had a splint inserted in an artery, but still he experienced difficulty. I told him about programmed dreams, gave him a set of the dream tapes to hear, and instructed him to wake up with the answer. Two days later I received a call from him. He was at the University of Pennsylvania Medical Center, saying that he had the dream and was told to "get it over with." So he went in for quadruple bypass surgery. I assured him he would not have received the answer if the operation were going to fail, because I had never known a programmed dream to be wrong.

The next night I visited him and learned the surgery already had been completed that morning. During sleep that night, I received a clear message. He was up and running around in my dream, and suddenly one of the arteries burst. The words I heard were "too soon." I knew this was a warning—not that it was *going* to happen, but that it *would* happen if he became active too soon. I cancelled half a day's worth of appointments to go see him and explain the dream. I explained to him that his arteries were made of very delicate 75-year-old tissue, and that he must not get up and rush around too soon—even if his doctors told him it would hasten recovery. His wife and son were there and agreed completely that it would be just like him to be up and dancing practically the next day. It is five years later, and he is alive and well.

I didn't program for the dream and I did not program to awaken with it, and I do not know how it came about—but I was thankful for it.

Editor's note: Techniques for programming dreams are beyond the confines of this brief presentation, but are taught in the basic course, and more information is available on www.DrMcKenzie.com.

CHAPTER 9
DIRECT HEALING ENERGY

BY JOSE LUIS (PEPE) ROMERO

There is more at work in correcting health problems mentally than just attitude and relaxation. Subjective communication plays a big part.

Cleve Backster, a polygraph expert, was the first to demonstrate scientifically and publicize the subjective connection that exists between humans and plants.

In 1966 Backster conducted an experiment with a dragon tree plant in his office one night. Its large leaves made it easy to attach electrodes to measure changes in the resistance to a small electrical current.

"For whatever reason," he explained, "it occurred to me that it would be interesting to see how long it took water to get from the root area of this plant, all the way up this long trunk and out and down to the leaves."

He was surprised at what he saw on the polygraph. Backster explained, "[The plant] had the contour of a human being tested, reacting when you are asking a question that could get him in trouble. So I forgot about the rising-water time and thought, *Wow, this thing wants to show me people-like reactions. What can I do that will be a threat to the well being of the plant, similar to the fact that a relevant question regarding a crime could be a threat to a person taking a polygraph test if they're lying?*"

Next, he decided to get some matches to burn the leaf. But before he had a chance to get the matches, there was a big reaction on the polygrah reading—whenhe just *thought* about burning the plant.

"I thought, *Wow! This thing read my mind!* It was that obvious to me right then," he said.

This startling observation started Backster on a new career. Since 1966 he has continued to conduct experiments with plants and with humans' white blood cells. They continue to react to his emotions and to his thoughts.

It is a new kind of research. It might not work if you are not serious and not a believer.

"When my partner in the polygraph school came in," he explained, "he was able to do the same thing also, as long as he *intended* to burn the plant leaf. If he *pretended* to burn the plant leaf, it wouldn't react."

According to Backster, living cells can tell the difference between *pretend* and *intend*. This has major implications for our subjective work.

Backster's work was featured in the book *The Secret Life of Plants* by Peter Tompkins and Christopher Bird (Harper and Row, 1973) and is the focus of the book by Robert B. Stone, *The Secret Life of Your Cells* (Whitford Press, 1989).

"The work that we've done in hundreds of hours of testing of the white cells is just absolutely fascinating," he said. "There's no doubt about it, that your thoughts can permeate every cell of your body, without going through any of the conventional communications systems."

"In other words," he continued, "if your thoughts, when your cells are separated from your body and being tested, under glass or in vitro, if they can react to your emotions when you are separated from them, you know in your body that they are going to react to emotional changes, particularly the negative emotions."

This research supports Jose Silva's work with holistic faith-healers and with distant healing. You can project your mind subjectively—while functioning at the alpha level—and influence the health of other people. At a distance, you cannot cause any harm; you can only help to change things back to normal. It takes physical force to break things; spiritual energy is an attractive energy—it attracts matter to conform to the original blueprint of perfection.

Backster said that it is sometimes difficult to persuade other scientists that the material you are working with—plants, white cells, yogurt—can determine what your real intentions are, and this affects how they react to your experiment.

One researcher complained that when he sat and thought about burning the leaves of a plant, using the same kind of plant and polygraph equipment that Backster had used, there was no reaction.

"I asked him if he actually intended to burn the plant," Cleve explained. "He said he didn't intend to burn it, because I hadn't burned my plant. But I pointed out to him that I had intended to burn my plant. The plant can tell the difference between *pretend* and *intend*."

You can read more about Cleve Backster's exciting research on the Ecumenical Society of Psychorientology's Web site, which Jose Silva established in 1975 to support research and education in the field of holistic faith healing. The address is www.ecumenical.org.

Scientist investigates "laying on of hands"

There was a research project reported on at a 1972 conference proceeding sponsored jointly by the Mind Science Foundation and Silva International, where a biologist, Dr. Bernard Grad, detailed his experiments to demonstrate that a healer could cure wounds and illnesses in laboratory mice by the "laying on of hands," transmitting healing energy to the mice.

Dr. Grad also conducted experiments with plants and with seeds. Both were positively affected by the healer's hands.

His final experiment involved water used to water the plants. Sure enough, the water could be programmed in a positive way, and plants would grow faster. When the container of water was held by a psychotically depressed person, the plants watered with that water showed slower growth than those watered with untreated water.

Water—and other matter—store energy from human beings. Dr. Grad noted that this has major implications for people who prepare food. They can help or hurt the people who eat the food they prepare.

Editor's Note: This report goes beyond the scope and space limitations of this chapter, but you can read Dr. Grad's full report on the Web site of the Ecumenical Society of Psychorientology.

Pepe Romero came to work at Silva International headquarters in 1971, shortly after graduating from college. He traveled extensively with Jose Silva, learning firsthand how to teach the holistic faith-healing techniques that Silva developed.

Chapter 10
Dealing with Disabilities

By Bill Sturdevant

There are several ways the Silva techniques can help persons with disabilities. Many people have used them very effectively—including myself.

The techniques help the individual in coping with the situation. Some people grow bitter when they are hit with a serious problem, but that doesn't help.

Improving our own attitude about the situation has enormous benefits. There is less stress on the person with the disability, and they have much more energy that they can use to cope and deal with life.

At level, you can come up with more ideas for circumventing the disability, for living life in as normal a way as possible.

Changing how people treat you

One of the big problems for many people with disabilities is public attitude, the way other people deal with those of us who have disabilities. People in wheelchairs feel more comfortable when the people they are talking with sit down, so that they are all on the same level.

We can use the Silva techniques to help influence other people's attitudes towards us in several ways.

You can use Mirror of the Mind to visualize and imagine people treating you the way you want to be treated.

Also, when you spend enough time at deep enough levels and learn to cope with your own situation, learn to turn it into an advantage and change your inner attitude and your inner pictures, then you project this new positive "can do" attitude instead of a "poor me" attitude, and this is much more pleasant to other people.

When you are projecting a negative attitude, one characterized by bitterness, disappointment, and helplessness, people are uncomfortable and do not want to be around you. When you have an attitude of optimism and joy, people love being around you.

Some personal experiences

The techniques are all highly adaptable. I encourage students to find new ways to use the techniques to help people (including themselves, of course), ways that the name of the technique might not suggest.

Who would have thought that multiple sclerosis (MS) symptoms could be corrected with the Habit Control Technique that I learned in the Basic Lecture Series? Something told me to try it, since my sister had MS, and it helped her stop her choking problem, to stop shaking her head, and to begin feeding herself again.

Attitude is everything. If I had had a "poor me" attitude, I have no question I would be dead now.

When the neuroophthalmologist told me that he thought I had MS, I was on my way to Laredo to become a Silva instructor, and I knew there was nothing I could not overcome with the techniques. I blew him away, because I think he expected me to be devastated by the diagnosis, considering my sister's situation.

Positive affirmations helped me a lot when I was correcting my eyesight. I had a whole sequence of affirmations I went through, at least three times a day, every day, along with my visualizations. I still repeat it occasionally.

Although Silva is a program of mind control, doing something physical is not cheating. I encourage people to do things like massage, physical therapy, or foot reflexology, or to take herbs if that will truly help the condition and not just alleviate symptoms.

I don't want people to become a lifetime subsidy for the pharmaceutical industry, but sometimes those things can help a person to concentrate on what they need to do for their healing. And as Jose Silva said, if you have a serious problem, throw everything at it that you've got.

The more I study this field, the more I understand that love is all there is.

I once heard a doctor say that he had never seen a person with an autoimmune disease who loved himself or herself. And I thought, "Yep, that's me." So now I also program to love myself more.

You have to love yourself enough to want to do the programming. You have to love yourself enough to believe that you are worthy of good health. And of course, the more you love yourself, the more you can love others and help them.

Finally, I have some caveats: First, there's the idea of being careful what you wish for because you might get it. This is how I got MS; I wished I had it so I could show my sister it could be healed.

Second, don't quit programming when you think you are recovered. Keep up a minimum "maintenance dose" of programming to be sure that things keep going the way you want them to go. This can prevent a relapse.

Third, okay stinks. I'd look at my sister's condition and think, *I'm not that bad yet—I'm doing okay*. It took me a long time to realize that I wasn't, and that "okay" isn't.

Bill Sturdevant has been a Silva instructor in Juneau, Alaska, for the past 15 years. He teaches both the basic and advanced Silva courses, is director of Silva activities in Alaska, and is especially interested in using the mind for healing.

Chapter 11
Grow better as you grow older

by Rebekah Hickman

A psychic friend of mine introduced me to Silva. We didn't have a Silva instructor in Charleston, West Virginia, at the time, but an instructor who was traveling around teaching Silva courses came to Charleston. My friend said, "This is a real good course. I took it 20 years ago and it changed my life."

I had been to a lot of workshops, and I thought, *This will be exciting for a couple of weeks, then I'll forget all about it and will have wasted my money.*

I asked my friend about the cost and the time involved. When she told me I said, "No, I don't have the money or the time to do that." Those are the standard excuses for folks who don't want to take the course. She said, "You've got the time, and I've got the money." She literally dragged me to that course, sat me down, and handed out the money to pay for it.

I thought, *This must be really something, that she would do this.* She didn't have much money, and I was sort of in awe that she did this.

Twenty years earlier the course changed her life. In November 1987, it did the same for me, and I will always thank her for it.

"This is not going to be the end of me."

When I had my heart attack, I thought, *This is not going to be the end of me.* When they took me to the hospital in the ambulance, I knew I wasn't going to die. I knew I had to live for something, that there was something else in life for me to live for.

I remember thinking, *I won't close my eyes; if I don't close my eyes I won't die.*

115

I didn't die. And as soon as I got out of the hospital, I took the Silva course. I felt like it was what I had been looking for all my life.

It all made sense immediately. As the instructor said, the right brain doesn't take a joke. And it doesn't. I remember that one of my favorite expressions was, "That really hurts my heart." I don't know what kind of messages I was sending to my body, but I sure got busy and stopped sending them right quick.

I learned all the techniques and used them all. I went to every class the instructor gave in Charleston, and drove four hours to her town to attend more.

One day when I was in her class, I told the instructor, "You know, if I was 20 years younger I would love to go to Laredo and take the instructor training." I really wanted to find out what was behind it, what made it work so well, what made all these good things happen.

She said, "That's the silliest excuse I've ever heard! You know you can go to Laredo and become an instructor if you want to!"

Then I began to think that maybe I could. My friends all told me I was too old. By that time I was 69 years old. What people are going to put you through the training and let you start at 69? Society doesn't accept that kind of thing. You know, you are supposed to get old and decrepit and end up in a nursing home by the time you are 70!

A sign from a higher power

Going to Laredo for instructor training began to sound like a wonderful idea. All kinds of fabulous things had been happening: I'd changed my life, I had helped my husband, and I had done so many good things. People still laughed at me because of some of the things I was doing, but when they found out what the results were, they became believers.

I decided to go to level and ask for a sign to let me know whether I should go or not. I knew that I was getting old, and I wanted to do more with my life. I didn't want to give up my life. I wanted to be involved, and I liked helping people.

I programmed that if I received money from an unknown source, it would be a sign to go. I didn't need money to make the trip to Laredo, but it would be a sign.

A couple of weeks later I got a letter from Nellie, a friend I grew up with, whom I hadn't heard from in 37 years. When I opened the envelope, there was a check in it from the Wells Fargo Bank in California. I thought, *I've never been to California.* I didn't know what Wells Fargo was. It looked to me like it was one of those fake checks that was just made to look like somebody was giving me $400 but was really just some kind of promotion.

In the letter, she said she knew I would be surprised hearing from her, and she used terms like, "I've been thinking a lot about you" and "I don't know how much money I really do owe you but this number keeps popping in my mind."

The way she wrote, it sounded like something or someone was sending her messages to do this, in order to send me a sign.

I wrote her a thank-you note. I would have sent the check back because I didn't feel like she owed me anything, even though she thought she did. But then I thought, *Well, I did ask the universe for it*, so I decided to accept it. I knew where it really came from.

That gave me my real sign, in the physical world. And it also paid my way to Laredo and back. I was very excited about that.

I went to Laredo and took the training, and I felt like I was in heaven. I didn't know enough about it to ask a lot of questions, but I knew that I would learn more as I went along. As I've gone along with it during the 12 years since I attended instructor training, I have learned more than I have ever given away. I know that.

When I introduced myself at the beginning of instructor training, they asked why I was there. I confessed that I thought maybe I was too old to start doing this. A lot of the instructors who were in that class have kidded me about that ever since. Twelve years later I'm still going strong, teaching at least one class a month, and involved in a lot more activities, such as writing a chapter for this book.

It was like a dream come true. I had mentally pictured going down and getting my certificate and being accepted as an instructor. I looked at Jose Silva—he was older than I was, and he was still so active! He was demonstrating a memory technique and could do it so well, I thought, *If he can do that at that age, I'm sure I am not old either*. He was a great inspiration.

I literally began to get younger every year—in my feeling, in my life, and in the way I could do things.

I found that I didn't have to get old. In fact, one of our instructors, Marcelino Alcala, used the Spanish phrase *y no contamos*, which means stop counting. I think that's a great idea.

Becky Hickman has 36 years of professional experience helping people as a schoolteacher and counselor. She has been a Silva instructor for 13 years, teaching both the basic and advanced courses.

Chapter 12
Build better relationships

BY ALEJANDRO (ALEX) GONZALEZ SILVA

There is nothing more important to our happiness in life than our relationships with others. I've gained valuable insight and guidance during my 65 years on this planet about how to improve your relations and relationships.

When I say relations, I mean the workplace—work for my boss, work with all the people on the staff; work with my banker. You have to have a kind of relations with these people. This is life.

Then we have relationships. This covers more intimate relations: your spouse, your family, your kids, and so forth.

I have conducted research on this for 45 years. The reason is that my wife and I have been married for 45 years.

I also spent 22 years in the Air Force and retired as a Senior Master Sergeant. I was assigned to military intelligence and worked with super-secret information, so for much of my career I reported directly to generals. Like any other Senior Master Sergeant, I supervised many enlisted personnel. I got a lot of experience in dealing with all kinds of people.

Good relationships

The ingredients I have for good relations and good relationships are:

> **Love.** You have to have love. But the word "love" is used too loosely nowadays. Everybody says to each other, "I love you." You say it, but what you have to do is to mean it. Sincerity is the key.

119

> **Forgiveness.** We are all human. We are all going to go through things we might not like. Nobody's perfect.
> **Understanding.**
> **Common sense.** Too many people go by what they read in books. They read books by psychiatrists, books written by nobodies, and see techniques. People are living by what they read and leaving common sense out.

Common sense

I was in Thailand on my last Air Force assignment. I was in charge of the intelligence operation there. I had people working on the day shift, swing shift, midnight shift, and so forth.

We had a log book where every shift wrote down everything they did, so the next shift could read the log.

I had complaints that the swing shift was not doing anything, that the men were taking too long to open the door, they were reading magazines, and so forth.

So I called in my sergeant in charge of the shift. He had a master's degree, so there was no doubting his intelligence. Unfortunately, the Air Force promoted based on test performance. That's unfortunate, because sometimes that's not the best way to promote. The guys who know how to do well on tests get promoted, while the guys who are good at doing the work don't.

I said to him, "Sergeant, there have been complaints about you and your guys not doing anything, taking too long to answer the door, reading magazines when the colonel comes in.

"From now on, when the colonel comes in, act like you are working. Make yourself busy. Answer the door quickly. And your crew, too." Then I left.

The next morning I came in, and the colonel was already there. He was looking at the log book, laughing. The colonel and I had a close relation. He said, "Speedy,"—my nickname—"come into my office."

I went in and he said, "Did you tell your sergeant that if I came in, to act like he was doing something?"

I said, "Yes, sir."

"Did you tell him to...?" and he read off what I had said.

"Yes, sir."

The sergeant wrote down everything I had said for the midnight shift. This is where common sense comes in. You have to use common sense to make decisions.

And do you know the one place where we are much more likely to use common sense and make good decisions? The alpha level.

There is more information available to us at the alpha level, and we should take advantage of it.

When you center yourself at the alpha level, it is easier for you to access all of the information that is stored in your memory banks, no matter where it is stored. When you are way up at the beta part of the brain, you are too far away from information stored in other parts of your brain. Center yourself at alpha and you have greater access to your memory storage areas.

In addition, when you function at the alpha level, you can become aware of information that has been impressed on other people's brains. They may have information or experiences that can help you. Wisdom is the ability to use experiences to guide you. Now you are not limited only to your own experiences; you can also use the experiences of others to guide you. Take advantage of this.

Better relations

What is it you have to do for better relations?

You have to hear. You have to understand. You don't do all the talking.

It's hard. If you go to a bank asking for a loan and they tell you no, it's hard to take a deep breath and relax, because you need the money.

These things I'm telling you are not that easy. You have to learn them, but you also have to apply them. Most of us forget this. You have to work at it. If you don't work at it, if you give up, you'll never be happy. You can program all of this at the alpha level, and it will be easier to make it all a part of your daily life.

To be liked, you have to be understood by your fellow man. The only way I have been able to do it is by being sincere and truthful.

That's another thing—don't be too truthful. A little white lie never ever hurt anybody. If your friend buys horrible-looking earrings, you're not going to tell her they look awful. Remember, use common sense.

For example, always look people in the eyes.

If you are looking for a job, look the interviewer in the eyes.

If you are looking for a boyfriend or girlfriend, look at their eyes and mentally say, "Happiness to you." You have to pass the message.

Without eye contact, you are not passing anything. Look right in their eyes and say, "You look beautiful." Look directly, firmly, and be sincere.

You can actually program people with your eyes. A lot of energy comes from your eyes, and other people can become aware of what you are communicating with your eyes. Be sure you are honest and sincere.

Relationships

The things that I am going to tell you about relationships will work most of the time. Not every time, but most of the time.

I have been around the world several times, lecturing, on business. People have told me, "These techniques will never work here."

You have to remember that human beings are all over the world and we all have a heart. We are all the same. Chinese, Mexicans, Americans, whatever—we are all the same; we all have a heart.

This heart is what you have to protect, not to break. By that I mean that you have to watch what you say. You shouldn't go up to a person and tell them that somebody doesn't like them. That's common sense, because you will be hurting the person by doing that. Even if it is true, you don't tell them.

Be careful. Always think about the person in front of you. Think about their feelings. Remember:

➤ Love.
➤ Forgiveness.
➤ Understanding.
➤ Common sense.

You can use your level to do these things:

➤ Tell somebody subjectively that you love them.
➤ Tell someone that you forgive them.
➤ At your level, why not imagine how other people perceive things. This can help you to better understand their point of view. You could imagine "putting their head on"—that is, imagine that you are superimposing their head over your own, as if you were putting on a helmet. Then you can "see things through their eyes," and experience what they are experiencing.

➤ If you made a mistake during the day and failed to use common sense, then correct it with the Mirror of the Mind. In the blue-framed mirror, review the foolish thing you did, erase it, and in the white- framed mirror imagine yourself using common sense and doing the right thing.

Programming for success

I recommend that if you want to go further in improving your relationships, use your Silva Method techniques. I'm going to give you a technique that I teach in the Silva Two-Day Ultra Seminar called the Three Scenes Technique, and you can use it for relationships.

Project an image of the problem onto your mental screen, directly in front of you. Visualize the problem. Do you want to work with your mother-in-law? Visualize her. What's the problem? You want to communicate better, so visualize it. You could also do this with your boss, or anyone else.

Once you visualize the problem, shift your attention toward your left, 15 degrees. On this part of your mental screen, imagine what you want to do to correct the problem. Here is where you work on the problem: You are talking to your mother-in-law, and she is receptive.

Then shift your attention further toward your left, another 15 degrees, and imagine the final results: Both of you are happy.

You use the Mirror of the Mind when you know the end result and you are not concerned with how you get there. You use the Three Scenes Technique when you know what you want to do and you know the result that you want to produce with this action.

Regarding imagination, in the second scene, whatever you are imagining, imagine it as exaggerated as you can. The more exaggeration that you use, the better. Exaggerate what you are doing to correct the problem. Build it up.

Alex Gonzalez Silva came to work for his uncle, Jose Silva, after retiring from the U.S. Air Force in 1976. Within a year he had been promoted to administrator and general manager of the company. He currently teaches the basic and advanced Silva courses throughout the world.

CHAPTER 13

THE CHILD OF YOUR DREAMS

BY KEN MITCHELL

There are so many good things happening in the world today—and they are happening so rapidly—that it is difficult for most people to even conceive of the kind of life our children can look forward to.

In 1966, when Jose Silva first taught his course to the public, the average person did not even believe in the existence of psychic ability. Three decades later businesses were sending employees to seminars in intuitive management, major medical schools were teaching spirituality healing courses, and people from every walk of life were discussing messages from angels and the way that they have learned to trust their hunches.

In the 1960s the Cold War frightened people on both sides of the mythical iron curtain. Road maps in Russia were filled with fictional highways to mislead enemy pilots that they feared would attack someday. Who could have imagined that in 1998 my wife and I would adopt a 2-year-old Russian girl with the blessings of the Russian government?

Our dreams come true

Jose Silva said that prospective parents can program to bring a genius to the planet. He recommended that the husband and wife go to level separately and decide at level what kind of child they want: one who will become a professional, a scientist, a government leader, and so forth. Then they should talk it over, continuing to go to level, making decisions, and talking with each other, until they are in agreement. Then they can program to conceive that kind of child.

I was not aware of that when my wife and I decided we wanted a child, but we did most of the things that he recommended, with outstanding results.

I guess that I always had pretty good intuition, judging from the results I got. By the time I was 35, I had a thriving real estate business. My family and I lived on a lovely 85-acre farm in central Illinois. We had race horses, a 5,000 square-foot home with a swimming pool, and nice cars.

Evidently my natural intuitive abilities left something to be desired, because in 1985 I found myself divorced and broke, with custody of our four small boys. I was lost in a fog of despair and confusion and about ready to give up when the first of many "coincidences" happened.

A close friend invited me to his church. As I was sitting there waiting for the service to start, I noticed a lady walking up the aisle and taking a seat in the front row. I was amazed when I turned to my friend Dave and said, "That's the girl I'm going to marry!" I was amazed because I was not even interested in dating at that time. And I didn't even know the woman.

After the service there was a christening, so we all stayed for the short ceremony. As I watched her, I had the strongest feeling that she wanted a child herself. I mentally said to her, "I'll get you a child some day, don't worry."

I learned that her name was Karen Kelly, and that she was a licensed teacher at Unity, so naturally I signed up for her class. In fact, I signed up for both of the classes she was teaching. I finally talked her into going out with me. I told her that my boys were actually my brother's kids—and I don't even have a brother!

In 1992 we married and purchased a house. By that time two of my sons were in college. Karen and I had discussed having a child of our own, but did not get serious about it until my youngest son moved out in 1997. Then she told me something she had not told her closest friends: that having a child was her heart's desire. My intuition had told me that back in 1985, the first time I saw her.

We wanted a girl, but despite all our efforts Karen did not get pregnant. Even working with a fertility specialist for several months did not produce the results we desired. We were both receptive to the idea of adoption. After all, my two oldest boys were adopted and were a joy in our lives.

I did not know why I had changed careers—I was now selling long-term-care insurance—but perhaps it was another instance of divine intervention, for one day in a client's office I saw a wall filled with children's pictures. It turned out that my client was the head of foreign adoptions for the state of Illinois. I told her our story, and she offered to help us any way she could.

I rushed home and told Karen and asked her if she thought that was a sign that we should go forward with the idea of adopting.

She agreed enthusiastically, so we set an appointment with my client and she gave us some adoption sources and information on what countries to consider.

Coincidences or not?

The coincidences kept coming, each one reassuring us that we were on the right track and should keep going. I noticed an ad in the local newspaper for home studies for foreign adoptions. When I called, they gave us the names of some of their clients. One of the agency's clients I called had just returned from Russia and referred us to the agency she had used, located in Falls Church, Virginia, just outside Washington, D.C. The agency in Virginia specialized in Russian children, which was perfect for us.

We got the paperwork to start the yearlong process, but simply set it aside until in early 1998 some money unexpectedly came into our lives. I thought back to the Silva class I had taken with Hans DeJong the previous November and how he had predicted that this might happen to us. In addition to tithing, paying off bills, and doing some redecorating, we got the strongest message that we should use the rest of the money for the adoption.

We called the agency and got started. We referred to our efforts as the "Kate Project." While we were trying to conceive, we had decided that we would name our daughter Kathleen Kelly Mitchell in memory of Karen's deceased sister. Throughout the adoption process, we had the feeling that Kathleen was helping us.

One day an ad in a magazine caught my attention. It contained a picture of a little girl in a beautiful outfit that struck me as rather Russian-looking. I cut the ad out, showed it to Karen, and put it in my planner where I kept my daily schedule and would see the picture often. The little girl was dark-complexioned—not the blue-eyed blonde that we planned to adopt, but I still used that picture to remind me of our Kate Project.

After months of effort and mountains of paperwork, we finally got a video showing two little Russian girls. One was the blonde infant we had asked for, while the other was a 2-year-old named Zemfira. "Zemfira is for you," our Russian contact told us. We agreed to look at the video but told our contact that we didn't think she'd be what we were hoping for.

We watched the three-minute preview of the 2-year-old girl, then the one of the 6-month-old infant. We were disappointed because the infant did not look well. The next day, an intense knowing came over me. I *knew* we were going to take Zemfira. I also knew I could not make that decision alone.

When I got home that evening, I told Karen about the message I received. She looked startled, and told me that her feeling was so strong that she was completely at peace with the other girl too. We had come to the same conclusion, independently. Another coincidence? According to Jose Silva, coincidence is God's way of guiding us.

We took a picture from the video to show friends. When I put a copy of it inside my planner, next to the picture of the ad, it was eerie how similar Zem was to the model in the ad! The darker complexion, the eyes, the telltale rose-petal lips—it was pure magic.

On August 12, 1998, we arrived back on American soil with our daughter.

And this could be just a coincidence, or it could be one more confirmation that we did the right thing: Zemfira's birthday is July 19, the same date that a daughter who died at birth was born to my ex-wife and me in 1972.

Over the next few months Zemfira adjusted beautifully to her new home. She speaks English very well, plays at the YMCA's "Gym and Swim" program, plays well with other children, and has a great sense of humor.

Zem has excellent intuition too, something we encourage in her. One night I told Zem after prayers, "You are our little angel, Zem."

"No, Papa," she answered, "I'm not an angel. But Mama's sister is an angel."

We never told Zem about Kathleen, or how we wanted to name our daughter Kate, or how we had always felt that Kathleen was helping us from the spiritual dimension with our adoption efforts. So how did Zem know Kathleen?

What I know now that I didn't know before is that you can use your intuition for more than detecting information that you can use in business, to help you make money and get what you want.

You can use your psychic ability to communicate with higher intelligence so that those who are helping us can guide us to do the right thing. Jose Silva called that having an invisible means of support.

Ken Mitchell is an experienced corporate trainer and a successful businessman. He has been using the Silva techniques for the past five years with such outstanding success that he decided to become an instructor.

CHAPTER 14
INSIGHTS FOR GUIDING CHILDREN

BY NELDA SHEETS

Our families are so important to us that ordinary politicians can be elected to the highest offices by proclaiming that they are for "family values." The way we think about what we want for our country has been changed by great leaders who reminded us that there can be a better and better world for our children by changing our laws and our concepts.

An example is Dr. Martin Luther King, who made people of all races think with our hearts when he proclaimed, "I have a dream!" His dream was for his children to live in a world free of racial discrimination, where all people have equal opportunities.

Nelson Mandela made a gigantic change for all African families because he wanted a better world for his daughter. He wrote to her, "There are few misfortunes in this world you cannot turn into personal triumph if you have an iron will and necessary skill."

In a discussion about how great people have made the world better, we should remember that Jose Silva created the Silva Method of Self-Mind Control because he, too, had a dream: a dream of providing inner skills for his family of 10 children so that they could reach their potential in school and in life.

We invited Jose to come to Amarillo to teach his Method to 125 artists who belonged to the Area Arts Association. We wanted to "get a handle on the creative levels" so we could become better artists. We learned in the first four hours that what he was teaching us was much more than that. We could learn to manage stress, use visualization for better memory and better health and to achieve our goals, and even develop our intuition for awareness of the universe. We practiced "case-working," using subjective communication to project our minds to problems and then verifying that we were accurate in the information we detected.

We wanted that for our family members, too. My son Steve was 16, and my daughter Dana was 14 at the time. We talked to Jose and convinced him to come back to Amarillo for an additional class for our family members. From there the Silva System spread around the world.

What do you want for your family? Now would be a good time to stop and make a list.

Here is a list of what I want for my family, now and for the rest of their lives:

1. Stress management.
2. Mental skills for fitness and wellness.
3. Creative problem-solving skills for all areas of life.
4. Creative expression skills in art as well as appreciation of the arts.
5. An education that leads to a fulfilling career and lifestyle.
6. Social and family values that bring a sense of well-being and also relationship skills.
7. A well-developed intuition that will bring about lucky and correct decisions.
8. A spiritual connection with higher intelligence, as well as a connection with all life on planet earth.
9. A belief in their own potential, and the mental tools to achieve it.

Now let me tell you how the Silva techniques have helped our family achieve all of that and more.

Stress management

When we ask kids what causes stress for them, they answer:

1. When parents are stressed out and cranky with us, yell at us, or argue with each other. For some children it is even worse, when the parents' stress leads to child abuse.
2. When no one listens to us.
3. When kids at school make fun of me or pick on me.
4. Beginning to date.
5. Divorce.
6. Problems of the world.

A study of Connecticut high schoolers by Dr. Alexander Tolor, as reported in the *New York Times*, showed that there is a big difference in what parents and teachers *think* causes teenagers stress, and what the high schoolers themselves say is stressful.

Teenagers listed not getting into the college they wanted, having to go to summer school, and the break-up of a romance.

Dr. Taylor says, "What would help most is for parents and teachers to psychically connect with teenagers and see their problems and their world in the eyes of the child."

Jose Silva provided a very effective technique for doing this: subjective communication—what he said is the most valuable technique in the course. At the end of the course we practice projecting our mind to detect information about illnesses and injuries to other people, and verify that we are accurate in our detection. Once you learn to do that, you can learn through practice to use your mind to detect information about any kind of problem—"if it is necessary and beneficial for humanity," as we say in the course. Here is an example:

When my son was 17, he became moody and seemed to be experiencing stress. When asked about what was bothering him, he told me nothing and obviously didn't want to discuss it. I used subjective communication to get a sense of what I could do to help.

I went to my level and imagined that he was there in front of me. Then I "put his head on." That is, I imagined superimposing his head over mine as if I were putting on a helmet.

While I had his head on, I had thoughts that he was bothered by his dad and me taking for granted that he would soon be leaving for college. He was concerned about possibly being drafted for military service, and he was also concerned about whether he should serve his country before he went to college.

I can remember thinking at the time that these thoughts that I was having could not be right! But at the same time, I had a feeling inside that this was for real.

After dinner that night, I mentioned to him that I noticed that some of his classmates were volunteering for service, and that it must be a very important decision to make. I asked if he had ever thought of that.

I wasn't surprised when he confirmed that he had.

I told him that I respected his decision, but I believed that he could get his college education first, then volunteer. By doing that, he would be more mature and would make a much better soldier.

I breathed a big sigh of relief when he said that he thought I was right.

In their book *Teenage Suicide*, authors Sandra and Dr. Gary Rosenberg say that what teenagers need most is to feel that there is a meaningful life to look forward to when they become adults. Listen carefully to their statement: "Not being able to cope with stress and pain is a key factor in teenage suicide."

For the sake of your family, learn and practice relaxation skills. And learn to use your intuition—subjective communication—to help you better understand what other members of your family are experiencing, so that you can help them cope and relieve some of the stress.

Mental skills for wellness and fitness

When my grandson Travis was five, I spent a week babysitting him while his parents vacationed. I gave him a plastic baseball bat and ball. We played a lot of ball that week, and I had a built-in opportunity to teach him that he could use his "magic mind" to mentally picture himself hitting the ball just right.

Throughout his school years we occasionally talked about how he could use his magic mind in sports, especially baseball. He became a star player on his high school team. In fact, in his senior year his high school team won the state championship in Texas and he was named one of the Most Valuable Players.

When he was interviewed after the championship game, he was asked, "Who taught you to play baseball, your dad?"

He answered, "No, it was my grandmother."

As you can imagine, there were a lot of surprised people, especially a very proud grandmother.

My children learned how to go to their level and program to relieve pain and to visualize injuries healing quickly and without pain.

Creative problem-solving skills

I want my family to have whole-brain thinking skills for fixing problems. The Mirror of the Mind Technique is basic for almost any situation.

One of the most spirit-fulfilling experiences that I had with a child was with Donnie, a nine-year-old student with cerebral palsy. His father, a Silva graduate, wanted his son to learn to relax at will, especially so that he could stop debilitating muscle spasms that are painful and can even be fatal. Donnie's father was also eager for him to learn to use his mind to help in any way possible.

I knew very little about cerebral palsy, so I went to Jose Silva for advice. His advice was simple: "Don't read anything about the disease. You will only read about problems of the disease, not possibilities. Use case-working when in doubt about how to proceed."

It turned out to be excellent advice, as born out by the results that we got.

Donnie did learn to relax completely at will, before spasms set in. And he learned much more.

One of the things that Donnie wanted to do was to learn to write. He especially wanted to write his name like the other kids. Since he couldn't even hold a pencil with his hands, I admit I was doubtful. I went to level, as Jose had suggested, and asked what to do. At level, I got the thought that rehearsing at level using the Mirror of the Mind Technique would work. And it did!

Once he could hold the pencil, we mentally rehearsed writing his name. Once he had succeeded at that, he wanted me to teach him to paint. It went through my mind that this could be a real *big* challenge. Since he was holding his pencil straight up with his fist wrapped around it, it would be very difficult for him to mix the oils that I used in the children's art classes.

Once again I went to level. There, I got the idea to show Donnie how to paint with watercolors. He could hold the paint brush the same way he held the pencil, and easily move the brush to the water, then to the watercolor pan, and then to the paper. It worked beautifully.

Creative artistic expression and appreciation

Art is nourishment for the spirit. It expands the heart. It is the global language that everyone can speak and understand. Art teaches us to care for the planet and its inhabitants.

There are several things you can do to block the creative spirit. One is to judge the work as "good" or "bad." To avoid this, you can praise the process instead of commenting on the product.

Dord Fitz, our art professor, who brought Jose Silva to Amarillo to speak to us and then to teach us his method, told us that the difference between a painter and an artist is that a painter can have expertise with skillful drawing and painting, but the picture lacks spirit; the artist is a psychic who expresses with paint the vision in his or her mind's eye. It's a subjective experience put into an objective form; the spirit of the painting is felt by the viewer. It is the same with all art forms.

When my oldest granddaughter Jill was six, she spent a week with me at the New Mexico ranch where we lived at the time. We had a painting lesson in my studio one morning and took a break by taking a walk.

As we walked down the tree-lined lane westward, there was a wonderful view of the Sangre de Cristo mountains. Both of us admired the wild flowers and the view of the pretty meadows in the foreground, a view of the town of Raton in the middle ground, and those great snow-capped peaks in the background.

Then Jill asked, "Mimi, where is God? Is He in the sky?"

I answered, "Jill, I find God everywhere. When I look at your sweet face, I see God. When I look at these pretty flowers, I see God."

When she looked a little puzzled, I suggested that we find a seat on the log and go to our level and imagine going inside the flower to a very deep level where the spirit of creativity was, and feel God's energy and love within the flower. Then we connected in the same way with the trees, the cattle, and the mountains.

When Jill opened her eyes, she enthusiastically proclaimed, "Oh, Mimi, now I know why everything is so-oo 'bootiful.' Let's go back to your studio and paint it!" She painted a wonderful landscape that now hangs in my current studio to remind me of the spiritual and creative process of painting.

Another creative thinking technique for solving problems is brainstorming. Jose Silva developed a variation of brainstorming he calls the Alpha Think Tank, where we all go to level together and work on problems as a group.

My family worked out a problem with this technique when the kids were still in high school. I was working in my office from 8 a.m. to 4 p.m., and I was teaching the Silva System several evenings a month. I depended on the kids to help me with the housework. They suggested I quit so they could be relieved of their chores. I suggested that we discuss it in an Alpha Think Tank session to find a win-win solution.

During the Alpha Think Tank session, they presented their views, my husband presented his views, and I presented my views. The result? The kids decided that having me work was not only okay, but it was good for them because it gave them spending money as well as the opportunity to learn how to run a household.

Kids as young as age five can participate in a family Alpha Think Tank. The rules are simple.

➤   All ideas are written down.
➤   There is no judgment until all ideas are presented.

➢ It lasts as long as anyone has something to share.

➢ Ideas are judged for workable solutions, and the participants select the one that is best for everyone.

Education

All of the Silva techniques are important to students and their success in the educational system.

In some cases it has been a matter of going to level in order to understand why the teachers acts so awful. In other cases it has been developing mnemonics for better test grades. In many cases it has been learning to expect positive results from oneself.

My experience with a boy named Charlie is a good example of how the creative insights and intuition at the alpha level can be beneficial to students who are having trouble in school.

Charlie's grandmother called and told me that Charlie had been diagnosed as having Attention Deficit Disorder (ADD) and wanted to know if we could help him. Teachers had told Charlie's parents that he couldn't read or concentrate for more than 15 minutes.

I told her to bring him to the children's class that I was holding to see how he responded. Charlie seemed to be fascinated with what we were saying, and I was amazed at him during the first break: He was explaining what I had said during the first hour to the younger kids—and he was explaining it accurately.

During class, he asked questions and joined in whenever we opened the class for a discussion. He was never unruly in any way, and he was a total delight to have in class.

During the afternoon break, I asked Charlie why he didn't like to read. I was very careful in how I asked the question. I didn't want to ask, "Why *can't* you read?"

He answered, "Have you seen the books they give us kids? They're *boring!*"

I asked what he liked to do. He said he enjoyed watching television and playing games. I asked him if he had thought about what he wanted to do when he grew up. He said that he wanted to do something with computers.

The next day, after the kids had worked health cases, I asked Charlie to project himself into the future, to imagine himself working with computers, and needing to read something. I asked him to tell me all the times he would need to read, and to feel the fun and excitement of learning new information by reading.

When he came out of level he simply said, "I want to read."

A year later when Charlie and his grandmother repeated the class he proudly reported that he had an A average that year.

Social and family values

Family values and social values are subjects that need our attention and consideration when we consider the things that we want for our children. Hillary Rodham Clinton says in her book *It Takes a Village to Raise a Child*, "One of the families' and the village's...most important tasks is to help children develop those habits of self-discipline and empathy...that which we call character."

It takes creative-thinking parents and teachers to raise creative-thinking children who will be prepared to raise the village, or as we say in the Silva class, to make the world a better place to live for those who follow.

I had the privilege of working on the island of Guam with Sister Naomi Curtin and Silva consultant Dr. George DeSau, who were involved in teaching the Silva System in the parochial school system. One of my assignments was to show the teachers how they could use the alpha level creatively in the classroom.

In a seventh grade social studies class, we studied the Sioux Indians of South Dakota. I did something a little different than they were accustomed to.

I had the children close their eyes and I guided them to level. Then I asked them to imagine taking a trip to South Dakota in the year of 1860, and to imagine that they were spending the day as a guest and a friend of the Sioux Indians. I suggested that they experience the way their new friends lived.

It took only 20 minutes for me to cover all of the information that their textbook chapter contained. When they came out of level they drew pictures and wrote a record of their experiences. Then they shared verbally with each other. They loved sharing this way. *Now* someone was listening to them, and they loved that it was their classmates.

The next day they had another chapter to study, another culture to learn about. But they were disappointed that they were not going back to South Dakota to visit the Sioux village.

"But we made friends," they said. "We like these people."

Of course, it was the same with all of the people they read about and experienced at the inner level. It is a way of learning to care. And that's something that we can all benefit from.

A well-developed intuition

Today's bookshelves are getting richer with books that tell us the importance of developing and using our intuition. Books that suggest ways for us to be safe in an unsafe world emphasize that our intuitive feelings are to be respected and followed. Studies of successful companies show that the best have intuitive leaders.

When is the best age to teach your children how to be intuitive?

Jose Silva said age seven is the ideal time to begin. From ages 7 to 14 children naturally function more at the alpha level than at any other level, so it is easy to teach them. He gave us these guidelines:

1. Practice visualization. Ask your child to close eyes, roll them slightly upward, and recall and describe in detail and in full color, people, things, and places. Do this for 15 minutes, once a week—every Sunday, for instance.

2. Practice imagination. With eyes closed, turned slightly upward, ask your child to alter objects or scenes they have seen. For instance, if they have seen a person wearing a green sweater, then mentally change the color to red. Practice visualization for three Sundays and imagination for one, until the child is 8 years old. Then alternate—practice visualization every other Sunday until the child is 9. At age 10, practice visualization once a month and imagination three times a month.

3. At age eight, they have practiced visualization for a year. If the parents are Silva graduates, they can now present health cases, which are the easiest kind of cases to do. Later you can give business, political, personal, or social problems as cases for them to work. When working cases, the psychic first mentally detects what the problem is. Then after they confirm that they are accurate in what they detected, they can mentally correct the problems.

4. It is best not to refer to psychic ability or clairvoyance. Children do not like to be considered different from their peers. But all children enjoy "guessing," so just have them guess.

5. When a child guesses wrong, do not tell them that they are wrong. Simply move forward and encourage successes.

6. When they guess right, have them review the feeling associated with the correct guess.

Spiritual connections with higher intelligence and all life

Entering level and working cases is how we connect with our spiritual evolution. There are many views of what being spiritual entails. Mother Theresa told us that spirituality is not preaching about God; it is *doing* that which is Godly.

Jose Silva said the same thing in the course when he advised us to "continue to strive to take part in constructive and creative activities to make the world a better place to live, so that when we move on, we shall have left behind a better world for those who follow."

UN Secretary General U Thant said he believed that spirituality will be the next state of evolution and will ultimately bring harmony to individuals and society. Jose Silva long referred to this as the "second phase of human evolution."

Because of the world's problems, there is an urgency for more parents, teachers, and concerned citizens to encourage the inclusion of consciousness education in the school curriculum, to encourage the artist within, to express the poet's language of sentiment, the mystical language of a spiritual connection.

Young people today lament that they missed the great causes of the 1960s—civil rights, peace, the women's movement. Yet today there is a cause that is even greater and more significant to humanity: spiritual development, so that all people can experience the reality that the similarities that bind us in the spiritual dimension are far more important than the superficial differences we see at the outer level.

Awareness of one's potential

There is no greater gift for you to give your children than the realization that with the use of their creative mind they can do anything they want.

Today's children have been born into the worst of times—and the best of times. It's the worst of times because of the problems that still plague humanity: war, disease, drugs, bigotry, pollution of the planet, and crime—including the very worst crimes: those committed against children.

It's also the best of times, though, because of the evolution of human awareness and consciousness.

Humanity's consciousness has been raised since the 1960s. Then, there were many people who wanted the world to be a better place. Today the average person realizes that we are not just physical beings, but we are also spiritual beings. We understand that the spiritual tools that we can use to improve conditions include visualization, imagination, psychic ability, and prophecy.

You are so fortunate to be living in a time like this when you can give your children and grandchildren such a wonderful gift. That fact that you are reading this book and developing your own ability in the spiritual dimension is evidence that you want the best for your biological family, and also for your greater family of humanity on this planet.

Congratulations and thank you for joining the millions of people who are already taking the first steps into the second phase of human evolution.

Nelda Sheets was the first person other than Jose Silva to start teaching the Silva System. She has taught numerous Silva courses to children and to families. She has also trained instructors to teach both the basic and advanced courses.

Chapter 15
Healing the Family

By Ginger Grancagnolo, Ed.D.

Wounds of the spirit and the soul can drain our energy and impede us from carrying out our life's work just as surely as physical wounds can stop us.

Fortunately, Jose Silva has given us a way to go deep within ourselves to the very best part of ourselves, where we can call on help from our higher self and a higher power to help us heal the hurt, rid ourselves of prejudice and disrespect for others, and by so doing, learn to love ourselves completely.

We do not live in the world alone. The last thing that we read to students in our mental training exercises before we bring them out of level is: "You are a superior human being; you have greater understanding, compassion, and patience with others." Jose put this at the place of honor, the very end of the conditioning cycle, the most powerful spot.

Family is how we got here in the first place. It is the most important relationship we have, yet it often seems like a case of "can't live with 'em, can't live without 'em." How can family issues be avoided, solved, or resolved? Can we heal our own families?

The last 25 years have been spent searching for solutions to societal problems, such as alcoholism, financial stress, lack of communication, control patterns, depression, and various kinds of abuse through self-help books, therapists, talk shows, and television sitcoms. Yet all these efforts seem to offer no real help.

Why are we still stuck in family residue, unable to see the purpose and power of this genetic dilemma? I believe we perpetuate these kinship issues because we don't really understand the function of family.

Family is a divinely ordained gateway so that we all emerge as independent children of God, able to use our full potential to create a life path that is personally

141

fulfilling and that serves the whole of humanity. That sounds idealistic, but it *is* the truth. Family is our first society, our first experience in learning how to fulfill our individual needs while also sharing and interacting with others.

This is obviously an important lesson, and one which applies to us as members of the family of humanity as well as to our biological family. Yet look at how people struggle over property, power, and greed. All too often we fight, argue, abandon, oppress, abuse, and fear each other.

Can we solve these problems? Can we learn to treat all people, depending on their ages, as fathers or mothers, brothers or sisters, sons or daughters?

Yes, we can. We can begin with our own families, and the healing will spread throughout the world.

One of the most effective ways to heal our relationships is through the Silva technique of working a case. You enter the alpha level and mentally detect a problem that someone else has. Then you mentally correct the problem.

The results can be amazing—not only for the person you are mentally sending the healing to, but for yourself as well.

Case-working heals a family

Carol, a Silva graduate from Arizona, shared her family's story. Here it is, in her own words:

"I completed the Silva training in April 1995. The next month I brought my 16-year-old daughter to her first class.

"In order to make the following event meaningful, you will need a brief history of family events prior to attending Silva.

"When she was 15, my daughter developed a serious relationship with an African-American boy, and would sneak out of the house at night to see him. I was married at the time, and my husband was adamantly against interracial dating.

"Our home became a battleground. My daughter refused to stop seeing the boy. Her stepfather could not change his feelings, and I didn't want to come home anymore. This situation was altered by divorce.

"A few months later my daughter told me she was pregnant. I was not understanding. I got restraining orders, no trespassing orders, and anything else I could legally get in writing to try and keep these two apart.

"*Our financial situation, which was precarious, meant nothing to my daughter. There was no way I wanted this unborn child to be linked to me, nor did I want to support it.*

"*Then came Silva—twice!*

"*My daughter went into labor May 30, 1995, and her baby was born the next day, two months early.*

"*The nurses tried to prepare us for all the physical problems the baby might have from being born premature. Throughout the night, I went to level and began working the physical issues that had been mentioned.*

"*At the end of these sessions I would picture the baby as a young child crossing the finish line in a foot race. Then I would hug him and hold his arms up in a sign of victory.*

"*My grandson had some of the physical issues to deal with, but not all of them. He finally came off the ventilator after our local Silva instructor Joan McGillicuddy explained one of Jose Silva's holistic faith-healing techniques that involves rubbing hands together and passing them over the baby seven times. All previous attempts to take him off the ventilator had failed.*

"*I know he has proven to be a bridge between me and his father. I can now see positive in a culture I thought was beneath me because it was different from the way I was raised.*

"*My life is much more rewarding and a whole new view of the world has opened up to me.*

"*I am deeply grateful to Silva instructors Joan McGillicuddy and Tony Estrada for making Silva available to me and my daughter.*"

The differences we see at the outer level are only superficial. At the spiritual alpha level we experience the reality that we are all creations of God who have been sent here for a purpose, and that we must pull together so that we can all fulfill our life's missions.

There is no better place for healing the family, healing ourselves, and healing the problems of the world than at alpha.

Ginger Grancagnolo is a former teacher and guidance counselor. She holds a doctorate in education, as well as master's degrees in theology and guidance counseling. She has been a Silva instructor for more than 20 years and also has a private counseling practice.

Chapter 16

A Medical Breakthrough

By Prof. Clancy D. McKenzie, M.D.

In September, 1969 I took my first Silva Mind Control class—spurred on by the guarantee of clairvoyance or a full money-back guarantee. The experience was exhilarating. No one asked for a refund, and skeptics like myself seemed particularly impressed.

The timing was just right. I had completed formal academic training, including adult and child psychiatry residency programs and adult and child psychoanalytic training courses. This left me free to study my patients and to apply methods of creative thinking as taught in the Silva course.

Looking back, I recognize four ingredients that were vital components for my discovery of new concepts in the field.

The first was the thorough background and formal training I received.

The second was a separation from that body of knowledge for a period of time. You cannot see a cloud when you are in it; you must first separate to catch its outline and see beyond.

The third was creative thinking, which Jose Silva taught me.

The fourth ingredient was love. All of my efforts at deciphering cause, mechanisms, and treatment for serious disorders were propelled strictly out of a sincere desire to help my patients. It is this propelling force that provides the energy, the clarity, and the insights for healing.

Jose Silva's course utilizes the same love energy for psychic diagnosis: Each trainee pictures the patient for the purpose of trying to help that individual, and according to Mr. Silva, it is largely because of this intended purpose that the trainee is able to do so much. As soon as the trainee begins thinking, "Look what I can do," it is gone! It then is necessary to change that thinking to "let me find out what is wrong with this person and what I can do to help." With that, the magic returns.

The creative techniques are taught well enough in the basic Silva course, and so there is no need to repeat them here—nor would this chapter allow enough space. Instead I will briefly summarize the findings for you.

The mystery solved

Often what is most profound, once revealed, is profoundly simple. I hope this is your experience as you read these next few pages, within which I describe a new origin for schizophrenia, depression, and other serious disorders.

Everyone understands posttraumatic stress disorder from combat. A car backfires next to a combat veteran, and he grabs a gun and hides in the woods for a few days. His reality and behavior change to that of wartime; even his body chemistry and physiology match that of the earlier time when his life was in extreme danger.

We "understand" because the earlier events associated with loud noise were so life-threatening that they were indelibly etched upon his mind and brain.

What we fail to recognize is that more terrifying than war trauma to a soldier is separation from the mother to an infant. To all mammalian infants, for the last 150 million years, separation from the mother has meant death. Thus the human infant is highly susceptible to what *it* considers to be a threat of separation.

This need not be an obvious threat of separation, such as one caused by the death of a parent or by parental divorce. Unsuspected events can overwhelm the infant and set the stage for the later development of a serious disorder. Such traumas might include the family moving to a new house and the mother busying herself making the new place look like home, or an older child becoming deathly ill and requiring all the mother's attention for a period of time. In pervious generations, the birth of a younger sibling was devastating because mothers spent five days in the hospital following delivery. These separations might not seem traumatic from the adult perspective, but from an infant's point of view they can be overwhelming. Any event that results in the mother's temporary absence or distraction, potentially, can frighten the infant very much and leave the indelible mark etched upon his or her mind and brain.

Then 10, 20, or 30 years later, instead of a loud noise precipitating the flashback, it is a separation from some other "most important person" (husband, wife, girlfriend, boyfriend, or group), which precipitates the initial step back in time.

And instead of combat reality and behavior, it is infant reality and behavior that we see. A full-grown man, for example, might sit in the middle of the floor, screaming, "Mommy! Mommy!"

The first time I witnessed this was nearly 60 years ago, when I was a young child. I saw an 18-year-old girl running nude through the lawn sprinkler in the front yard, squealing with delight. As a young child I thought, *What's wrong with her? Grown-ups don't do that.*

It took a quarter of a century for me to realize that this was perfectly normal behavior, but transposed in time. Had she been 18 *months* old instead of 18 years old, no one would have thought anything odd about her behavior.

With careful examination, virtually every piece of bizarre reality and behavior of the person with schizophrenia matches in some way that of the infant—and when you have studied this as carefully, and for as long as I have, you will realize that it matches the reality and behavior of the infant at the *precise time* or age that the original trauma occurred.

Simple so far? Just like posttraumatic stress disorder from combat. A loud noise 20 years after the original trauma precipitates a flashback to war experience and behavior because loud noise was associated with terrifying experiences of war. A separation from a "most important person" 20 years after the original trauma precipitates a flashback to the infant experience and behavior because the infant feared separation and felt equally overwhelmed.

The difference

The most important difference between the combat veteran and the person with schizophrenia is that while the veteran flashes back to the brain structures he was using as an adult, the person with schizophrenia flashes back to the brain structures he was using as an infant.

These are the earlier developmental regions of the brain, the parts of the brain we were using before we became so smart. Depending on how early the original trauma occurred, these are the parts of the brain we were using before we learned to walk or talk.

These earlier developmental structures are the ones that produce more of the neurotransmitters involved in the disease process, such as Dopamine. In schizophrenia, when they are reactivated as a result of shifting to infancy, they produce more! Is this not obvious? Why has no one suspected this? Why has everyone looked only from the opposite direction and wondered how Dopamine causes schizophrenia?

Likewise there is a shift of brain activity away from the later developmental structures. Remember the grown man sitting in the middle of the floor screaming for his mommy? Was he using the part of his brain that developed in adult life? Obviously not. And what happens to a part of the body that becomes less active? It *atrophies*. This is much like the common expression "use it or lose it." So the brain atrophies as the result of the disease process.

So why hasn't anyone even entertained the thought that schizophrenia causes brain atrophy? Why do researchers only look at brain changes and wonder how these cause schizophrenia? Why isn't disuse atrophy the first thing they question? With any other part of the body that atrophies, one thinks of disuse atrophy first.

I have long puzzled over the reason why such obvious questions were never considered. Researchers look at the multitude of biological changes that occur with schizophrenia and take them as evidence of biological cause, when common sense would dictate that it more likely represents evidence of biological *results* due to an underlying problem. It stands to reason that if biological change is the result of the disease process, then biological change should be present in great abundance.

One reason for the myopia could be the large amount of funds devoted to the search for biological cause. The powers that be have $970 million allocated for the year 2000, largely to be used to find the biological cause of mental illness. Would they be interested in doing something other than what already is bringing in $970 million?

Aside from the search for biological cause, there is yet another area of investigation that continues to take center stage over and over again: the search for genetic cause. According to Kaplan and Saddock, a leading psychiatric resource book, nearly half of the chromosomes have been implicated in a genetic cause for schizophrenia. Several times each year, for as many decades as I remember, we have seen newspaper headlines about scientists at Ivy League universities identifying the gene that causes schizophrenia. It's the same story each time; only the the university and the identity of the chromosome differ. If such a gene truly were identified, why would they come out with a different one several times each year? If one percent of those research dollars was spent identifying the peak age of origin and age range of origin for each psychiatric symptom or disorder, there no longer would be a question as to origin of mental and emotional problems.

The truth of the matter is that if we combine genetic factors plus familial factors (traits that run in families as well as in the genes), only 10 percent of people with schizophrenia have a first-degree relative with the disorder. It is a fact that some, possibly even most, of this 10 percent have nothing to do with heredity, since familial factors invariably are included among genetic studies as though they were genetic.

This does not mean that I disagree with genetic predisposition. But contrast the 10 percent with our finding of delayed posttraumatic stress disorder. Delayed posttraumatic stress disorder cannot occur without an original trauma. This is a one-to-one ratio!

The Unification Theory of Mental Illness

What we have been describing thus far is a comprehensive formulation for the origin and mechanism of schizophrenia, which applies to all serious mental and emotional disorders that I have studied, and for which the noted late Dr. O. Spurgeon English coined the name, the Unification Theory of Mental Illness.

The Unification Model neither refutes biological change nor precludes genetic predisposition. I have no quarrel with any biological finding. The researchers have done their jobs very well. And their findings are important, because just as a chain can be broken at any link, so can schizophrenia be interrupted at many levels. Biological findings also confirm psychological origin, since nearly every biological change studied is precisely what we would expect to find when persons shift brain activity away from adult brain structures and back to regions of the brain that were active and developing during infancy. Thus biological change is important in confirming traumatic origin.

Genetic factors are a part of the model as well, but they represent predisposition, and their degree of contribution is not yet determined to my satisfaction. This does not change traumatic origin. It is possible that infant trauma and genetic predisposition both could be necessary in some cases. If proven, I shall accept this most readily. The Unification Model encompasses all possibilities. It provides the framework in which all findings are accommodated and given due measure of importance.

Summary

You now have an overview of the origin of schizophrenia. There may or may not be a significant genetic predisposition. Regardless of this factor, in order to develop the disorder later in life, there must be an infant separation trauma. I have not seen this to be otherwise, whenever the history is known. There are thousands of events that can cause the infant to feel threatened with separation and overwhelmed, and most of these are not obvious to the adult. This is no one's fault, and the events are unintentional.

But then years later a spouse, partner, or group rejects or leaves the person. If this experience is sufficiently intense and similar to the first, then that individual flashes back to the time of the original trauma. He begins behaving the way he did as a young child, and he begins using the brain structures he was using then as well. These structures produce more of the neurotransmitters involved in the disease process, and when reactivated that is what they do. Likewise, since there is a shift of brain activity away from the later developmental structures, there develops a disuse atrophy—as would occur in any other part of the body not used. Thus we have a neurobiological disorder.

This is the essence of the Unification Theory of Mental Illness, and if you understand this much, then in my opinion you understand more than most physicians, more than most researchers, and more than the National Institute of Mental Health. You certainly do not know more *about* the disorder, but you have a better understanding of its origin and how it works. This is very important, because with this understanding you will be able to understand why it is unnecessary to have the disorder.

Editor's note: Such insights, those that change an entire field of thought, come only through enlightenment techniques. With the help of the creative insights that he gained at the alpha level, Dr. McKenzie made a major medical breakthrough in understanding the cause of schizophrenia and depression. His findings as to origin have been tested and confirmed on 9,000 patients with schizophrenia, and his treatment methods—based on that insight—are so effective that many patients no longer need medication after the first few months. More of Dr. McKenzie's work, including his new treatment methods and his textbook, are featured on www.DrMcKenzie.com.

CHAPTER 17

SILVA TECHNIQUES IN MENTAL HEALTH

BY SAM GONZALEZ SILVA

Psychologists need to have understanding, insight, compassion, patience, and endurance. Often, that's not enough. There is no greater challenge than understanding another human being. It is especially important to be able to make quick, accurate evaluations when working in crisis situations, such as I have done for the last 21 years.

I've gotten calls in the middle of the night, and I've been paged while presenting Silva classes, to come and evaluate somebody to decide if they need to be committed or not. The wrong choice could mean losing them.

I have had to make many quick decisions in the emergency room when people were brought in with bleeding wrists resulting from a suicide attempt. Many counselors will simply play it safe by confining all of these people. But I use my intuition to sense whether this is just a one-time incident because they were depressed over some particular thing, or if they are chronically depressed and will attempt suicide again. I've sent a lot of people home, and have never lost one yet. I've made the correct choice every time.

You can also lose a person if you select the wrong method of treatment. Sometimes you do need to use a confrontational approach, but if you use it at the wrong time, you can lose all of the rapport that you have established.

A parole officer confronted one of his parolees about getting a job. He told the parolee he was tired of hearing excuses, and that if he didn't get a job right away, the parole officer would have him sent back to prison.

Late that night the parole officer received a call from a deputy sheriff. The parolee had hanged himself, and in his pocket they found the parole officer's card.

The parole officer did what he thought he should, but he still carries the guilt over that decision. I am so grateful that I have been able to use my intuition to avoid situations like that.

There are many other examples of intuition helping psychologists help their patients. A particularly moving story follows.

Establishing better rapport

A psychologist in New York told us about something that happened while he was conducting a group counseling session. One member of the group was a paranoid schizophrenic, and he started acting out. The patient jumped up, started talking rapidly, gesturing excitedly, and causing concern among the other patients.

Previously the therapist would have tried to regain control and calm the patient down. Instead, he tried a technique that he had learned in Silva training that allows you to find out exactly what the other person is experiencing. At your level, you imagine that you are superimposing the subject's head over your own, as though you were putting on a helmet. Then you can test the subject's senses by testing your own senses. Whatever you sense is what your subject is sensing.

The psychologist stayed in his seat and mentally superimposed the patient's head over his own and began thinking about what the patient was experiencing.

Suddenly the patient stopped and looked directly at the psychologist. "You know what I'm thinking, don't you?" the patient asked.

The therapist cautiously acknowledged that he did.

"You have the same thoughts in your head that I have in mine, don't you?" the patient asked.

Once again, the psychologist cautiously confirmed that he believed he did.

"Then that means that I'm not crazy, doesn't it? Because if I'm crazy, you're crazy, too!"

The effect of this realization was spectacular, the psychologist reported. When the patient discovered that somebody else knew what he was experiencing, and was experiencing the same thing, he didn't feel so alone anymore, he didn't feel so different, so abnormal.

Shared experience is very powerful. In this instance, it turned out to be a healing experience.

The patient made more progress as a result of that one experience than he had made in the previous year of therapy.

Sam Gonzalez Silva has worked with Southern Nevada Adult Mental Health Services since retiring from the U.S. Air Force in 1978. He has also been a Silva instructor during that time. He first learned the Silva techniques as a child from his uncle, Jose Silva, and is one of the most knowledgeable Silva instructors in the world.

Chapter 18

ESP for Executives

BY JOHN MIHALASKY, ED.D

In the last few years it has become increasingly difficult for business and industry to stay competitive. Critics charge that there is too much reliance on short-term thinking and on the fear of taking risks.

With more data being generated by more and more computers, there has been a tendency to slip into a posture of "managing by the numbers." The emphasis has been on the use of rationality and logic in problem-solving and decision-making—operations research, management science, modeling, and the development of computers that "think."

Unfortunately, all this has given us more and more incorrect, invalid, and/or unreliable data, faster, to make decisions whose outcomes have been correct about as many times as when we made decisions by holding a wet finger up to the wind.

It is my contention that this state of affairs is due to the fact that not enough has been done to investigate the application of illogical, nonrational, unconscious thinking. We have spent most of our time on rational, logical, conscious thinking. It is (and has been for a long time) necessary to delve into the use of the unconscious.

The purpose of the matieral in this chapter is to explore the basis for the use of the unconscious—ESP, if you will—in the problem-solving and decision-making processes.

The precognitive decision-maker

The PSI Communications Project at the Newark College of Engineering (now the New Jersey Institute of Technology) researched the phenomenon of precognition and the nature of the precognitive decision-maker in the 1960s and 1970s.

There is now evidence to suggest that the successful "hunch player"—a person who makes decisions based on hunches rather than fact or evidence—may have something more solid going for him or her than the odds of chance.

Experiments indicate that what the texts call illogical (and what managers privately call "lucky") decisions have some scientific—that is observable, dependable, and explainable—support.

The research project strongly supports the idea that some executives have more precognitive ability than others—that is, they are better able to anticipate the future intuitively rather than logically and thus, when put in positions where strong data support may not always exist, will make better decisions.

Moreover, a valid test has been developed for determining which people do, and which do not, have this ability.

The test consists of asking the participants to guess at a 100-digit number not currently in existence. (The numbers would later be computer-generated using random-number techniques.) Each of the 100 digits can take on any value from zero to nine. A computer generates a specific target for each participant.

As expected, some people guess above the chance level of 10 correct guesses out of the 100 digits, while others guess at, or below, the chance level.

That some people score above chance on this test would, by itself, not prove they have precognitive ability. But the research has revealed some interesting and significant relationships between high scores on this simple guessing game and other kinds of data.

For example, participants are asked to rank their preferences among five metaphors (such as "a motionless ocean," "a dashing horseman," and so forth) that have been adapted from a psychological test.

Based on their choices, the subjects are divided into "dynamic" and "nondynamic" types. Admittedly, this is not a very sophisticated classification. But invariably, those classified as dynamic by this relatively simple means also tend to score above chance in predicting the computer's random numbers.

In tests on 27 different groups, ranging from four members to 100, dynamic people outscored nondynamic people in 22 of the groups. Statistically, the chances of this happening by accident are fewer than five in 1,000. Many other groups were tested after this initial 27.

But what does a dynamic executive mean? Whatever it connotes, it must also be measured somehow by performance.

Four groups of chief operating officers of corporations, all of them in their present jobs for at least five years, were asked to take the tests. These men had held office long enough to assume responsibility for the reliability of their decisions and the recent performance of their companies.

The first two groups of chief executives were divided into two classes: those who had at least doubled profits in the past five years, and those who had not. The second group included some who had lost money.

Of the 12 men whose companies doubled their profits, 11 scored above the chance level on the computer guessing game. One scored at the chance level, and not a single one fell below chance.

Of the 13 who had not doubled profits, seven scored below chance, one scored at chance, and five scored above chance. This last five had improved profits by 50 to 100 percent. Of the seven who scored below chance, five had improved profits less than 50 percent. Only two of those who scored below chance had improved profits more substantially than that.

The chief executives who had more than doubled their companies' profits in five years had an average score of 12.8.

Those who had not met this criteria scored an average of 8.3, well below what they should have achieved even on a random basis.

To give one striking example of the difference between the two groups: Over a five-year period, one president had increased his company's annual profit from $1.3 million to $19.4 million. His test score was 16. Another had been able to increase his profit by only $374,000. His score was eight.

The third group of participants consisted of 41 members of the Steel Distributors Association. Of the 41, 11 had been a company president for at least a five-year tenure. Of those 11, nine had at least doubled their company's profits over the last five years. Eight of these nine scored above chance. Their average was 11.44 percent. The remaining two, who had not at least doubled their company profits, averaged 9.5 percent, with both scoring at chance or less.

The fourth group was composed of 20 Canadians. Of them, six had been company presidents in their current job for at least five years. Five of the six at least doubled the profits, while one fell into the 50-to-95 percent improvement class. Of the five profit-doublers, three scored above chance; the other two were below chance. The sixth person scored at chance level.

This finding has interesting implications for selection of executives for the "top spot." Given a group of people who have the usual traits needed for such a position, which one should be selected?

I feel that it should be the person with the something "extra"—in this case the ability to make good decisions under conditions of uncertainty.

In the groups of company presidents tested, had the selection been made on the basis of their scores, there would have been an 81.5 percent chance of choosing a person who at least doubled the company's profits, while if someone who scored below chance had been chosen, there would have been only a 27.3 percent chance of choosing a person who would have doubled the company's profits.

Development of precognition abilities

Precognition is not a mystical origin, but rather an energy or information transfer using senses currently not recognizable or known. I believe that everyone has this ability. It is thus not a question of having precognitive ability but rather one of developing the use of the precognitive ability we all possess.

Precognitive information comes in many forms—dreams at night, daydreams, flashes, hunches, and "gut feelings." The user has to first be aware of these various forms and then look for their appearance.

With precognition abilities, usage sharpens the talent.

With executives, it has been found that they believe in precognition, use it, and then build a rationale to justify the idea they used, or the decision they made, so as "to not look foolish."

Precognitive information is usually obtained concerning a matter in which the problem-solver has been deeply and emotionally involved. It also tends to arrive at times when the mind is supposedly resting and not thinking specifically about the problem.

Problem-solvers accept and use such information to make decisions, find solutions, and form ideas. There are many engineers and scientists, but the number of those who can come up with good ideas is very small.

These superior idea-generators review the same hard data that others have, but they must contribute something extra to come up with their ideas. Could not part of this something extra be their ability to gather information through what is loosely called ESP?

The utilization of precognition ability

Research on precognition ability does not support the idea that this ability is a unique trait. However, it does support the idea that some people have more of this ability—and make better use of it—than others.

The executive who wishes to avail himself of the ability to use precognition must first understand the nature and form of this phenomenon.

Precognition is a part of the unconscious process. As such, it is not bound by the usual limitations of space and time.

The ideal condition for the utilization of precognition information is when it does not require decoding or interpretation. The interpretation process, which tends to be logical and rational, can rework the illogical, but incorrect, information.

An example of getting precognition information would be the sudden thought that comes to an automobile driver to take a side road rather than the usual straight and shorter highway. The thought is not heeded, and later on down the highway, the motorist runs into a traffic jam.

Sir Winston Churchill is reported to have "gotten a feeling" that caused him to sit on the side of the car that he never uses. Later on during the auto trip, as the auto was speeding down the road, a bomb exploded, causing the auto to rise up on two side wheels. Due to Churchill's weight, the auto did not turn over but righted itself. Had Churchill not heeded the information that came to him, he would probably have been killed.

The executives studied not only had to be able to recognize the format of precognition information, but they also had to be prepared to get it any time. For them, this was not an ability that could be turned on and off at will.

Next, the user of precognition information has to have the faith and "guts" to use it. It is necessary to accept the existence of the phenomenon, whether or not the user knows how or why it happens.

Finally, the "practice makes perfect" rule should be followed. The intuitive decision-maker has to make using precognition information a habit.

Each decision-maker has to test the existence of precognition for himself with an open and positive mental attitude.

If you deny its existence you are, in effect, repressing it, and it will go away. We tend, out of fear, to resist anything we do not understand. Our research indicates that the best results were achieved when resistance was at a minimum. For ESP abilities to function, we have to overcome any resistance we may have.

Several individuals I know had precognition abilities, were frightened of them, and ultimately managed to suppress them. When they realized that the ability could be very useful, a more relaxed attitude resulted and the ability began to return.

Common sense dictates that in any situation where knowledge is incomplete, the approach should be gentle. This is probably the best advice one can offer concerning precognition.

Be willing to believe that it exists. Have the courage to use it.

Do not expect to get good intuitive action under stressful conditions. When test subjects are under stress, the results follow the inverse hypothesis—that is, the dynamic managers who should have scored above chance did not do so. In fact, they scored below chance.

Similarly, you should not expect good results when you are tired or physically under par. Precognition tests consistently indicate that better results are achieved when tests are held early in the day.

Alcohol may also impair precognitive ability. After a three-martini lunch, dynamics from a group of production engineers scored 9.9 on average, and nondynamics scored 9.3 on average. The entire group, in other words, scored below chance. While we cannot with certainty blame the martinis, much evidence already exists concerning alcohol's effect on mental processes. I would suspect that ESP is no exception.

Lastly, you should probably try not to make intuitive decisions in any environment where you feel dominated. If you do, it is possible you may "intentionally" predict the future incorrectly.

It appears that if you are assured of a dominant role in the environment, and have precognitive ability, you will probably score high, almost as if validating the status quo. We call this the dominance effect.

But if your role is a dominated one, you may reinforce the existing hierarchical structure by "deliberately" scoring low.

During tests with mixed-sex groups the dominating sex followed the hypothesis; dynamics scored higher than nondynamics. But the dominated sex produced a mirror image—that is, dynamics scored lower.

In another case, executives/owners who were fathers or fathers-in-law dominated their sons and sons-in-law. (By dominance we do not mean numerical superiority. It might better be termed environmental.)

In tests in groups where the environment was discernibly dominated by one sex, the dominance effect was noted. In groups where the sexes met on an equal footing there was no mirror imaging or following of the inverse hypothesis.

Using precognition for good business

Here is a story from Silva instructor Nelda Sheets about a time when she used precognition abilities to obtain information to help her employer make a major business decision, in her own words:

"When you practice using your intuition enough, you learn to recognize that special feeling of being right. Jose Silva referred to this as an emotional feeling.

"I was the office-manager and a salesperson for a John Deere dealership. My boss and I had taken the Silva training together and used it for such things as mentally encouraging people to pay their bills. If we reached a certain sales quota, we'd win a trip to Nassau in the Bahamas. Our goal was 50 tractors.

"When it was time to place our next order, my boss and I worked a case to determine what kind of tractors our customers would need. Normally I was the orientologist, but this time he was. I was the psychic. I went to level and asked how many diesel tractors we should order but was interrupted by a sign on my mental screen flashing the words "order all 50 tractors now" over and over. I told Gene, my boss, and he tried to talk me out of it. (We normally ordered five tractors at a time.) Gene had another concern: our bank balance.

"I took a deep breath, relaxed, and did some deepening exercises to make sure I was at a good deep level. I mentally asked the question again. In response, I got the same neon sign flashing, telling me to order all 50 tractors. This time, I got that familiar feeling that I was right. I knew I was right, and I told Gene. Gene agreed this time, but because of a tax incentive he knew about. Having tractors in stock once a tax break was announced would help the business.

"We ordered all 50 tractors. The John Deere people called me, thinking it was a mistake, since we always order just five at a time. The tractors were delivered, but our lot would only hold five! We had tractors parked in every empty space we could find. The local paper even came to do a story on us.

"About a week later we got a call from the John Deere office saying that their workers had gone on strike and that no more equipment would be available. We had our tractors, and we sold all 50. And we enjoyed Nassau!"

Professor Emeritus John Mihalasky taught industrial engineering at New Jersey Institute of Technology (formerly Newark College of Engineering) for 31 years. He was the director of the PSI Communications Project. Although he retired in 1987, he continues to teach part-time. He is one of the authors of Executive ESP, *the book about the landmark research project on precognition (Prentice Hall, 1974).*

Chapter 19
Intuitive
Management

by Hans DeJong

Imagine that you are working for a corporation and you do your job so well that your efforts produced several millions of dollars in new revenue. How would that make you feel?

And suppose at the same time that your efforts are bringing in that kind of new revenue, the product you developed was saving people's lives. How would that make you feel? What do you suppose the leaders of the company would think of you? You'd be a hero in that company, wouldn't you? And imagine how proud your family would feel of your tremendous success.

The head of the research department at New Dimensions in Medicine (NDM), based in Ohio, didn't have to imagine it. He experienced it firsthand after using a Silva technique to help him find the solution to a problem.

Probably the most common problem in business is making the correct decision. Jose Silva always reminded us that there is no such thing as a problem without a solution. If you have enough information, it is easy to make decisions. If you could tell in advance what the results of your decision would be, imagine how much easier it would be to make decisions.

In the case of the research director at NDM, he needed more information to complete his project, which was to create a formula for artificial arteries. (At the time, doctors had to transplant arteries from other parts of the patient's body to replace bad arteries in the heart. If they could use artificial arteries, it would be much easier on patients, and would undoubtedly extend their lives in many cases.)

The researcher had already developed four new formulas at his beta level, but there was still a problem with the body rejecting the "foreign" material.

The researcher attended a Silva course. Instructor Ken Obermeyer explained that there is more information available at alpha than at beta, and that you can gain access to the information that you need by going to your level. Another common way to access information in this creative dimension is in dreams.

The NDM researcher reasoned that there was nothing to lose and perhaps something to gain, so he programmed to have a dream that would contain information that he could use to solve his problem—how to create the best formula for artificial arteries.

He awakened sometime during the night and wrote out a formula. Then he went back to sleep.

When he awakened in the morning, he saw the formula, went into the laboratory, put a sample together, and found that the human body would accept the plastic used to create the artificial arteries.

"One interesting note about this creative solution," Obermeyer reminds us, "is that, according to the researcher, if he had considered the formula with his beta information, he wouldn't believe it to be one the body would accept." In other words, reason and logic would not have led him to this solution.

This is not to say that reason and logic should be ignored, Obermeyer is quick to point out. We all need the logical, objective beta level for analysis and reasoning—but we also need the creative and intuitive alpha level for the creative insight that it offers, and for the help and guidance that higher intelligence can provide to us.

Where did the researcher's idea come from? Was it from his own subconscious mind? Or did the idea come from higher intelligence?

Whatever the source, the idea solved the problem at hand and has provided many benefits for humanity.

Alpha functioning proves valuable

Several years ago, 25 RCA Records executives took the Silva training. Naturally, they hoped to observe improvements in their ability to perform their jobs.

Silva International organized a research project to measure changes in the executives' personality traits using a standard psychological test that has proven its value through the years in accurately assessing personality traits. The executives answered the test questions before and after completing the Silva training.

J.K. Mangini, Divisional Vice President, Occupational Services for RCA Records, liked what he observed. He called it "an outstanding experience that left a positive mark on all who participated."

He also said, "The Silva Method has provided a definitive way to allow people to be self-motivated."

The research report on the personality testing stated that "indications of change were very positive in terms of personal development as well as viewed from the perspective of characteristics that should make for effective management."

"The group showed significant change in skills reflective of positive self- and organizational management," the report continued. "Indeed, if one were to hand-pick factors to increase relating to management, it would have been a task to select more appropriate dynamics."

Mangini echoed the praise: "The course clearly depicted a way for all to enrich their lives, to gain better control of circumstances that, in the past, may have negatively affected them. I am grateful for understanding this rather uncomplicated way of approaching my job and personal life and I know that RCA Corporation will come out a winner also for having endorsed such a positive program."

Read the stories and books about almost any successful businessperson and you will see places in their careers where they made decisions that were not entirely logical, but that proved to guide them to their greatest success.

This happens because they are natural alpha-thinkers.

Now you are an alpha-thinker with an advantage over the "naturals." You are a *trained* alpha-thinker. You now know how to manage the process—to do what the researcher at New Dimensions in Medicine did and enter the alpha level whenever you desire to take advantage of the creative insights and new information that's available there.

Once you make your decision with the help of the insight you gained at alpha, test it, observe the results, make any necessary adjustments, and become a hero in your company and to your family with your success.

Hans DeJong has introduced more people to the Silva programs than any other instructor in the United States since 1976. Since 1995 he has been consulting one-on-one with business owners and professionals, routinely doubling and even tripling their income.

CHAPTER 20
INTUITIVE SELLING

BY DENNIS HIGGINS

To increase your sales, learn to ask questions on a subjective, intuitive level. Before you meet with a person, you can earn the right to ask them subjective questions by "working a health case" on them. That's a moral feeling on my part. (Working a health case means checking a person out physically to determine if they have any health problems. If so, then you mentally correct them.)

First you help them, and that will tune you in to them. In the Silva courses, you get all kinds of points of reference by projecting into metals, plants, and animals.

Have you been getting points of reference in your sales field?

➢   Are you getting points of reference on desire?

➢   Are you getting points of reference on why people want to buy?

➢   Are you getting points of reference on when it's time to close a deal?

How would you do that? How would you get points of reference on when someone is ready to close?

You could go to level, go back over sales that you have made, follow that person, and see when it was that he or she was ready to say yes. That becomes a point of reference for you.

Feel it. Feel what it felt like to sit there. Listen to what the person is saying and the meaning behind the words. Replay the conversation, and make that point of reference yours.

Then recall another sale when somebody bought from you, and make that a point of reference.

Everyone wants to know, "How do I handle objections?"

Your job is to find out what they want, and to find out how your product can help them attain it.

So when somebody comes up with an objection, what is the first thing you would do, as a Silva grad? Go to level. Put your three fingers together. Defocus your vision. Take a deep breath. Mentally ask them, "What's your real objection?"

Using the Silva Method while you are on your feet is very simple. Use the tools that you have.

If I am going to go talk to a group of people that I don't know, I try to get points of reference. Where is the building where you will be making the presentation? Look it up on the map. Visit the building. Get some points of reference. Who are these people? What are their names? At least get the name of the company. If you know where the building is, then you can go see what kind of people go in there every day.

The night before a big talk, you can program yourself to wake up automatically at the exact time when most of those people are going to be the most receptive. Then program them. And program yourself.

Then when you walk into the room, make your talk a needs-based talk. In fact, it would be great to make your life a needs-based life, so that you can leave this a better world, as Jose Silva said.

If you really care about the people that you do business with, it shows.

Dealing with fear

Some people are afraid to go see big clients, or to go see a lot of clients. It's okay to admit that you are afraid. That's why we have the blue-framed mirror. At level, you can identify what it is you fear.

Let's say you don't like making cold calls on the telephone. If you don't know why, then enter your level and mentally picture yourself calling someone. See what happens, what the person's response is, and what you might be afraid of.

Perhaps you don't want to bother people, because you know that they are busy. You want to be liked, so you don't want to be a bother. If this is the case, go to level and ask what the reasons are that someone would want to talk to you and would like you. Instead of focusing on yourself, focus on your client.

Maybe you are afraid that they will say no because of a lack of money. Enter your level and ask yourself how many of the people that you are going to sell to really can buy your product. Ask yourself why they would buy your product.

Perhaps you are afraid of being rejected. Go to your level and think about whether clients are rejecting you or rejecting the product. Don't make yourself the issue. As long as you are concentrating on the client's needs, you are not the issue.

When you enter your level yourself, and you ask yourself these types of questions, then you will come up with the answers that are right for you. One of the greatest discoveries of Jose Silva's research is that nobody can do it for you as well as you can do it for yourself. Not a hypnotist. Not a sales manager. Not a psychologist. You can help yourself more effectively and quickly than anyone.

How to establish instant rapport

When we taught the first Silva Sales Lecture Series, Jose sat in to see how we were doing. He was so enthusiastic that he gave us a new technique on the spot.

It is a technique that you can use to establish instant rapport with a person, even if you are meeting them for the first time. Here's what he taught us to do:

At night, when you are ready to go to sleep, enter your level and program yourself to automatically wake up at the ideal time to use the technique. Then the first time you wake up during the night, or in the morning, enter your level and program it.

At your level, bring together the tips of the thumb and first two fingers of either hand. Then tell yourself that when you meet the person you have in mind, all you need to do is to relax and apply your Three Fingers Technique, as you are doing while at your level, and the person will sense that you are there to help them, that you are being honest with them, and that they can trust you.

Just one cautionary note: Tell the truth. They will sense what you really feel, so if you are planning to take advantage of them in some way, they'll sense that very quickly and you won't make a sale. The law of cause and effect works.

But if you sincerely want to help people, and you are willing to do what is best for your client because that is the right thing to do, then they will sense it and will immediately like you and trust you.

Dennis Higgins used the Silva techniques he learned in 1971 to become a top salesman, selling executive-development training to banks, corporations, and marketing companies. He worked on Sales Power *with Jose Silva and developed the Silva Sales Power home-study course.*

Chapter 21
Stress-free Telemarketing

By Katherine L. Sandusky

The Silva techniques have been a big help to me in my career. They helped me become a star in the very stressful job of telemarketing.

When I got my first job, shortly after finishing high school, some people wondered if I even had a chance of succeeding. But I was lucky, because that job was with Silva International.

The first thing they told me to do was to file some invoices. "What's an invoice?" I asked. That kind of shook them up, because I was supposed to be handling the accounts for instructors throughout the United States.

One of the benefits of working for Silva International is that you can take the course for free. I took advantage of that and signed up for the next course they offered. Ed Bernd Jr. was my instructor.

At the time I took the course, Ed was working on *Sales Power* with Jose Silva and Dennis Higgins, our sales trainer. That was a very lucky coincidence for me. The combination of Jose Silva's training with the things Dennis and Ed taught me about selling, soon had me doing more than just taking orders for materials from Silva instructors. I was selling them additional merchandise.

Ed noticed this, and he asked me if I was interested in coming to his next class to take orders for books and tapes from the students. *Take orders for merchandise?* I thought. *I could do better than that—I could* sell *merchandise!* I went to level and imagined that I would sell so much merchandies that Ed would ask, "How did you *do* that?"

And it worked! The combination of my programming and using the sales tips that I had gotten impressed Ed so much that he insisted I come to all of his classes and sell merchandise.

After five years of working for Silva International, I moved to Austin, Texas, about 250 miles from Laredo and got a job working for the State of Texas, as well as working part-time job for the local newspaper.

The job with the newspaper was one that few people succeed at: telemarketing.

My job was to make phone calls for four hours each evening, either to sell subscriptions to the newspaper, get people to accept a free trial that would turn into a paid subscription after the trial period ended, or get people to renew and upgrade subscriptions.

If you've ever worked that kind of job, you know how difficult it can be. You are calling people who don't especially want to talk to you. It is not like selling to students who have come to the class because they are interested in what you have to offer. Many of the people you call are not interested in reading a newspaper at all, much less paying to do so.

Some reps are lucky to make two or three sales per hour. In fact, I have read that good telemarketers usually average about 15 to 18 completed calls per hour— and that says nothing about how many sales result from those calls.

I knew I had to do better than that. And I knew I *could* do better than that. So I recalled how I had programmed myself when Ed asked me to sell merchandise during the class. I recalled the feelings I had when I programmed, and again when the programming was working so well and people were buying so many items from me. I also recalled how good it felt when Ed was so surprised and delighted at how much I had sold.

He had taught me to recall my past successes. Dennis Higgins had suggested establishing "sales points of reference" at my level. That's what I did. I recalled what I had done before, the results I had gotten, and how great it felt, and I referred back to those experiences—my "points of reference."

It really paid off. This is what Sharon, my sales manager, wrote in a letter dated July 7, 1997, to document my successes:

"One week, working part-time (15 hours), Kathy had a total of 132 sales. This is more than any other salesperson I've ever seen, including myself. She typically makes more than 100 sales per week.

"She sold 88 conversions over a two-night period, persuading subscribers to the weekend paper to upgrade to daily subscriptions, and reactivating prior customers whose subscriptions had expired. One time, she sold 61 conversions in a four-hour shift."

One reason Sharon was so impressed with my results is because she knew I had never taken a sales course. *"If you ask her what kind of 'close' she uses when she's selling, she'll probably talk about what she's wearing,"* she wrote.

Sharon wasn't quite sure what I was doing, but she saw the results. Her letter continued, *"Kathy has a way of sensing just the right thing to say, in order to persuade people to buy. She projects a sincerity and enthusiasm—even over the telephone—that people respond to."*

Sharon concluded her letter by syaing, *"Kathy said it was a program called 'Silva Mind Control' that helped her become such a persuasive salesperson, and I believe her because I can't account for her outstanding success in any other way."*

The case-working part of the Silva course—where you mentally detect what kind of problems people have, and then after confirming that you were accurate, you imagine correcting the problems—opened up my intuition where I could tell quickly whether to spend time trying to sell to that person, or whether I should move on to another call.

One thing I noticed is that a lot of our sales reps stayed on the phone too long. I guess they were trying to avoid being rejected. They probably are not in too big a hurry to call somebody else, who might reject them.

But the way I see it is that the more calls you can make, the more chances you have of finding people who will accept your offer. Sure, you may get rejected by more people if you make more calls, but you will also find more people who accept. As soon as I got the feeling that the person wasn't going to accept my offer, I thanked them and moved on to the next call.

It really helped me to be able to sense whether the person was going to buy or not. There is a story in *Sales Power*, a book by Jose Silva and Ed Bernd Jr. (Putnam Berkley Group, 1992) about how Paulette Temple, a Silva graduate in Oklahoma City, used visualization when she was on the telephone with people. She was a dismissal clerk at a hospital and had the difficult job of collecting the difference between a patient's total bill and what the insurance paid.

"Nobody likes to be asked for money when they are sick or hurting," she said, "so you have some idea what I was up against. After going through the Silva course I began using my Mirror of the Mind Technique and picturing every patient surrounded by love. Then I imagined myself asking the patient to give whatever it was I needed to complete his dismissal."

She did such a good job that she was promoted to a collector. There were three other ladies in the department, all with many years of experience, while Paulette had none. When she told the story, she had been in the new job for seven months, and had been the office's top collector every month.

Carrying mental projection a step further

I learned from Dennis Higgins that his mother Ruby had carried the idea of mentally projecting to your customers a step further. Ruby Higgins is a bubbly, happy, 75-year-old redheaded fireball with a knack of making everybody feel good. She has adapted one of Jose Silva's techniques called the Alpha Uni-Mold. With that technique, you imagine a mold in the shape of a perfect human being. Then you imagine all of the people who are sick or hurt backing into the mold, so that you can mentally correct all of the problems of all of the people at one time.

Ruby imagines a similar mold for the people she calls. She imagines them in the mold, filled with positive white light that will bring health, happiness, love, peace, contentment, and abundant success.

How well does this work? It works so well that she is able to keep the CEOs of the nation's biggest computer businesses on the phone for a survey for 30 to 45 minutes. When she is through with the survey they even thank her! Some executives have remembered her from a 30-minute phone call more than a year ago.

Ruby says, "You can use this mold in any situation you encounter in your career, family, school, or any relationship. It helps *you* while you're helping others because *you* are in the mold too. That's why I have so much energy at the end of the day after making all these calls."

Kathy Sandusky first came to work for Silva International in 1989. She now owns her own marketing company, CS Marketing, Inc., in Austin, Texas, specializing in selling Silva courses and products.

Chapter 22

Direct-marketing success

By Dr. John M. La Tourrette, Ph.D.

Guidance from higher intelligence can take many forms. I should know; one message to me came as a kick in the groin.

I was operating a karate school at the time, and the message was delivered by one of my lower-ranking students, a brown belt! It was during a training session, and he shouldn't have been able to land a kick like that—certainly not three times. I'd have been terribly embarrassed if I hadn't been so busy hurting.

And what was the message? Review my career choice—and my life.

Do-it-yourself method doesn't work

I was brought up by my parents to be a hard worker. So after I found my niche in life as a martial arts instructor, I worked hard at doing what I loved to do. In fact, I was working 60 to 70 hours a week, 52 weeks a year, doing what I loved to do. After six years of pounding away hour after long hour, my chosen field wasn't fun anymore; it was just hard work. So I looked for something that would help make my life better.

I'd studied the popular money-making courses and the current self-help books. Some of them were good, especially *Think and Grow Rich* by Napoleon Hill, but they were all missing something. I read books that told me I could program my brain to become a money magnet, but they never told me how.

I first heard about Silva in 1970, after my release from the army. I was a Korean-language code-breaker and a translator, and I'd served three years in

Korea. During my stay there I also earned the third-degree black belt in tae kwon do, a Korean form of specialized self-defense that emphasizes the kicking arts.

At first I was only looking for something that would help enhance my martial- arts ability. The Silva System seemed to be an answer; it fit with my logical precise mind. I wanted to get much, much better at martial arts, so I programmed my unconscious to give me that skill. Notice that I left out the step of the higher intelligence connection, or the "deserving." Well, what you don't deserve and have not earned, you can't get. But I didn't know that—at least, not at first.

Then I got that painful message by way of my brown-belt student.

That night I went to level and asked mentally how it happened, since I was programming to be better, not worse!

The answer that came back was simple: I didn't deserve to be better.

I was shocked. What did "deserve" have to do with anything. I thought all I needed was proper programming. My next step was to ask, "What do I need to do to *deserve* to be better?"

A major attitude adjustment

The answer that came back was a real shocker: to stop drinking alcohol and stop smoking cigarettes, and then to ask again.

I couldn't believe it; my inner-conscious mind was talking back to me!

I decided to ignore it. The Christmas party was only two days away, and I didn't want to miss that party (and all that booze) because of voices in my head.

I had a great time at the party. At about 2:30 a.m., Mary, the wife of the man hosting the party, asked me to take the last case of beer home with me. Otherwise her husband would drink it all and be sicker than a dog. I agreed and grabbed the last case on my way out the door. Before I'd gotten five steps towards my Jeep I heard the screen door slam open and this drunk was running out the door after me.

"You can't take my beer—I'll kill you," he screamed at me.

I just looked at him totally amazed, because for the first time I didn't see a friend. Instead I saw a fat old man with vomit running down his chest and fresh urine stains on his trousers.

Just then, a voice spoke in my right ear, saying, "That's *you* in 10 years!"

It wasn't my conscious mind. It wasn't a voice from my unconscious mind. It was a voice from outside those two minds, the voice of higher intelligence, that gave me the information and also the motivation I need to change and to adopt a better living style so I could *deserve* what I was programming for.

I haven't touched a drop of alcohol since that night.

My point is this: Higher intelligence works in ways that we mere mortals have trouble understanding. So I don't bother trying to understand any more; I just accept the blessings that fall my way after proper programming.

I now know that if I program properly I will either get what I program for, or I will get a training methodology that I can undertake so I *will* deserve what I've programmed for. I just need to allow my mind to release so it will recognize the opportunities when they come—for they surely will come.

Life changes produce surprising results

Something really scary happened to my martial arts because of the Silva System. And I had no clue it was happening until after it happened.

Except for general programming, I'd never used the psychic skills specifically to enhance my martial arts. I'd say things like, "Every day in every way I'm going to get better and better at sparring."

Then one day I entered a tournament in Pocatello, Idaho.

I attacked my opponent, whomped on him, then broke away. He seemed slower than slow molasses.

Now here comes the scary part: Not one of the four judges, nor the referee, had seen me score a point!

So I did it again. And again. And again. I did it four different times and the judges made no notice of what I was doing.

By this time I was getting a bit annoyed, so I attacked my poor opponent, actually penetrating his mouth twice and his body once with a three-shot combination. As I retreated, he counterattacked with a reverse punch that I easily saw coming and deflected with my elbow.

The judges did not see my three punches. The judges did not see my block. But they did see my opponent's punch, and he was awarded a point.

After he was awarded the point, the referee saw blood dripping down from his lower lip where I'd rammed two teeth through it. The bright red blood was running down his chin onto his white uniform.

In a karate tournament, drawing an opponent's blood gets you disqualified.

And what was I disqualified for? The judges disqualified me for drawing blood with a blow *that they never saw!*

That night I went to level and asked for an explanation of what had really happened. Here's the answer that came through: "You are now so fast that no one trained in 'normal' karate can see what you are doing. If they see anything at all, they are seeing only a blur."

After that, I created four tournament fighting drills that were visual enough so that the judges and refs could actually see them, but that the actual opponent, from his different head-to-head perspective, couldn't. Then my team went out and kicked butt!

Business guidance proves profitable

So how does the above story relate to guidance from higher intelligence for business and marketing? Good question.

No matter how much you know about a subject, no matter how good you are at something, it doesn't mean a thing until somebody wants it. You don't make any money, and it doesn't help anybody, until you market it.

This is true of anybody applying for a job. You've got to sell yourself—you've got to convince the interviewer that you are strong enough to lift the load, that you can type fast enough to get all the letters done on time, that you can dance well enough, manage well enough, learn well enough, and so forth, to do the job he or she wants done.

In 1980 I retired from my first business for two reasons. First, I was burnt out from doing all that physical training. Second, I realized that people wanted to learn what I had to teach and would buy books if I wrote them.

So I went to level and asked higher intelligence for a book topic that would really help martial artists and would also help me to evolve positively in the process of writing the book.

Two days later I was in The BookShop, a great bookstore in Boise, Idaho. I ran across a tiny 23-page pamphlet titled *Principles of Personal Handgun Defense* by Jeff Cooper while browsing in the martial arts section.

I picked it up and looked at it, then put it back on the rack. I didn't buy the pamphlet, despite several impulses to do so. I let my conscious mind talk me out of it. The further away from the bookstore I got, though, the stronger the impulse to buy the pamphlet became.

I didn't know then that higher intelligence guides us by arranging coincidences in our lives, but I had learned to trust my intuition, so I grudgingly went back and got it.

Principles of Personal Handgun Defense is a small report on mental training principles for police officers, Special Forces and mercenaries, or anyone else that might encounter handguns in their job.

As I read it, I wondered why I'd even paid the $5 for it. I read the pamphlet over and over again. Finally the light flashed on in my head. What higher intelligence was trying to tell me finally broke through. I realized that no one else in the world had ever written a martial arts book on mental training.

That's how my first book, *Mental Training of a Warrior* came about. I expanded on Jeff Cooper's concept, making it applicable to martial arts athletes.

I also wanted to make decent money and gain positive recognition from those who really counted in the martial arts field. So once again I went to level and asked for guidance.

I was told to send a copy of the manuscript to Grand Master Ed Parker for my thesis requirements for fifth-degree black belt. He loved it and agreed to write the book's preface. He also promoted me to fifth-degree black belt. This was back when a fifth-degree black belt was a rare and prized commodity.

I didn't get an answer at that time to the part of the question about making money. The next day, though, I was having some karate brochures printed at the local print shop and I mentioned my manuscript to the printer. He told me to publish the book myself and that he would print it.

That sounded good to me, so we talked numbers. He wanted $7 per book and a minimum of 1,000 copies printed before he'd agree to do the job. There was no way I wanted to pay that much money—$7,000 up front. It didn't seem right to me, so I backed off quickly.

I went to level again. This time the answer was to talk to other printers. The next day I called around until I found a printer that had an answer that just felt right to me. He told me that he didn't print books but that he knew of a company that did, with reasonable prices.

I had my first book printed for $1.52 per copy, and in the first six months I made more than $26,000. That book, *Mental Training of a Warrior*, is still in print today and remains one of our best-sellers.

That was the beginning of my second business, which I named Warrior Publications. Two years later I sold my first karate studio and retired for the first time. It was 1980. In the next three years I wrote three more books, and all of them were written without the conscious guidance of higher intelligence. They were not best-sellers either. I was still learning.

Finally finding the perfect niche

In 1987 the sale of my books fell drastically. I went to level to find a solution.

My higher self gave me the answer I needed through Lynn, my wife, the next day. She said, "John, it's easy. You've got to remember that people don't read much anymore, especially teenagers and young adults. They are the television generation. Just do an advertisement and see if they'll buy the videos you've been selling to the karate studios."

What a concept! It was something I'd never have thought of.

I went to level and asked higher intelligence if it would give me an answer on what specifically to sell to people.

The short, curt answer came back instantly: Pick up the telephone, call some of your students, and find out for yourself.

So I did. The next day I called one of my black belts and asked him if he'd be interested in some self-defense videos on the kenpo techniques. He hesitated and tried to get out of buying anything. He just was not interested.

He then mentioned that if I had anything on tournament fighting, he might be interested.

Out of nowhere a thought popped into my head. I told him that I was thinking about doing a video on speed.

"Speed! Speed! You've got something on speed? I want it! I want it as soon as it's ready!"

I hung up and called another one of my black belts. It sounded like a tape recording of the first student's response. Their enthusiasm was enough to convince me, and I decided to write an advertisement for *Black Belt* magazine.

Guided to the perfect ad on the first attempt

Writing that ad was tough. After several hours of effort, I relaxed, went to level, and asked again for guidance. The answer was to get John Caples' books down from my shelf and go through them until I found the correct model for my ad. Higher intelligence told me that when I found it, I'd know it. (John Caples was the first to "test" advertising by measuring how many sales were made as a direct result of the advertising—the principle on which the entire direct-marketing industry is based.)

I found a classic ad that fit the format of what I wanted to say, and in about three hours I'd adapted the concept to work for speed enhancement for martial arts athletes. The headline was "Speed Hitting: How to Hit a Man 11 Times or More in One Second or Less!"

That ad produced $1.2 million in its first year!

A worldwide reputation for writing winning ads was also part of the success.

The more you do the alpha training drills the better you get at receiving the guidance from higher intelligence. Now I almost feel as if there is a telephone hookup between us. If they want me to contact them, I'll get a gut feeling that something is not right.

You can claim success if you use the alpha level properly, with the correct attitude. If you have the desire and you feel you deserve it, then you can get it with the help of higher intelligence.

John La Tourrette has written 18 books and produced 247 videos about martial arts and sports psychology, and he is recognized as the nation's leading expert in the field of mind training for martial arts. He has a doctorate in sports psychology and founded his own publishing company in 1978. He has been a Silva instructor since 1985.

Chapter 23
The complete
PR agency

BY LINDA ARNOLD

The Silva techniques have become part of the daily routine at The Arnold Agency. They help in every aspect of agency work: the creative work that we do, business management, client relationships, and help us stay healthy in this stressful business.

If I didn't know better, I would think that the Silva people had custom designed a program especially for us.

A creative dimension

The first thing we learned in the Silva training was how to enter the alpha brain wave level where we could think with the right-brain hemisphere. That is where we find creativity.

Many people have gotten in touch with their creative abilities simply by entering their level and practicing as we are taught in the class.

Even more exciting to me is the list of highly creative people who have found value in entering level the Silva way and doing their creative work there:

> ➤ Best-selling author of *Jonathan Livingston Seagull* Richard Bach praised the course publicly. "Mental discipline and creative visualization are what's behind the power of the Silva Method," he said in an article in *Harper's Bazaar* magazine. Shakti Gawain said in her book, *Living in the Light*, "I took the course and was amazed." She added, "The most important technique I learned in that course was the basic technique of creative visualization."

183

➤ Band leader Doc Severinsen has composed music while at his level. An article that ran in the *Laredo News* in 1980 said that he told them it helped him to be better in touch with his own spiritual life and in doing so he was a much better person.

➤ World-renowned sculptor Harry Jackson said it brought him the peace of mind he had been searching for.

➤ Singers Vicki Carr and Metropolitan Opera star Marguerite Piazza are Silva graduates, as are actresses Carol Lawrence and Loretta Swit, to mention just a few.

Intuitive management

The agency business is very creative, but it's still a *business*.

All of the Silva tools and techniques that other businesses find valuable are worthwhile here. The ability to make decisions at the alpha level, to smooth out conflicts within the office, to forecast and make projections for the future, to manage our money better, to determine the best way to prospect for new clients—all of these are valuable to us.

A creative business like ours is different from many other businesses because we are constantly being pulled in two different directions.

Creative people are open and spontaneous; they don't keep their emotions under tight control because this cuts off the creative flow. They express whatever they're feeling or thinking at the moment because that's what creativity is all about.

Management, on the other hand, is about control. Managers control budgets, work flow, schedules, and projects. They prefer predictability and certainty over spontaneity. They control their emotions. When they express emotion, they are sending a message, and they assume that other people are doing the same.

There are outstanding creative people who are good managers of course, and there are managers who are very creative. The ideal situation is to have people who can switch back and forth between managing and controlling and being completely open and spontaneous.

Through Silva, we have been able to understand this process better. When we are talking with someone, we quickly identify whether they are in a management mode or a creative mode. If a person is thinking creatively, then we know that the scowl on their face may not have anything to do with what we are talking about, but might be the result of a creative thought they just had.

Managers learn that they can step back from being strict managers and use their intuition and creativity to seek innovative ways of managing the business.

Silva is helping us to experience the best of both worlds.

Intuitively improving client relationships

Someone once referred to the Silva course as "a course in human relationships." That's really what it is when you stop and think about it.

- ➤ We are able to communicate mentally with other people. Students in the first half of the course learn how to mentally ask their professor for the correct answer to a test question.
- ➤ We are able to sense how other people feel; we can actually detect their emotional state and experience it ourselves.
- ➤ We are able to mentally detect health problems that people have, and then program to correct those problems.
- ➤ We can "work a case" on a person's relationship with somebody else, determine where the problem areas are, and program to correct them.

All of those things can certainly help to improve human relationships. And all of those things prove very valuable in agency work.

We work health cases on clients and prospective clients, whether we get their business or not. If we find out that they have a problem, we program to correct it. We don't tell them we are doing this, because we are not doing it in order to get credit for it or to gain business as a result of doing it. We do it because we can, and it is the right thing to do.

We do find benefits, of course. We find that it is easier to resolve differences with clients. We find that we can settle disagreements more easily. We are more forgiving of one another when we make mistakes. And the work we do for our clients benefits as a result.

Relax, it's good for you

Anyone who knows anything about public relations or advertising knows the stresses of deadlines, client expectations, uncooperative media contacts, unexpected catastrophes, long hours, the frustration of having your ideas rejected—you get the idea: It is a very stressful business.

And stress is at the root of many of the health problems that people experience. Stress can harm your health, ruin your relationships, interfere with your ability to think clearly and make good decisions, and generally degrade the quality of your life.

So the first thing to do to protect your health is to relax occasionally.

But you say there isn't time to relax during your hectic day. And even if there was, how could you sit at your desk with your eyes closed while you spend 15 minutes at your level? Your colleagues and your boss would think you were goofing off. They would not understand that you are recharging yourself so that you will be more productive.

I'm not going to let you get away with that excuse. I am going to tell you how to do it. All you have to do is to use the room that your company built just for going to level and relaxing for a few minutes: the restroom.

Go in there, close the door, and nobody will know what you are doing.

Just remember to program yourself to remain awake. One of our graduates, an officer of a major corporation, learned that the hard way. He had meetings each afternoon, and each afternoon he had a headache after the meeting. So he went to the rest room each day, went to level, rid himself of the headache, relaxed, and then programmed for the rest of the day to go smoothly. One day he fell asleep and fell off the seat in the executive washroom—and other executives were in there wondering what happened!

You can use your level to correct any problem and reach any goal, as long as your goals are of a constructive and creative nature. And that's what the agency business is all about.

Linda Arnold is founder, chairman, and CEO of The Arnold Agency, a full-service advertising and public relations agency in Charleston, West Virginia. A former press secretary to Senator Jay Rockefeller, Linda has been instrumental in the development of the Wisdom Media Group, a television, radio, and Internet network, and regularly conducts on-air interviews with leaders in the self-improvement field.

Chapter 24
The intuitive entrepreneur

BY A. VICTOR KOVENS

Starting and operating your own small business can be one of life's greatest experiences. It certainly has been for me. But it takes a certain kind of person— one with initiative, confidence, self-discipline, and a lot of determination. It also takes a person who enjoys overcoming many, many different kinds of challenges.

The Silva techniques have made my experiences as a small-business entrepreneur much easier and a lot more enjoyable. I use the alpha level daily to analyze problems and make decisions, and the more I practice, the more often I make the right decision.

I first took the Silva course in 1974. The following year I made the *Guinness Book of World Records* by flying around the world on commercial airlines in less time than anybody had ever done before.

In 1979 I followed my intuitive guidance and traveled 240 miles to go on a blind date. My intuitive guidance was correct—my date and I have been happily married for more than 20 years.

In 1987, through the intuitive guidance I got in a dream, I opened a cruise-only travel agency, specializing in group cruises. This has worked out especially well as I now organize several cruises every year for Silva groups. We hold classes and special workshops, and everybody loves it. The instructors who sponsor the cruises get to go for free, we spread the word about Silva, and we help Silva students learn to use even more of their mental abilities.

The biggest, most important, and most satisfying thing I've done in Silva, though, was to help organize a class for homeless people in my hometown of Baltimore. After completing the class, these homeless people had a 70-percent success rate in finding homes or jobs within one week! (You can read about the project in Chapter 28.)

If you think I'm dedicated to the Silva ideas and techniques, you're right:

➤ I've attended 23 of the 25 Silva International Annual Conventions in Laredo.

➤ I am the only Silva Method Newsletter subscriber with a lifetime subscription.

➤ I attended Jose Silva's 10-day Ultimate Seminar the last seven times he taught it.

➤ I've organized and sponsored the Silva courses here in Baltimore.

Better business decisions

Through the years, I have learned the value of going to my level every day in order to make better decisions in my business and personal life, and to get the guidance I need to continue to achieve even more success.

Every small-business-owner must find ways to promote his or her business. With a little help from Silva, I found a great way to promote my travel business: As I mentioned, in 1975 I made the *Guinness Book of World Records* by flying around the world on commercial airlines in less than two days.

It took me just 47 hours, 48 minutes, and 7 seconds to complete the 25,000-mile trip. I crossed the equator twice, landed in nine countries, and touched points exactly 180 degrees opposite each other on the globe: Lima, Peru, and Bangkok, Thailand.

I visualized and used mental projection to smooth the way. Every step went just as I programmed it. It was almost as though people were waiting for me, like they had been prepared by my mental projection and were ready to help me continue my record-setting journey. This made getting through customs easy.

Making all of the connections from one flight to the next wasn't a problem either. I started in Lima and flew to Bogota, Caracas, Madrid, Rome, Bangkok, Hong Kong, Tokyo, Los Angeles, and back to Lima.

After the flight, I visualized getting into the record book. I think that was the most important thing. When I was in Los Angeles, I called the book's editor in London to ask him whether I should continue on, and he told me to continue. Before calling, I entered my level and imagined the telephone conversation. The one we actually had made the conversation I imagined seem like a rehearsal, because the editor used the exact words I imagined he would!

When I was back on the airplane for the last leg of the trip, back to Lima, the pilot invited me to sit in the cockpit. He asked me which direction I wanted to land in Lima. I told him to land whichever way he thought was fastest and best.

What was the secret of my programming success? One of the most important elements was the feelings that I incorporated into my programming. Every time I was at my level programming, I thought about how I would feel if I were already in the *Guinness Book of World Records*. I imagined seeing my name in the book and made it so real that I could actually feel the pride and sense of accomplishment seeing my name there.

Even though there were some problems to overcome, the project was a big success. For example, one flight was an hour late because the pilot had to fly an extra 600 miles around Vietnam out of fear of being shot down. I just kept programming and projecting, and it worked.

Everything begins in the mind

As you can see, there are many, many ways that you can use the creative alpha dimension to help you start and run a small business.

Those of us who operate small businesses seldom have the kind of support that large corporations can afford. That makes it all the more important that we nurture our "invisible means of support," as Jose Silva called it.

There is plenty of information available to help you meet every challenge, and you can use your mind to retrieve that information, no matter where it is.

And as long as you are doing what you were sent here to do, you will find it easy to get help from higher intelligence to keep you moving along at a rapid pace.

Victor Kovens has been such a big Silva supporter during the last 25 years that Silva International officials refer to him as a goodwill ambassador. He has promoted many of the Silva courses in Baltimore and has introduced countless people to the Silva programs.

CHAPTER 25
ADVANCED
COMMUNICATIONS

BY MICHAEL WICKETT

There are many ways that you can communicate with people: your words, tone of voice, gestures, body language, pacing, and timing. You can learn those skills in any public speaking class.

There is another skill that public speaking classes don't teach you, but Jose Silva's system does: subjective communication.

You can learn to actually use your mind to detect what other people are thinking and feeling. Just imagine how much more effective your communication can be if you develop this skill.

This advanced form of communication can be used in both your business and your personal life. It will benefit a salesperson or a business manager just as much as it will benefit a public-speaker or a parent. I know, because I am all of those things.

Before I tell you about one of the most profound experiences that I ever had with subjective communication, let me pass on to you a couple of the many stories that I've heard about some of the ways that you can call on your intuition for guidance.

Subjective communication makes public-speaking easy

Pepe Romero has been a fixture at Silva International since shortly after graduating from college in 1972. He recounts a couple of his experiences with subjective communication this way:

"Over the years I saw letters Silva graduates would write thanking Jose Silva for creating the Silva System and telling him how it had changed their lives for the better. Many of them said it had actually saved their lives. This made me feel very good about working there.

"When I casually mentioned to Ed Bernd Jr. that I wanted to take a more active role in the business, he encouraged me to consider becoming an instructor. I hadn't done much public-speaking, and wasn't too sure that I was suited for it.

"Ed was developing a program to teach the Silva techniques to salespeople, and I had a part-time sales job at the time. Ed assured me that he wouldn't ask me to do anything I wasn't ready to do.

"So we went out together and convinced more than two dozen people to attend the class. Ed taught the Silva techniques and asked me to say a few things about selling from time to time.

"Ed especially liked one story that I had told him, about a married couple I was selling to. He asked me to tell it to the class.

"As Ed listened from the audience, he realized that he'd made a small mistake. The point that he wanted to make to the students was that it was important to learn how to ask the right questions. In my story, the husband and wife were both telling me what they wanted in the product without my having to ask any questions.

"Ed thought to himself, 'I wish I had suggested to Pepe that he say: It is great when your clients give you all the information that you need, but when they don't, it is important to know how to ask the right questions.'

"The strange thing was that as soon as Ed thought it, I said it aloud! I recall wondering at the time why I had inserted that into the middle of my story.

"We were tape-recording the class, so we could evaluate it later. When Ed got to that part of the tape, he came to my office and played it for me. It was so strange. I was telling my story in a soft voice, with little emotion. Suddenly my voice changed. It became alert and firm, and I said, 'It's great when your clients give you all the information that you need, but when they don't, it is important to know how to ask the right questions.'

"We still have that tape. It was amazing confirmation of how quickly I detected his thought about what needed to be said to the class.

"When I was ready to teach my first class on my own (without Jose Silva there), that incident inspired me and gave me confidence that what Mr. Silva had told me was true. He'd told me, 'Just open your mind and all the information you need will be there for you when you need it.'

"Throughout that first class, information came to me so often that I even impressed myself!

"It's important that we be aware of the subjective communication between you and your audience. Ed Bernd Jr. said that in the first few Silva classes he taught, he wasn't aware of how open his mind was and how much information he was receiving from the audience.

"But invariably, as he taught many of the self-programming techniques of the Silva System, people responded to them. By the end of the class, as he saw the excitement on people's faces as they realized that they had been functioning as psychics, he was ready to start teaching another class immediately.

"He said that he finally figured out what was happening: 'On the first day,' he explained, 'I was detecting the audience's insecurities, their concern about whether they had made a good investment when they registered for the course, whether they would be able to learn all the things we had talked about. That was making me insecure. By the next day, they were feeling better, and so was I.

"'Once I figured that out it was easy to correct the problem. I simply programmed myself to project confidence and enthusiasm to the audience. I programmed to get rid of the feelings of frustration and insecurity just like you would program to get rid of a headache with our Headache Control Technique.'"

Ed said that he noticed two big changes after he did that: First, he felt better. He enjoyed *all* of the class rather than just the second day. Second, the people listening to him felt better. They no longer showed any signs of concern or insecurity. Evidently his confidence and enthusiasm rubbed off on them.

All that it took was an awareness of the problem, a formula for correcting it, and some practice using subjective communication to help correct problems.

Using subjective communication in your personal life

You can use your psychic ability to establish better relationships with your audience—whether it be clients, students, your family, or someone else.

A year ago, I decided that I wanted to be closer to my daughter, Kristen. Even more important to me than becoming wealthy and famous within my industry—which is a dream of mine—was to deepen my relationship with my daughter.

I had flipped through some books on ways to be a better father, because I love learning. Now I decided to access my intuition to decide what to do. I went to a deep meditative level and asked what I could do to get close to my daughter.

At level, my intuition told me to ask Kristen. (Not real profound, but I hadn't thought of it at beta.)

That afternoon we were riding in the car and I asked, "Honey, what could I do to be a better father to you?"

Without hesitation she said, "Dad, you could take me on some of your trips."

It just so happened that I had a speaking engagement for a major pharmaceutical company at a resort that was one of Kristen's favorite places. I told her about it, and asked her if she understood that if I took her that she couldn't come and interrupt me while I was in meetings, unless it was an emergency.

"Dad," she answered, "once you start the meeting I won't even bother you. As a matter of fact, Dad, just give me the charge card and I'll go shopping."

I let Kristen bring a friend with her, and before we all went to sleep the night before my speech, I reminded them that I'd be up very early to set up for the speech and that once the speech began at 8:30, they couldn't interrupt me unless there was an emergency.

When I got up in the morning, it was pitch dark. When I came out of the bathroom after showering and getting dressed, Kristen was standing there in the dark, dressed and holding my briefcase. She said, "Dad, I want to go with you and help you set up."

I was so stunned. She went up to the room with me, helped me set out my handouts, and asked me what they were for. The client came in, the vice president of the company whose employees I'd be speaking to, and I introduced him to her. Then she said, "Dad, I'll go now. I'll come back in three hours, and we won't interrupt you."

After she walked out, the client turned to me and said, "That child got up this early to come and help you? That's really wonderful. You must be doing something right." That was one of the most magical moments of my life.

There were a couple of benefits that resulted from the experience that I had not expected. One was the reaction of the vice president. You might expect him to be concerned that I had brought two young girls with me who might come in and take me away from the meeting with his staff.

And it was an important meeting. Two large pharmaceutical companies had merged. This is always a difficult time, as people struggle to adjust to new responsibilities, new co-workers, and a whole lot of uncertainty. My speech was about working together for the good of the company, accepting new roles, and finding ways to cooperate and make the transition period as smooth as possible.

The pharmaceutical executive realized that if I could forge such a good relationship with my adolescent daughter, I was just the kind of person he needed to help his employees build better relationships with each other.

The second surprise was that this has become a regular event for Kristen and me. Ever since that happened three years ago, I take Kristen and a friend with me once each summer. And every fall, just the two of us go to a nice resort by ourselves to spend some quality time together.

I now have a whole new dimension of closeness with my daughter.

How did all of this happen for me? It happened because of a simple question that came to me out of my intuition when I was at level.

Michael Wickett conducts business-building programs across the United States for companies such as Ford Motors, State Farm Insurance, Merrill-Lynch, Trans-America, Hyatt Hotels, and IBM. He has recorded more than two dozen very successful audiocassette learning programs, more than any business speaker in the world, and has been a main speaker at several Silva International Conventions.

CHAPTER 26
SUBJECTIVE EDUCATION

BY SISTER NAOMI CURTIN, SSND, PH. D.

At the alpha level, information can be impressed with more brain energy, which makes stronger impressions on neurons so that it is easier to recall the information. If you want to improve test scores, you can make stronger impressions on your brain, making recall easier.

This can enhance your IQ, because the more information you recall, the more questions you will answer correctly, the more problems you will solve, and the higher your score will be on the IQ test.

There is another advantage to using the alpha level to make stronger impressions of information. When you have impressed information more strongly, it is then easier to use your intuition—your psychic abilit—to supplement the information that is already impressed on your own brain; you'll have even more information available for problem-solving. This enhances your IQ even more.

Jose Silva explained the process this way:

> *"We thought that our intelligence, human intelligence, could only sense information on its own brain cells. We now know that human intelligence, at beta or at alpha, can detect information on your own brain cells. At alpha, you can detect that information but also any information on any neuron, wherever it is. That's subjective communication.*
>
> *"If you are able to become aware of information impressed on some other brain, then you can make use of that information, or those experiences, as though they were your own. You do not need to be limited to your own impressions on your own brain cells.*
>
> *"You can also improve your IQ factor by sensing how to use the information and using others' experiences to determine how to use your own information. This is wisdom."*

Naturally Intuitive

Children are naturally intuitive. That became obvious to Jose Silva early in his research, when children began "guessing" what questions he was going to ask them just before he asked. He soon learned that all of his young research subjects had this ability, and that all he had to do was to draw it out of them.

Unfortunately, as people mature, most lose this ability. The brain matures and functions at higher frequencies most of the time, and since grownups no longer have the ability to function psychically, they deny its existence in children, too.

For so many years these gifts were explained away through denial of the children's experiences. Parents, teachers, and others would say things like "Stop lying to me!"; "Who told you that? You couldn't know that by yourself!"; and "You're just making up stories." And very quickly children learn that there are certain things they should not talk about if they do not want to be punished.

Thank goodness Jose Silva paid attention when the children he was working with began to reveal their psychic abilities to him. Intuition truly flourished during those years of research as the students learned many ways of tapping into their intuitive gifting.

Children functioning as geniuses

"The first time I ever tried the Silva techniques was when my mom misplaced a purse filled with money," Dawn C., a student in grade six, reported. "When I went to sleep, I dreamt where it was. The next day when I woke up, I ran to the back kitchen and found the purse. I gave it to my mom and she asked how I found it. I told her all about the Silva course and now she wants to take it!"

If a child can project her mind to locate her mother's lost purse, then she can project her mind to obtain the information she needs to answer a question or solve a problem—even if that information has not been impressed upon her own brain cells.

When this young girl grows up, she'll be able to use her mind the same way to detect information that she can use to solve problems she encounters as an adult. The more opportunities children have to practice as students and as children, the better able they'll be to use this skill as adults.

Research provides objective evidence of success

There have been many research projects to demonstrate the effectiveness of Jose Silva's techniques in helping students achieve higher grades. One project was conducted at the Autonomous University of Tlaxcala, in Tlaxcala, Mexico, to measure the effect of the Silva System in the learning process, intelligence quotient, and personality factors amongst university students.

After completing the Silva BLS, the report reveals, the results of IQ tests "indicate that 67.7 percent of the subjects improved their IQ classification."

"From my perspective, and as result of my work with young people, the Silva Method could and should be taught to students in all academic levels in every country, in order to contribute to the betterment of humanity," urges Lillia Alcira Vacca, who authored a report of the project. (Excerpts from the report are available on our Web site.)

A Silva technique improved scores one letter grade

An article published in the *Journal of the Society of Accelerative Learning and Teaching* reported that students at the University of Tasmania in Hobart, Tasmania, Australia, raised their grades by one letter grade when they used the Three Fingers Technique.

Those students who had learned the Three Fingers Technique improved their scores by nine percentage points, while the scores of the control group (students who were not taught the technique) actually dropped by a percentage point.

"From the results of this study, it would seem reasonable to conclude that the Three Fingers Technique is able to facilitate short-term improvement in second year high school students' examination performance," according to Dr. Harry E. Stanton, who conducted the research project.

Stanton also stated, in the same article, "The technique is a very simple one, which students have no trouble in learning."

Trouble-makers find it's more fun to behave

Shortly after completing the Silva training, Marie Buckingham (now Burleson) found herself faced with a challenge in a junior-high school classroom.

There were four trouble-makers in one of her classes, four girls who disrupted the rest of the students so that no one could participate. It was not limited to just Marie's classroom. These same girls had a reputation among the faculty and the school counselor for causing similar trouble in all of their classes.

For one week, Marie programmed herself to wake up earlier than usual so that she could project to these girls while they were still asleep. Here's Marie's story, in her own words:

"I would get up, maybe 15 minutes early, and project each one on my mental screen. I'd spend five minutes, maybe less, on each one. I told them that it's more fun to be good than bad and reminded each one that I thought she was a wonderful person.

"And they were all nice girls, and they were all intelligent.

"I told them that I hoped they would cooperate in class so that they, and their classmates and I, could all enjoy the class. I told them I looked forward to having them do this and that I would appreciate it. Then I thanked them.

"After the next class, I asked them to stay behind for a minute. I told them that they were creating problems in the class, but that I knew they were nice people.

"When they came to class the next time, the ring-leader refused to let herself become involved in the antics of the other three. She sat apart from them.

"During the next class, she asked a question. The other students looked at her in disbelief Pretty soon, though, she came up with some ideas, and by the end of class, all four girls were participating in class.

"As they left the room at the end of class, the ring-leader looked at me, smiled, and said, 'You know, I think it's more fun being good than bad. '

"That was the end of my trouble with the trouble-makers. "

Benefiting from others' knowledge and talent

Silva instructor Carol Callahan of Vermont taught her students the test-taking technique. Here's her story, in her own words:

"First I tell the students to do the standard things we always say: Stop and think for a minute, go back, let it go, and go on to something else and then go back to it. But the most profound thing I say to them is this: Close your eyes, picture me in your mind, and ask me, in your mind, for the answer. They really like that one. And it works!

"When we're drawing, I tell them to close their eyes. Children are primarily at alpha between the ages of 7 and 14, so this is really easy for them.

"They tell me, 'I can't draw this, I can't do that.

"So I ask them who the best artist is in the room. They tell me it's Sally. I then tell them, 'All right, you know what to do.'

"They close their eyes, and they can 'put Sally's head on' and 'put Sally's hands on. ' They get great big smiles on their faces and are able to draw beautiful pictures like Sally can.

"In all areas of our lives, whatever we do, we can do better if we use alpha. "

The future is in our hands

It is up to parents and teachers to guide young people and to help them gain the skills that will help them to fulfill their purpose in life. I believe there is no higher calling than this.

As you can see throughout this book, in every field—from medicine to business to athletics to the arts—intuition has proven an indispensable tool for the most successful practitioners in those fields. And now you can learn it. We have observed it in our own experience, and research has confirmed it.

A research project conduct by Dr. George Maycock at Appalachian State University in North Carolina demonstrated that students who completed the Silva training showed a significant increase in creative- and intuitive-functioning.

Of the 30 students who participated, 25 showed gains in intuitive abilities. Four of the other five (who did not show improvement) were already functioning in a high intuitive mode before the training.

Intuition is valuable for students—and for adults, too. One researcher found that 70 percent of gifted or high-IQ students were predominantly intuitive, while only 39 percent of students in regular classes were intuitive.

There are plenty of anecdotal reports, plenty of real-world experience, and plenty of research. What is needed now is to teach students how to learn, how to gain greater self-control, and how to use their inborn, God-given genius abilities. It is our responsibility to teach them.

Sister Naomi Curtin is a member of the School Sisters of Notre Dame congregation. She has been an educator since 1943, teaching at all levels from elementary through college, as well as professional and adult groups. Since 1975 she has taught the Silva techniques to thousands of children and adults. She received the Silva World Cup in 1982 for her work with children in the Catholic school system in Guam.

CHAPTER 27
THE INTUITIVE ATHLETE

BY GIUSEPPINA (VIDHEYA) DEL VICARIO

Sporting activities are very valuable to society for many reasons. Athletes are role models, at every level from childhood to the pros. Sports teach the value and benefits of teamwork, doing your job, practice, persistence, and concentration. You can see how hard work pays off.

An army instructor at the U.S. Military Academy at West Point put it this way when he spoke of mental training for their athletes: "It's a part of their leadership development, because this is no different really than the ability of a leader to think, problem-solve, react, and eliminate distractions in combat." He added, "The ability to maintain focus, to maintain a calm state, and to make critical decisions is paramount to our profession."

Top athletes have great anticipation

Top athletes throughout the world report that intuition and mental projection help them in many ways.

The ability to correctly anticipate what your opponent is going to do gives you a definite edge in competition. In fact, the ability to use your intuition to get information and to anticipate future events is the real secret to outstanding success in every area of life. If you can use your intuition to sense the best training routine, you will get into better shape more quickly and easily than if you are limited only to random guessing. Any time you can sense what other people are thinking or what they are likely to do, you know exactly how to prepare so that you will be ready for them.

Imagine sensing what someone is willing to pay for your services. You'd know exactly what price you can negotiate. Imagine sensing what your opponents' game plans are. And imagine being able to send a message to your teammates to let them know mentally what you are going to do next. Basketball player Walt Frazier said that he and teammate Bill Bradley could do this. "Sometimes he has passed the ball before I've taken the first step. It's like telepathy," Frazier said in the book *Clyde*, which he wrote with Joe Jares (Grosset and Dunlap, 1970).

Olympic fencers sense opponents' strategies

To help his fencers develop a strategy, Andrzej Wojcikiewicz, a sports psychologist and former coach of the Canadian National Fencing Team, used a special technique taught in the Silva courses, where you imagine that you are putting another person's head over your own, as though you were putting on a helmet. You can then experience what that person is experiencing.

"This was used by some fencers before unusually difficult bouts in order to instinctively plan the correct strategy for the fencing match," Wojcikiewicz explained. "One fencer imagined putting on the head of a world champion before a match, got the feeling, took off the 'helmet,' and then fenced the match with a great success."

Know when to shoot

Lance Miller, an international shooting coach at the U.S. Olympic Training Center, said that one of the most important things in the Silva course to help his athletes is intuition.

There are a number of factors that shooters cannot detect objectively, such as the wind direction and velocity, which can influence the bullet's path, a nick in a bullet that you can't see with the naked eye, or even tiny variations in the size of the power charge. "The athletes need to be able to sense these things," Miller said. "I tell my guys and girls that if everything doesn't feel right, don't shoot. When they learn to project their minds to detect problems, this helps them tremendously."

Miller is teaching his athletes how to use some of the Silva techniques to help them in their quest for world and Olympic championships. The same idea applies to other sports as well, where variables such as wind or precision manufacture of equipment could be factors that influence the success of the athlete's effort.

How to program to be in a "special state of mind"

Have you ever had a day when everything you did was right, every movement was smooth and precise, when you felt that nobody could defeat you?

Some athletes call that "being in the zone." It is a time of great anticipation, when you seem to know in advance what is going to happen so that your reactions are always right. Jose Silva called it being in a "special state of mind."

You can condition yourself to be in this special state of mind more often by using your alpha level. Jose Silva explained it this way:

"First, enter your level and recall a time when you were 'in the groove,' when you were 'in the zone,' when you performed perfectly, when everything you did was right, when you could feel yourself achieving your best, when you knew that you would achieve just what you desired. Recall how you felt at this time. This feeling is the result of a special state of mind. Recall exactly how you felt, physically, mentally, and emotionally, when you had this special state of mind.

"Any time in the future when you need to have this same state of mind again, all you need to do is to use the words 'special state of mind' as a trigger mechanism to help you get into that state of mind where you will be just as successful again, and more so every time you do this.

"Eventually you will establish enough points of reference for the feeling of being 'in the groove,' 'in the zone,' so that it will then be automatic. At that time, all you need to do is to recall that state of mind, of being 'in the groove,' 'in the zone,' and you will be there.

"Every time that you perform in a superior manner, every time that you have a very good training session or performance, then enter your level and reinforce that success at level, so that you will continue to get better and better every time you practice."

Giuseppina Del Vicario, who competed under the name Vidheya, won the Italian martial arts national championship in tai chi chuan three consecutive years, competing against both men and women, and retired undefeated. She has been a Silva instructor in Italy since 1995, and she currently directs all Silva activities in the Milano area and in southern Italy.

Chapter 28

Silva techniques in social work

BY JONELL MONACO LYTLE

I had been thinking on and off for quite a while that I wanted to work with the homeless. The Silva System had given me so much over the years, so many blessings, that I wanted to give something back. It would be my way of tithing.

In the 26 years that I have taught the Silva techniques, I have given numerous scholarships to children whose families could not afford the tuition. I have given equally as many to adults who were poor. I now wanted to share it with the truly poor, the homeless. This was in November 1995.

A plan is born

My plan was to work with people in Virginia Beach, where I live. One cold, windy, and rainy November day I was visiting a friend's church. I was feeling sorry for myself because of some recent financial difficulty and I was worrying about making my mortgage payment. I was looking for sympathy when I shared this feeling with Linda, a woman I met at my friend's church.

She commented, "I wish I had a house and a house payment to worry about. My husband, son, and I are living in the woods a few blocks from here."

She was not fishing for sympathy; it was just a statement.

That night when I went to bed it was 35 degrees, raining, and there were winds of 25 to 30 miles per hour. The temperature was supposed to dip into the 20s, and that, of course, meant snow. It was about 60 degrees in my bedroom. The howling wind was so noisy I had trouble getting to sleep.

A commitment is made

But it wasn't just the noise that kept me awake; a simple Silva technique could have handled that.

It was my thoughts of Linda and her family. Even her dog, Buddy, was living in the woods with them.

Within an hour or so I had made a full-blown commitment to God that I would use Silva to help the homeless.

Guided by coincidence

Through a series of "coincidences" I ended up in a Silva System Sales Lecture Series in Baltimore, Maryland, about five hours from my home. When I arrived, Victor Kovens, a dedicated Silva supporter and sponsor of the Silva Cruises, introduced me to the class and mentioned that I was a Silva instructor.

During a break Truxon Sykes, someone I had never met, made a beeline for me. He had his hand extended to shake mine. His handshake didn't seem to be one of introduction; it was more like a handshake between people who had just made a deal of some kind. His first words were, "I've been thinking of doing some research on how fast the Silva Method could mainstream the homeless back into society."

As he spoke I noticed that he was wearing a big red button that said, "Homeless, Not Hopeless." We connected mentally. We were each fulfilling each other's plan—well, we thought the plan was ours, but we both knew and discussed later how it was actually God's plan.

Truxon Sykes is the president of The Baltimore Homeless Union. We spent several hours that night after class talking with each other.

Bigger than expected

When he told me that Baltimore had the largest homeless population in the United States, I knew that I had to begin there—especially now that I had someone to organize the class for me.

When he told me there were 32,000 homeless in Baltimore, I corrected him, as I thought he meant to say 3,200. In fact, even 32 sounded like a lot!

So, when *he* corrected *me* and explained that it was 32,000, I knew then why God had guided me to Baltimore.

I figured if I could train just one percent, which would be 320 people, that might be the critical mass. I believed that it would also affect the homeless throughout the planet. I guess I'm a born optimist.

We made plans for me to return to Baltimore the next month to give an introductory lecture to as many homeless as Truxon could gather in the hope of getting them to sign up for a class where I'd teach some Silva techniques.

Praying for guidance

On my return trip to Virginia Beach, I had a lot of time to think about what I had just committed myself to. There was a part of me that thought I had bitten off more than I could chew.

Then I realized it had nothing to do with me. Silva could help anyone and everyone. The system was successful worldwide.

The first night back at the beach I did some heavy-duty praying. I begged God to give me the trigger words I would need to inspire each and every person who showed up at the introduction to have the desire to be in the class.

Do it mentally first

I started really getting excited. In the time leading up to the lecture I found myself talking to these homeless people, who I hadn't even met yet, all day long in my mind. There was so much to share with them. I could only picture success and happiness for them. After a few days, I could even picture their faces. I couldn't wait to meet them.

How many would attend?

Fifty homeless people came to the lecture. Truxon passed around sign-up sheets, and 49 of the 50 signed up for the class that we'd hold in January!

About 15 minutes after starting time on the first day in January, one homeless person wandered in. He came to inform me that he didn't think anyone would show up because one of them had frozen to death that morning when the electricity went off in a federal building.

Getting recommitted

I excused myself, went to the ladies room, cried, and then prayed. I told God that I was perfectly willing to work with just one student if that was His will.

Within 15 minutes two more people joined the class. Then a few more came, and by 11:30 we had 23 in the class!

Over the next five days we always had between 11 and 23 people in the class. I was thrilled to see that the Silva books that Victor Kovens so generously donated were always with them.

My message to the class

As I prepared for the class in the weeks leading up to it, I was inspired over and over by the following words, so I used them as my introduction to the class:

"I just want you to know, before we begin, what a privilege it is for me to be your Silva trainer.

"Somehow in my heart I know that you are very wise souls to have chosen this most difficult path that you have been on.

"When you use these Silva techniques you are about to learn this week, you will be an inspiration to your fellow homeless and to the rest of the world.

"I admire you for who you are and what you have been through, and that at some level you have chosen to suffer through your survival.

"Thanks to a great man named Jose Silva and his years of research and sharing, you won't have to suffer anymore. I hope you know I speak this truth from the bottom of my heart and the very essence of who I am.

"And who I am is one of God's servants serving His children in the best manner I know: the Silva System. I thank God daily for that.

"May I be the first to congratulate you on the beginning of the best of the rest of your life. Let's begin!"

So many who needed my help

On Tuesday, one of the "students" brought in a magazine with an article about homelessness. I turned to the page with the article and there was a photograph of a dignified-looking man wearing a suit. He looked successful and sophisticated. He held a sign in his lap that read, "I am not a bum. I am not lazy. I am 74 years old. I have worked all of my life. I would like to work for food. I do not want a handout."

My eyes filled with tears, and I used the Three Fingers Technique to regain control of my emotions. It was so sad that this man felt that he had to defend who he was and what he was doing. I knew at that moment that I would dedicate a portion of the rest of my life to using Silva to help the homeless.

At that moment I reminded the class of something I had told them earlier, "I said to you at the beginning of this class that I had a sneaky and almost guilty suspicion that I would get more out of this week than you will, and that I will learn more from you than you will learn from me."

Slow going

By Tuesday afternoon they only had the intro and a few of the very first techniques. It is important for me to emphasize how little of the Silva training they had so you can fully understand the miracle that occurred on Wednesday morning.

When I got into my van to drive to the class Wednesday morning, I noticed that one of the windows was broken. Almost all of my Silva materials were gone, including a large suitcase with books written and signed by Jose Silva.

A bold experiment

When I arrived at class I immediately put two six-foot tables together. The 17 students and I sat around the tables. I put the rock in the center of the table and told them to write down anything that came to their minds, because anything could be a clue as to where the Silva materials were.

Much information detected

By 11:45 a number of us were able to describe what the person who broke into the van was wearing, right down to the shoes. Several people came up with the name of a street—the same street. Several came up with a different street, and one person had written down the intersection of those two streets.

Three more homeless walked in just as we were finishing up the exercise. When we related the story, they immediately set off on foot, before I could stop them. I was so moved I almost cried.

A few minutes later two more came in. They were familiar with the neighborhood we were talking about and went to check it out. As they were leaving I had a vision of the two of them returning with my big suitcase.

At 2:30 that afternoon we were taking our lunch break. Victor Kovens had generously supplied lunch for us all week. While I had my eyes closed and was energizing my lunch I heard one of the ladies at the other end of the room, near the long corridor which led to the exit, scream, "Oh, my God, look at you!"

Results produced

When I opened my eyes, to my surprise there were two of the men who had gone searching, coming down the hall toward the room with my Silva suitcase!

The books were missing, and a lot of what I did get back was damaged. They found some materials in the street and some in trash cans and dumpsters.

We celebrated—and not just the return of my materials. The thing we celebrated the most was how they had used their faculties of genius so effectively with so little Silva training behind them. They were all so proud.

Warren's first success

By the Thursday afternoon break a man I will call Warren came up to me with a big smile and said, "I can't wait to tell you this, I can't wait any longer. I want you to know that last night for the first time in two years I slept in a real bed—not on cement, but a real bed. The reason I can't wait any longer to tell you is because I won't be here tomorrow."

He saw the happiness in my face when he told me about the bed, but he also saw my disappointment when he said he wouldn't complete the course.

He grinned and said, "The reason I won't be here tomorrow is because I have to start my new job."

Warren's story

At this point I did something I hadn't done up to now, mainly because I thought it was none of my business. I asked, "Warren, you don't have to answer this if you don't want to, but I am curious. Why have you been on the street?"

He told me that he, his wife, and their 14-year-old daughter had been living in California in a $200,000 home. They had a truck, two cars, and a boat. Between Warren and his wife, they were making about $80,000 a year.

Three summers before, when they returned to Baltimore for a vacation, Warren's 19-year-old son, from a previous marriage, was shot and killed.

He felt guilty for his son's death and experienced pain that could only be numbed by prescription pain killers. This worked for a time. When the prescription drugs no longer worked he turned to illegal ones.

In just 10 months he lost everything. His wife and daughter left, and he never returned to California.

He told me that when I gave the introductory lecture, there was something I said that made him think there was this "little ray of hope that I don't have to live on the street forever."

He came to the class out of curiosity. (Remember my prayer for trigger words?)

Another success for Warren

In a class several months later, Warren joined us for an afternoon. He shared what he had achieved with the help of the Silva techniques.

He had used the Three Fingers Technique, Mirror of the Mind, Habit Control, and Sleep Control. He signed himself into a rehab clinic and he had *totally recovered* from the crack-cocaine habit. He planned to rejoin his family later that summer.

Many happy endings

Truxon Sykes told me that 70 percent of the homeless that we trained found jobs and homes! Warren's story and others inspired people to believe that Silva techniques could help them overcome their problems. Every day I thank God for the many blessings the Silva Method has brought me.

JoNell Monaco Lytle is willing to go anywhere in the world to help any Silva instructor or graduate with their first Silva Homeless class. She will do it free of charge as long as you provide her airfare and lodging.

CHAPTER 29
SPIRITUAL
LEADERSHIP

BY REV. JAMES R. MURRAY

Before Jose Silva ever thought of teaching his method to the public, he offered all of his research to the churches. Why did he do this? Because he realized the great value it would have to religious leaders and religions themselves.

"All religions should be teaching this," he said. "God is not physical; God is spiritual. The mind is not physical. It is said that we were made in the image of the Creator. Image is of the mind, it is not physical, it is spiritual. It does not mean that we all look like God. It means that we can do what God did."

Since God is not physical, we do not use physical words to communicate with God. We use the mind: visualization and imagination. We communicate with mental pictures. Everyone can understand a picture; it is the universal language.

The more we understand about the mind and the better able we are to use the mind, the better we can serve God.

Prayer seems to be more effective

Jose Silva reported on a minister in the *Silva Method Newsletter*. The minister told Silva that his prayer seemed to be much more effective than it had been for the 12 years he'd been a minister after learning Silva and practicing it for several months. He asked Jose why he thought this was happening.

Here is Jose's explanation:

"Success in communicating with the other side is a direct result of functioning at the alpha level. It is something like this: We use our objective senses to communicate in the objective dimension. That is, we

use our eyesight, our ability to talk and listen, our senses of touch, taste, and smell, to communicate with one another physically.

"But to communicate with the other side, the physical senses are useless. The other side is the place that we came from when we were born and is the place that we go back to when we leave this planet.

"That spiritual dimension cannot detect our physical dimension directly. Spiritual means nonphysical. So we must find a way to make a connection with the spiritual dimension, and convert our information from a physical form to a spiritual form.

"If you attempt to communicate with the other side while you are functioning only in the physical dimension, you will not make the con-nection. When you enter the alpha level, you make a connection with the spiritual dimension."

Many benefits received

After the churches declined Jose's offer to turn over his research to them, he still did all he could to help. For many years he gave full scholarships to religious people—ministers, priests, rabbis, nuns, and anyone else working in religion.

The benefits to these people and to those whom they serve have been great. Silva's techniques can be used for things as simple as helping you to prepare your place of worship, as important as counseling and guiding young people, and as pragmatic as obtaining the finances necessary for continuing your work.

Author Robert B. Stone gave an example in his book *The Jesus Legacy* (Sum Press, 1993) of how information came to a minister in a dream. He wrote, "Friezes created for a church ceiling would not stick no matter what glue was used. The minister asked for a dream. He dreamt he used Elmer's glue with a hot iron. It sounded ridiculous but he tried it. The artwork is still up."

Helping youself means being better able to help others

Rev. Myrtle A. Ridgeway, an ordained Unity minister with more than 20 years experience in teaching, counseling, and lecturing and success as a spiritual healer, said that she really didn't expect to get much out of the Silva course when she took it in 1979 at the urging of her friend Tag Powell. She reported that mental projection at the alpha level brought people to her ministry as if by magic. Here is Myrtle's story, in her own words:

"What a pleasant surprise was in store for me! In a very short time I was able to completely relax my body, quiet my mind, and still be in absolute control of my own thoughts and feelings.

"Using the Silva techniques, I improved my personal health, my ability to concentrate, and my finances. I used the Mirror of the Mind technique to bring more students to my new class, and I had more attendance than I had during my entire career!

"From the very beginning, my healing practice improved 100 percent. It's almost eerie how many times I'm accurate and how many healing there have been.

"I also used the Mirror of the Mind to picture myself married to the one person in the world who is right for me, and me for him. Our wedding was April 25th of last year!"

Practice at alpha leads to a better life

Sister Charlotte Bruck was working as a counselor in the Catholic school system in Florida when she took the Silva course with Marie Buckingham in 1974. A pioneer in elementary and junior high guidance and author of several books on the subject, Sister Charlotte said that the Silva techniques enabled her to help children even more. Here's what she had to say about the Silve System:

"Learning the Silva technique is only the beginning of a new life. The daily practice of meditation and atonement is just as necessary for well-being as exercise, rest, and health foods.

"I begin my day with meditation and placing myself in the presence of God, as if it were my 'hotline' to the Holy Spirit.

"Then I begin to project the things that I need for that particular day. As each projection becomes a reality, I thank God for it, and add one more to my accumulated list of blessings.

"It has taken some time and much concentration to develop the belief factor to arrive at my present state of mind. Now it is almost automatic and well worth the effort I have spent on it. I now expect all of my projections to become reality."

"Believing the old adage that 'If you give a child a fish, you feed him for one meal; but if you teach him how to fish, you provide him with food for a lifetime,' I am teaching children how to project for good things to happen, and suggest that they, too, begin to count their blessings.

"How many people really follow through I may never know; I have no need to know, for I am only planting seeds. I leave it to the Holy Spirit to nurture the seed and bring it to fruition. I simply project that they will follow through 'if it is for their own good or the good of humanity.' For me, I know it must be 'for my good and the good of humanity,' and hence I shall never turn back."

More revelations to come

It is in the nature of human beings to be apprehensive about change. It is part of our survival programming; we never know whether the unknown will be beneficial or a threat to our survival. Some people use this energy to discover ways to improve conditions on the planet, while others take a defensive posture.

This was true in Jesus' day, when the religious establishment opposed the brash young man who dared to suggest that there was new knowledge that could be beneficial to humanity.

Shortly after Columbus sailed to America and proved that the earth is round, Galileo, a scientist, confirmed Copernicus' discovery that the earth and the other planets rotate around the sun.

But the religious leaders of the time believed that the earth was the center of the universe. It had to be so, they reasoned, since man was a divine creation. This had become part of their doctrine, their dogma.

Galileo's assertion upset church leaders so much that they tortured him to force him to recant. Eventually he succumbed to the pain and did as they wished. But this did not change reality. Earth and the other planets, in fact, do revolve around the sun.

In the mid-20th century Jose Silva encountered similar opposition from church leaders, as well as scientists and even leaders in the business community.

Jose never claimed to know everything. He saw and described his research findings as "semi-conclusions"—because more will surely be added in the future.

Silva told attendees at a Silva International Convention, "We learned how to activate our brain within the subconscious, by guiding—orienting—the mind to look for a different brain frequency and to learn to use it. That's what *psychorientology* means: orienting the psyche—your mind—to look for and find that specific dimension and then to use it. That's what we call psychorientology. Right-brain use.

"Science is open-ended all the time. It is like telescopes: If you get a better telescope, you discover more planets, more solar systems, more galaxies."

Surely someone will "get a better telescope" someday and learn even more in Jose Silva's field, but it will not negate what Jose Silva discovered.

Jose Silva always insisted that he was not trying to hurt or replace religion. He simply wanted to add some knew discoveries to what was already known. The experiences of millions of people over the last 55 years, since he began his research, certainly indicate that his discoveries have tremendous value.

Universal appeal

Whether they are creating a reverent environment, helping church members, or doing good works in the community, religious leaders of all kinds are finding that Jose Silva's methods and techniques can help them do their job better and can help them understand their own religion better.

This science has universal appeal. Jose Silva's books have been translated into more than a dozen languages. The benefits are available to all, no matter what our religion, age, background, race, gender, cultural background, how much—or how little—education you have.

We are all creatures of the Creator; we have far more similarities than differences. Jose Silva said that we have been given some of the abilities and powers that the Creator has; one of these is the ability to correct problems and to create solutions on planet earth.

"We are made in the image of God," Jose used to say, "because we have the power to use our minds to detect information and correct problems. That is our mission; it is why we were sent here."

Whatever *you* believe, as long as you are striving to take part in constructive and creative activities to make this a better world to live in, you can use the Silva techniques to help you do it.

I believe that all of the power comes from God and can only be used for good. That is my experience. If it comes from God, and is used for good, then we should use it every chance we get.

James Murray is the founder and leader of The New Thought Learning Center in Houston, Texas. He holds a doctorate in religion and is an ordained minister in the United Church of Religious Science. He began teaching the Silva techniques in 1972.

Chapter 30
Claim Your
Creative Heritage

by Nelda Sheets

The first Silva class was formed back in 1966 because a group of 125 artists was interested in getting a handle on creativity.

We had studied the creative levels. We had studied meditation of different forms (yoga, hypnosis, and so forth), and we had studied Carl Jung. We were looking for a way to get a handle on reaching the inner-conscious levels, where we knew creativity springs from.

We were blessed with an art professor named Dord Fitz who told us in every lesson, "Kids, claim your creative heritage. It is more important for you to learn to be a creative being than learning to mix paint, learning perspective, learning colors. First, learn to be a creative being."

Dord heard about Jose Silva and invited him to come to northern Texas to speak to us. We knew when we heard him that we wanted to learn his method. Dord Fitz told us later that when he met Jose Silva, he found what he had been searching for his entire life.

As soon as we learned Mr. Silva's techniques, we began looking for ways to apply them to being more creative, which is what we were originally looking for.

First we wanted to get to the level where we could paint. Thirty years ago we had the expression to get "in the mood" to paint. It was a matter of whether we were in the right level of mind to paint creativity, to take care of the blocks and achieve what we wanted.

It has been an adventure studying the Silva System to learn the techniques that are appropriate for us: which techniques take care of the blocks to creative thinking and which techniques we can use to enhance creativity.

Creativity from my perspective is expressing from within. It is a subjective experience you put on canvass, or put into a song or melody, or write out in words, or perform in dance or theater, or bring a new invention to enhance humanity, or find a better way of doing business that serves more people.

Some ways to claim your creative heritage

1. Dare to be original. Thomas Edison and Henry Ford dared to try "crazy" ideas.

2. Discover your own song and dare to sing it, for someone will come along and listen.

3. Practice exercises that "fine tune" your right brain:

    ➢   Listen to great classical music and translate the sounds into shapes and colors.

    ➢   Make doodles.

    ➢   Use Dream Control and keep a record of your dreams with stories and drawings.

    ➢   Use the Silva case-working technique to attune to creative thinkers, such as artists, writers, inventors, and performers.

4. Keep creative thinking agile by thinking like a child. Practice this at your level. Wonder about everything. As Pablo Picasso said, "Every child is an artist. The problem is how to remain an artist once he grows up." *Everyone* has an inner child.

5. Use art as a way of getting in touch with your most truthful being. Art is so much more than a hobby or diversion; it is a way of discovering your spiritual self. It is a way of sharing insight.

Two kinds of creativity

Jose Silva was a very creative individual, to say the least. His keen insight is legendary. He said there are two kinds of creativity: rearranging what already exists into a new form, and bringing something brand new to the planet.

Both techniques spring from the alpha level. The second kind obviously requires psychic ability. Great creative people are able to project their minds to other dimensions and then express what they find there.

Great classical music is an example of this. That's why it affects people so deeply; it is communication from another dimension. People who have never cared for classical music often find that when they listen to it while at their level, it brings them great enjoyment.

Great literature inspires us because the author is bringing us something from another dimension, which enables us to learn something new about ourselves.

Painting, dance—in fact, every kind of creative expression can achieve a similar effect.

Nelda Sheets: tips from an artist

I believe that wild and wacky ideas very often lead to profound creative expression. Here are some of the techniques I have learned to use over the last 33 years to help me to paint and sell paintings for several thousand dollars each.

Dord Fitz said the difference between a painter and an artist is that an artist is able to create from within, so my goal is to get in touch with the heart and soul of the subject. I go to level and really attune—feel a connection—with whatever subject I am going to paint.

Many times a painter has an assignment to paint something. Whatever it is, you can use your level to go into that subject and reach its "heart and soul" and let it connect with yours. Then the connection appears on the canvas.

Dord Fitz said that a true artist is a psychic. That's why we were so excited when we met Jose Silva, because we were looking for a way to become psychic. The Silva graduate works a case—as we learn in the Silva course—on the subject that we want to portray, and whatever experience we have at level, any intuitive insight we may have, we portray that on canvass.

When I am going to do a portrait, I attune myself to my subject by "putting their head on," another Silva technique. I imagine that I have the person's head on, and I imagine, while at my level, what kind of person they are, what they are passionate about.

With certain subjects, it's important for me to get in touch with my "inner child." I enter my level and go back in time to look at the subject the way I would when I was five, so I have that fresh childlike approach. In working with my grandchildren, I have come to really appreciate the creativity that children possess, and I want that, too.

I also use the Three Fingers Technique to later remember what comes to me when I get inspired.

When I took the Silva course, I was painting portraits by commission. I decided I wanted to do Jose Silva's portrait. He had mentioned a lot of painters, and told us how much he admired them. I decided it would be appropriate to paint Jose's portrait in the style of Rembrandt—with a dark background behind him, and his face in the light. That would be an expression of some part of Jose. I worked on the idea for his portrait, but was not entirely comfortable with it. I thought about the project at a very deep level—I was so deep that I felt I had been napping when I came out of level. The thought I had was to start over and do the portrait in *my* style. I attuned to him and painted his portrait in my own style, in an hour and a half. It became his favorite portrait.

I get blocked when I get concerned about whether the person who commissioned the painting is going to like it. I go to level and tell myself how much fun it is to paint. I have found that there *must* be some connection between having fun and expressing pleasure creatively. I get rid of the idea that this is a job I *have* to do, and think about how much fun it is, and not be concerned about whether that person is going to like it or not.

Uncreative people or negative people are blocks to creative flow, or could be if you let them be. It is really good to be around other creative people.

It is valuable—probably essential—to have an understanding spouse. Creative people are accustomed to doing "wild and wacky" things. People who are accustomed to having everything under control, doing everything logically, may have a difficult time with this. I've been blessed with a wonderful marriage to my husband, Willis. We just celebrated our 50th wedding anniversary. That might not have happened if we had not both been Silva graduates.

It is really helpful to understand how the right and left brain hemispheres work, and to learn what can activate the right brain hemisphere, the creative level, and what can turn it off. If the left hemisphere makes a judgment too soon, it turns off the creative flow. In the early stages of a project, you want to give your right brain the freedom to express all the ideas that you have, and save the judgement until later.

Everyone is creative. If you have not been doing any creative work yet, then make it a point sometime this week to go to level and attune, feel connected to, a subject: a flower, a person, an idea, and express that in some form—a song, or a sketch, for example—anything where you make a record of it. It is not creativity until it is in an objective form. It is a creative idea until you do something with it. Then send me a report and let me know what you have done.

Alan Phillips: tips from a composer and performer

Alan Phillips wrote a song titled *Better and Better* that has become a favorite of Silva grads around the world. Silva International declared it the official anthem of the Silva Method. For 10 years, Alan has performed the song at the close of the Silva International Convention. He has also provided the music for several of the Silva audiotape and videotape programs. Here are some tips from Alan.

For me, creativity is inherently wedded with passion. It is much more likely for me to be able to be creative, successfully producing music or some other project, if I feel compelled or passionate about the issue. I am a strong advocate of having as much passion in your life as you can.

I also feel that creativity is inherently structureless. As a matter of necessity, we have to create a certain amount of structure in our lives. We have patterns and routines, but I think the vast majority of us overuse the benefit of structure. What we inadvertently do is fall into our structured patterns; we are looking for predictability because we think predictability is safe. Creativity is inherently unpredictable, but you can set up parameters. I wanted to write this song for Silva; that was my parameter. I sat down with my guitar and started strumming chords. I could in no way have predicted what would have emerged ahead of time. That would be contradictory to creativity.

I urge you to look for and find the things in your life that you can become passionate about, anything that stirs you emotionally, anything that moves you: a painting, music, a movie, a trip through the woods, whatever it is for you.

You can set up structured time when you can do your creative work. Sometimes you have to do that out of necessity, but do allow structurelessness. Look for ways to purposely vary your routine, even if they are impractical. Don't drive the same way to work every day, for example.

Another thing that to me seems to be inherent about creativity is that you don't sit around and wait for it to happen. You have to take some initiative. When I started to work on Better and Better, I sat down and started randomly playing chords, grasping for words, and pulling it together. I wasn't thrilled with the result at all, but in the process of doing that, I experienced a sensation that I can best describe as "something dropped in." I sincerely believe that this occurred because I took the initiative to set the gears in motion. I wanted to write something, because Silva is something I am passionate about and something that can benefit people. I was in there heart and soul even before I started working on the song.

I think that practicing any of the Silva techniques will enhance creativity in general in your life. The techniques are inherently right-brain; creativity is inherently a right-brain activity.

Find the things that inspire you—music, painting, or whatever it may be— and incorporate them into your life.

I don't acknowledge the existence of "blocks." I have a lot of songs that are unfinished, but I will always do something—even if it's just strum chords. My experience is that when you take the initiative to do something, even if it is totally off the mark, you have already started the creative process.

I find creativity to be a wonderful interactive process. A number of years ago I sat down with a friend to cowrite a song. The collaboration didn't work as we expected. He'd make suggestions that didn't work, but they triggered ideas to try something else. In the end, my friend hadn't contributed one word or one chord to the final product, but his ideas sparked every one of mine. The experience was completely based on our interaction.

Ed Bernd Jr.: tips from a writer

Ed grew up in the newspaper business and describes himself as a reporter with many years of experience as both a news photographer, when he was young, and more than 10 years as a staff writer for metropolitan daily newspapers. He is also an author. He coauthored Jose Silva's last four books, and he is an excellent poet, too. Here are some of his suggestions that apply to all forms of creativity:

Think it through at alpha; alpha is the ideal level for thinking because it's the creative level.

Dream Control works wonders—just ask best-selling author Robert Louis Stevenson, who said that many of his stories came to him in dreams.

Bring a mentor to your level to advise you. Bring in any expert. At your level, imagine asking you favorite author (or lecturer, artist, or producer) how he or she would handle the situation or solve the problem.

Your body radiates energy, and this energy is stored in matter that is within range of your aura. If you find yourself getting more creative ideas in a certain room, while relaxing in a particular chair, while using a certain computer or paintbrush or camera, then keep using it. There is probably a record of your successes stored within the object.

You can definitely be inspired to do better work by other creative people. Listening to great classical music, reading great literature, studying great art, and enjoying a great performance can all be very inspiring and elevate the quality of your work. Imagine how much more help it is to surround yourself with other creative people. Not only will you communicate with the words you speak to one another, your minds will also communicate with each other's minds, even if you are not consciously aware of it.

Learn from those you admire, but always, always be yourself. A copy is never as good as the original. You have something unique to give to the world, so use your level and the Silva techniques to determine what it is.

How Juan Silva became an inventor

Juan Silva is cofounder of the Silva Method with his brother Jose. During their research, they wanted to see if they could use the Silva techniques to help them invent something that could be of value.

They were extremely successful. Jose programmed Juan to have a *desire* to invent something that would be of some benefit, some value. The result was that he invented a vending machine. He sold the patent to a company in Mexico and agreed to go to work for the company to set up and supervise the production of the machine. Juan held that job for more than a decade. In addition to running the factory, he was also teaching the Silva techniques in his spare time. He considers those years to be the best of his life.

A sea gull guides an author to a best-seller

Where do creative ideas come from? From your own brain? From somebody else's brain? From higher intelligence? They can come from all these sources—and more. Best-selling author Richard Bach's idea came from a bird.

"It was the weirdest experience of my life," Bach said in a November 1972 interview in *Harper's Bazaar*. "I was walking along one night, worrying about the rent money, when I heard this voice say 'Jonathan Livingston Seagull.' But no one was there. I had absolutely no idea what it meant. When I got home, I suddenly had a vision of a sea gull flying along, and I began to write. The story certainly didn't spring from any conscious invention on my part. I just put down what I saw."

Silva instructor Wingate Paine told us the rest of the story during an instructor training session in Laredo not long after the book became a best-seller.

Wingate told the group that Bach had written the first two-thirds of the book from a dream-like experience where a big sea gull appeared to him and said, "Take dictation; I have a story for you." But the bird faded away before the completion of the story. Wingate said that Bach told him he did not know how to get the bird to come back so that he could finish the book until he took the Silva course. Then he knew how to get to that dream-like level and how to invite Jonathan Livingston Seagull to this creative level to tell him the rest of the story.

Bach said in the *Harper's Bazaar* article that even before taking the Silva training, he'd come to assume that "there are certain 'hidden' capacities and powers which can be taught. I think there is a terrifically pleasant principle behind existence—do what you love to do and you'll be guided. It's a lot like flying a plane: You have to trust what you can't see."

At the top of their field

Silva techniques are not just for struggling artists. Even those at the very top of their field can benefit in many ways.

Dord Fitz, who was an outstanding artist, art teacher, and art historian, inspired thousands to claim our creative heritage. He did not need help to become a great artist, but he was thrilled with the benefits he got in his personal life from Jose Silva's techniques. "It is what I had been looking for my entire life," he said.

There are two steps that proved so valuable to Fitz and countless others:

1. Learning to enter the alpha level and to activate your mind, thereby using the subconscious consciously, and converting the subconscious into an inner-conscious dimension.

2. The mental projection exercises that are featured in the Silva UltraMind ESP System and the Silva Basic Lecture Series. These "mental calisthenics," as Mr. Silva liked to call them, provide you with points of reference—a roadmap to guide you while functioning in the creative, spiritual dimension.

When Doc Severinsen took the course back in 1980, he was one of the most famous band leaders in America, appearing nightly on late-night television. He told us that he used the alpha level to compose music, to help him with personal relationships, and much more.

Harry Jackson, "Sculptor of the American West," was the main speaker at the 1981 Silva International Convention. Evidence of his success as an artist comes not only from the critical international acclaim he receives; it is confirmed by the fact that he earned $5 million the previous year.

After dropping out of high school, Jackson moved west and became a cowboy. He was "killed" during service in World War II and then revived, but the head wound left him with epileptic seizures—and a lot of anger and resentment for the next three decades.

It was only after he attended the Silva course with instructor Paul Grivas in New York City in 1980 that Jackson finally found peace and an understanding of how his life's events shaped him into the man he is today: a man of great spiritual depth. He has carried a copy of the *Bagavad Gita*—the most spiritual writings of the Hindu religion—in his pocket ever since World War II. But it took the Silva System to help him find peace with himself.

Speaking at the 1981 Silva International Convention, he said that Silva is the most powerful method he has found for "helping the human soul to find itself."

That's also what Dord Fitz was looking for through art—and teaching to his art students—when he met Jose Silva and found what he had been seeking his entire life.

We have been told that we were made in the image of our Creator. That means that we are creative beings. Claim your creative heritage. It is the very essence of life. It is essential that we function creatively in order to come up with creative solutions to the many problems that plague the world today.

Jose Silva always believed that's what we were sent here to do. He concluded each mental training exercise this way:

"You will continue to strive to take part in constructive and creative activities to make this a better world to live in, so that when we move on we shall have left behind a better world for those who follow. You will consider the whole of humanity, depending on their ages, as fathers or mothers, brothers or sisters, sons or daughters. You are a superior human being; you have greater understanding, compassion, and patience with others."

Nelda Sheets is a highly acclaimed artist whose paintings sell for thousands of dollars. She has been one of the most active Silva instructors and supporters since she attended Jose Silva's first public class in 1966.

Chapter 31

Developing Your Psychic Ability

By Jose Luis (Pepe) Romero

Some people are naturally psychic, but most need to be trained.

While most people—90 percent, according to the research—are not able to function psychically on demand, they have, nevertheless, had psychic experiences. You probably have, too.

Many people have had some kind of psychic experience in their dreams. Have you ever had a dream that contained information that helped you to solve a problem? Have you ever had a precognitive dream—that is, you dreamed of something and then the next day, or a few days later, it happened?

Perhaps you had a déjà vu experience—you went to a new place and had the feeling you had been there before, or you met a stranger and felt like you already knew them, or something happened that you seemed to have a memory of having happened before.

Many people have had the experience of thinking about somebody that they had not thought of in a long time, and shortly thereafter, receiving a letter or a phone call from that person. And have you ever "known" who was calling when you heard the phone ring?

A very strong psychic connection exists between mother and child. This is true of all animals, not just humans. There are numerous documented stories during World War II of mothers waking up in the middle of the night, their hearts filled with fear. Days later, they would learn that their sons had been killed in battle at the exact time that they woke up.

How can these psychic experiences take place in people who have not learned how to enter the alpha level with conscious awareness?

Your brain automatically dips into alpha approximately 30 times every minute, even when you are wide awake and very active. The problem is that these trips into alpha are very brief—just fractions of a second. Sometimes this is enough.

Once you learn to enter alpha and practice functioning at that level as you learn in the Silva training, you will find that these brief trips to alpha will last longer and longer. In addition, the experiences you have using your psychic ability while at the alpha level will make it easier for you to take advantage of brief excursions into alpha even when you are not consciously doing it. Your practice and experience will give you points of reference that you can recognize in a fraction of a second.

How to develop psychic ability

The only sure way that we know of to develop your own psychic ability is to take the Silva training. You need a live instructor to guide you. Why? Because your mind needs another mind to guide it and teach it what to do.

If you want to try to learn on your own, you can do so, but we cannot guarantee what kind of results you will get or how fast your progress will be.

Here is what to do.

First, be observant. Notice any time that you seem to have had a psychic experience—whether it be a hunch that turned out to be correct, a feeling about something that proved to be right, or any of the things that we mentioned earlier in this chapter.

As soon as you notice an intuitive experience, as soon as possible, find a place where you can relax and enter your level. At your level, review everything about the experience—especially how you felt. Jose Silva always reminded us that feelings are a powerful part of our programming experience.

After that, whenever you go to level in the future, review the experience again. Recall exactly what happened and especially how you felt. Any time you review something at your level it is almost as if you were having another experience. The more experiences you accumulate, the faster your progress will be.

If you are not satisfied with your progress, remember that in just two eight-hour days in a Silva seminar, you will learn to function as a psychic. We guarantee it. In fact, we have *always* guaranteed it. How successful are we? It is very rare that anyone ever asks for a refund; not even one person out of a hundred wants his or her money back.

Practicing to be a better psychic

In the last part of the Silva course we instruct students to form small groups of two or three students. One will function as a psychic, one as an orientologist (or director), and one as an observer who takes notes. The three can talk to each other at any time.

The orientologist gives the psychic the name, age, gender, and location of a person who has a problem. The psychic, who is at the alpha level, attempts to detect information about the case. In the UltraMind ESP System, the first thing the psychic does is determine what kind of case it is: health, relationship, business, and so forth.

Then the psychic zooms in on details. If it is a health case, for instance, the psychic determines which part of the body is affected. Then the psychic determines how the illness is affecting the body. It is much like what a doctor might do if examining the person physically. The psychic can even ask the person questions, just as a physician would do. The only difference is that the psychic imagines what the person would answer.

During all of this, the orientologist encourages the psychic to keep investigating, but does not give any feedback—that is, he or she does not tell the psychic if his or her information is accurate or not—until after the psychic has given a complete report.

Once the psychic has given a complete report, *then* the orientologist tells the psychic about the case, confirming information that is accurate. After that, the psychic mentally corrects the problem.

Psychics will usually work three cases while at level, one after another, detecting information, getting feedback, reviewing the case in order to establish points of reference to help in future cases, and correcting all problems. Then the psychic comes out of level and trades places with someone in the group, allowing someone else to practice using their psychic ability.

All students work at least 10 cases in this manner, so that they will be thoroughly convinced that they really do have psychic ability and know how to use it.

We encourage them to continue to practice working cases on their own after they complete the seminar. By the time they have worked 50 cases and are satisfied with their results, psychic functioning will come easily to them. They will even be able to use their psychic ability with their eyes open when necessary.

One word of caution: It is important that you work on real problems. Some people suggest that you develop your psychic ability by guessing what is inside a box, or guessing what card a person is looking at, or guessing what number will come up when dice are rolled.

These kinds of guessing games were done for many years by Dr. J.B. Rhine at Duke University. He brought naturally developed psychics into his laboratory and conducted these tests with them. In the beginning the results were quite accurate, but eventually the psychics seemed to lose the ability to "guess" correctly.

Why did this happen? Jose Silva explained that the human mind is supposed to solve problems and correct abnormalities. It is not designed to play games. So it quickly gets bored when playing games, since there are no beneficial end results, and stops playing.

When you work on real problem cases, though, the mind gets better and better at detecting information, as long as you are using that information to correct problems.

It is all right, in the very beginning, to test yourself a few times by guessing who is calling when the telephone rings. Your need to develop confidence in your ability could be considered a problem, and accurately detecting the information could be a solution in itself. But once you have done this and know that you can, then it ceases to be a problem. From that time on you need to use your psychic ability to find solutions for real problems.

The message seems to be use it *correctly* or lose it.

A medical intuitive helps a surgeon

Ricardo Floyd, a psychiatric social worker in Laredo who worked with Jose Silva in the 1960s, is grateful that a trained psychic got to the correct level to help him with a problem.

Ricardo's young son, Bobby, darted into the street and was hit by a car one Halloween night. Fortunately the hospital was just a few blocks away. Here is Ricardo's story, in his own words:

"When I got to the hospital, I was too upset to go to level and program. I used my Three Fingers Technique, calling mentally for Jose Silva to come to the hospital.

"Suddenly Jose arrived with his daughter, Isabel, who is an excellent psychic. Jose had a child in his arms who had been struck by a car in front of their house. The boy looked the same age as Bobby, and I asked Jose and Isabel to work on Bobby as soon as possible.

"Jose and Isabel went to work on Bobby, mentally repairing the damage to his body and especially to his head. But something concerned Isabel.

"She said that he kept 'slipping away.' She continued working with the doctors. She noticed that the doctor repositioned a piece of Bobby's fractured skull—'closed it,' she said—but she could see inside that something was pressing against Bobby's brain. She kept telling the doctor mentally to check inside. Finally, she felt relieved. She had the feeling that Bobby was going to be all right.

"Later that night, the doctor explained to me what he had done. It was just what Isabel had told me. The doctor said the medical team almost lost Bobby. A couple of days later I talked with the surgeon, who explained just what had been done. He told me, 'Originally when I repositioned that piece of bone, it looked pretty good. Then I felt uncomfortable and decided to go inside and check to be sure.' That's when he found that something was pressing on the brain, and he repositioned it.

"Bobby recovered fully and developed normally. He played high school football, served in the navy, and is now an electronics technician."

Trained psychics, like Isabel, have the ability to enter their level any time they desire and also the ability to correct any problem they detect. As this book goes to press, articles are beginning to appear in magazines about how doctors are working with "medical intuitives," psychics who are able to detect health problems in patients.

Isabel may very well have been the first medical intuitive in the world. For more than 30 years, she has been a nurse anesthetist. She has worked with doctors all over the world, introducing them to her unique abilities.

Detecting a health problem that doctors miss

Elaine P. Millen says that she has always been sensitive to others' pain. "Silva helped me refine my sensitivity and put it to use by working on others. I used it before, during, and after surgery to help with my own healing, and I used it to help others as well."

Right after taking the course with Silva instructor Rick Bridges in North Carolina, Elaine began to put her psychic ability to use. One particular case involved her sister.

"One Friday night, I dreamt that my oldest sister had cancer," Elaine recalled. "In the dream I was compelled to shout, 'Check the right side!' Her doctors were only concerned with the left side."

What Elaine did not know at the time was that her sister had asked her doctor to perform a CAT scan after she read about the effect of teenage smoking and lung cancer in people 60 years old and older. Elaine's sister received the diagnosis that same day: lung cancer in the left lobe.

"On Sunday, I got the news," Elaine said. "There was a possible indication that there might be something in the right lung as well. She had a needle biopsy later in that week, and the tumors were found to be nondeterminent. I still had a nagging feeling inside."

Elaine programmed for her sister's doctors to check the right lung carefully.

"Finally the day of the surgery arrived, and when the surgeon looked at the right side, there were three tumors. Two were malignant, and one was benign. She had been asymptomatic."

Prophecy

It is more difficult to detect the future than it is to detect the past. That is because the past is already impressed on psychics; the future is not.

According to Jose Silva, the past is composed of materialized thoughts, the present is the process of materializing thoughts, and the future is made up of thoughts that have been conceived but not yet materialized. The future can be changed.

Jose Silva conducted research on prophecy but had only limited success. He would have his research subjects enter their level and imagine that they were present when the Mexican lottery numbers were being drawn. They would mentally project themselves to be standing right next to the people who were drawing the numbers.

The drawings were held three times a week, so there were many opportunities to try to predict the winning numbers. On a couple of occasions the researchers got correct numbers but for the wrong date.

Since time exists in the physical dimension, and the drawings had not yet taken place, they could not find a way to correlate the time with the event. It is easy to do in the past, since the past is already impressed on psychics.

Changing the future

One question that comes up about prophecy is: Are we able to change the future?

The answer is yes—in a manner of speaking. The future is made up of thoughts that have been conceived but not yet materialized. So if the thoughts are changed, the results will be changed also.

Here is an example: Suppose a train is going down the track at 50 miles per hour, and there is a stalled car on the tracks 25 miles away.

What is going to happen in half an hour?

If nothing changes, the train will hit the car.

But if we know the situation, then we have a chance to avoid the pending destruction. We can stop the train, switch it to a different track, or get help to move the car off the track.

Whenever a Silva graduate detects something bad lurking in the future, he or she then programs to correct the problem.

The only thing is, if the graduate is successful, there may not be any evidence of the success. If you imagine a plane crash that takes the lives of 250 people, for instance, and you change this mentally so that the pilots notice the problem, correct it, and land safely, and none of the passengers every knows that they were in danger, then that is a wonderful success. But nobody will ever know.

Awakened by a prophetic dream

Marina Niemeijer, director of Silva activities in The Netherlands, told us how a prophetic dream saved her life. Here is her story in her own words:

"A few days before I would be driving from France to my home in Holland I woke up in the middle of the night from a terrible dream.

"I dreamt that I sat in the car next to my husband, who was driving. We drove in the left lane and my husband gave way to a green van. The color green was very peculiar, and therefore memorable. All of a sudden the dream went on in slow motion and in very vivid colors.

"When the green van was just in front of us the traffic stopped and there was a terrible collision. My husband turned towards me and I put my hand on his head to let him rest on my shoulders. We hit the green van. Then everything became very quiet, and I realized my husband was dead. I woke up loudly shouting, 'No!'

"You can imagine that I was very shocked by this dream—especially because I had never experienced such vividness in my dreams before.

"I went to my level and asked higher intelligence not to let this happen. I reprogrammed the story in such a way that we were not in this terrible accident but that we drove past a place where a minor accident had occurred.

"A little apprehensive but with the reprogrammed picture in my head, I started the 12-hour drive to Holland very attentively. It was the first time I'd be making the trip alone.

"Halfway into the trip the driver of a car in front of me put his alarm lights on. I slowed down and, as I got closer, I noticed a green van in the right lane—the same color as in my dream.

"I became even more cautious after seeing the van. Not even a minute later I drove past a number of cars who had had a collision. One car had turned around 180 degrees.

"A bit shaken, I stopped my car and went to my level to thank higher intelligence for helping me. I hope that my programming may have also helped others.

"I am very grateful for this experience, which showed me that the future consists of a set of possibilities, which, with the help of higher intelligence, we can direct."

Pepe Romero is director of the Silva UltraMind ESP Systems and teaches courses throughout the United States and overseas.

CHAPTER 32
SILVA TECHNIQUES
IN OTHER FIELDS

BY JOSE SILVA JR.

Even though my father had not originally started his research in order to train people to be psychic, he did not call it an accident. He often said that he was guided by higher intelligence to make the discoveries that he made.

After he realized that he could train anybody to be a psychic, he began to think about all of the ways that this ability could be of value. Silva graduates have used psychic ability in a wide variety of fields over the years. This chapter includes a few of my favorites.

Police officers project calm in tense situations

Silva graduate Denis McKeon, a retired police officer from New Orleans, Louisiana, used mental projection to help him deal with violent hostility. The Silva System seemed to hold hope, so he repeated the program, seeking techniques to help him achieve his goal. He found a technique for dealing with confrontations that he considers ideal. Here's his story, in his own words:

"I wanted to find a way to prevent crime and violence instead of constantly dealing with the aftermath of these incidents.

"When an individual or a small group of people confront you and are angry or projecting hatred and insults, remain calm. When they insult you, just smile and say, 'Thank you.' This will surprise them.

"While they are confused, mentally project love, peace, and brotherhood toward them. The majority of the time this tactic will break the tension and either

239

end the situation or allow you to deal with these people in a rational way. This will eliminate the possibility of violence.

"I discovered this method when I was confronted by an individual who was very angry, calling me vile names and threatening violence.

"I remembered the beneficial statement that 'Negative thoughts and actions will have no influence over me at any level of the mind.' I decided to try to avoid violence by using positive mental projection, but first I had to stop his advance.

"I smiled and said, 'Thank you. That's the nicest thing anyone has said to me today.' This stopped him in his tracks with a bewildered look on his face. This gave me the few seconds I needed to mentally project love, peace, and brotherhood toward him.

"The result was that he slowly started to smile and he said, 'You know, you're okay,' and then he wanted to shake my hand. The potential for a violent situation had passed.

"By using the method I have described, violence may be avoided most of the time. I found this technique to be effective in about 80 percent of these types of confrontations."

One other technique he has used involves mental projection at a distance.

McKeon said that he would mentally project to every area of his post each day before he started his rounds. He would visualize everything peaceful and harmonious. Here's how he explains it:

"After I had been using this technique for a while, I started to observe that the residents of my post were beginning to act less fearful, there was much less anxiety present, and the people were happier in general.

"Their attitude toward me changed also. They became very friendly toward me and were always glad to see me. They gave me the nickname of 'Smiley, the happy cop.' This did wonders for me also. At the end of my day I felt a sense of accomplishment and satisfaction, whereas before, I had felt frustrated and depressed.

"I know this method works. I have used it successfully for many years. At the same time, the surrounding posts had all kinds of problems."

Psychic ability aids attorneys

Marcelino Alcala has been a Silva instructor in the Caribbean for more than 20 years. He is also an attorney, and he reports that psychic ability has helped him in many ways.

Lawyers usually prefer to reach a settlement rather than deal with the uncertainty of a trial. Marcelino uses the creative insights and information of the alpha level to help him come up with ways to settle cases that are acceptable to all parties. This is exactly like one of the affirmations that my father included in the Silva UltraMind System: "The solution must be the best for all concerned."

Diana Navarro, an attorney in Laredo, Texas, said that a client of hers was trying to negotiate an agreement but ran into trouble. Acting on a verbal agreement, her client invested money in a project. After he made the investment, the supposed partner wanted to add several conditions to the verbal agreement they had previously made.

"They were not making any progress," Diana said, "and my client was getting very frustrated. I told him I'd see what I could do to help."

The next day the client called to say that everything was resolved. "All I had done the night before," Diana said, "was to enter my level, visualize the parties to the agreement—I knew both of them—and program that the other person would tell my client what it was that he *really* wanted. And that's exactly what he did the next morning."

There are no secrets at alpha. Psychics can detect the truth, no matter how hard you try to conceal it. Marcelino said that's been a big help to him when he is cross-examining witnesses. "When you can sense that a witness is lying, then you know what areas to delve into," he explained.

A pilot sees into the future

In 1986 a woman named Tweet Coleman joined us in Amarillo, Texas, to celebrate the 20th anniversary of the first commercial Silva class. A year earlier, Tweet had gotten a job as a pilot for a major airline.

When flying, she uses her mind to check for problems. Here is Tweet's story, in her own words:

"Sometimes when you're flying you will hear things in the airplane, or the flight attendants will come up and they will hear things, and you have to go back and check it out.

"A couple of weeks ago, a flight attendant told us that on takeoff it appeared that the hubcap on the right tire was making a noise.

"I went to level and I mentally pictured the tire and the mechanism around the tire. Plane tires don't have hubcaps, but something else could have been wrong.

"I sensed that two of the four cotter pins around the wheel were missing. There was nothing I could do in the air, so I went ahead to our destination. On landing, the flight attendant reported the same situation again. After the flight, a mechanic and I checked, and, sure enough, the cotter pins had fallen out.

"Another way psychic ability helps me is with the weather. We have radar in the airplanes, and it is about 95 percent reliable. Sometimes there are problems. An airplane pilot needs to know whether to go left or right, up or down.

"You need to use your intuition and your radar. I think they are about equal in importance. So I have used it a lot of times to see through the clouds and see through the weather to make the right decision. That's really helped a lot.

"I fly from Guam to Japan, Manilla, and so on. You are not always in radar control. It is not like on the mainland where you are always talking to somebody. You make a report about every 30 minutes, but other than that, you are not talking to anybody.

"So if you see some weather in front of you, it is up to you to determine what to do. By visualizing the weather, picturing the movement of the weather, then you can make right or left turns as necessary. This is pretty exciting."

The International Society of Women Airline Pilots lists Tweet Coleman as a member of the first all-female B727 flight crew in the world.

Tweet believes in doing something for those who will follow in her foot-steps. She has established the Tweet Coleman Aviation Scholarship through the American Association of University Women. This provides several thousands of dollars in scholarships each year to young women who want to pursue careers as active cockpit crew members.

Tweet credits the Silva techniques, which she learned in the 1970s, with helping her to achieve so much success. And she has certainly taken my father's guidance to heart: to leave behind a better world for those who follow.

Jose Silva Jr. helped his father with the Silva seminar business since its inception. He is a director of the Silva UltraMind systems and has also served as president of Silva International, Inc. since 1995.

APPENDIX A
CONTACT
INFORMATION

We have included as many different subjects as possible to introduce readers to as much of the exciting research that exists in this field as possible. For more information, check out the Web sites provided in this appendix or contact the people and organizations mentioned throughout this book.

➢ Avlis Publishing (publishers of Silva home study courses)
P.O. Box 1815
Laredo, TX 78044-1815
(800) 579-4108 or (956) 727-3412
E-mail: edbernd@juno.com
www.SilvaMind.com
You can reach Ed Bernd Jr. at this address.

➢ Robert Collier Publications, Inc.
1248 N. Lamont Drive
Oak Harbor, WA 98277

(360) 679-8981 (phone and fax)

➤ CS Marketing, Inc., specializing in Silva products
P.O. Box 16669
Austin, TX 78761-6669
(888) 322-8547 or (512) 419-9074
E-mail: CSKathy@juno.com

You can reach Kathy Sandusky at this address.

➤ Ecumenical Society of Psychorientology, Inc.
P.O. Box 1806
Laredo, TX 78044-1806
(888) 879-2168
E-mail: mail@ecumenical.org

www.ecumenical.org

➤ Clancy McKenzie, M.D.
Philadelphia Psychiatric Consultation Service
P.O. Box 345
Bala Cynwyd, PA 19004

www.Dr.McKenzie.com

➤ Silva International Graduate Association (Silva alumni association)
P.O. Box 1815
Laredo, TX 78044-1815
(800) 579-4108 or (956) 727-3412
E-mail: siga-us@juno.com

www.siga.org

➢ Silva International, Inc. (presenting the Silva System BLS)
P.O. Box 2249
Laredo, TX 78044-2249
(800) 545-6463 or (956) 722-6391

E-mail: silva@silvamethod.com

➢ Silva UltraMind Systems LLC
P.O. Box 1638
Laredo, TX 78044-1638
(888) 882-7866 or (956) 796-1246
Email: mail@SilvaUltraMind.com
www.SilvaUltraMind.com
You can reach Jose Luis Romero, Alex Gonzalez Silva, and Jose Silva Jr. at this address. We also have contact information for all of the other contributing authors in this book.

➢ Warrior Publications, Inc.
6252 Dark Hollow Rd.
Medford, OR 97501
(541) 535-3188
E-mail: docspeed@cdsnet.net
You can reach Dr. John La Tourrette at this address.

➢ H. Michael Wickett
5005 Lancaster Bay
Suite 164
Clarkston, MI 48346-4406
(800) 968-4955

APPENDIX B
SUGGESTED
READING

Some of these titles are out of print but may still be available in your local library.

"Ace" Any Test, 4th Edition by Ron Fry
(Career Press)

Ask the Right Questions by Ron Fry
(Career Press, 2000)

Creative Visualization by Shatki Gawain
(Bantam Books, 1983)

Dream Telepathy by Montague Ullman, M.D. and Stanley Krippner, Ph.D.
(Macmillan, 1973)

Executive ESP by Douglas Dean and John Mihalasky
(Prentice Hall, 1975)

Get Organized, 4th Edition by Ron Fry
(Career Press, 2000)

Healing Words by Larry Dossey
(Harper San Francisco, 1995)

How to Study, 5th Edition by Ron Fry
(Career Press, 2000)

I Have a Hunch: The Autobiography of Jose Silva edited by Ed Bernd Jr.
(The Institute of Psychorientology, 1984)
Available from Silva International.

Improve Your Memory, 4th Edition by Ron Fry
(Career Press, 2000)

Improve Your Reading, 4th Edition by Ron Fry
(Career Press, 2000)

Improve Your Writing, 4th Edition by Ron Fry
(Career Press, 2000)

The Jesus Legacy by Robert B. Stone
(Sum Press, 1993)

Jonathan Livingston Seagull by Richard Bach
(Buccaneer Books, 1991)

Kinship with All Life by J. Allen Boone
(Harper and Row, 1954)
A fascinating account of how humans can communicate psychically with animals.

Living in the Light by Shatki Gawain
(Bantam Books, 1993)

Reading Course in the Law of Success by Napoleon Hill
(Revised edition: Success Unlimited, 1979)

Real Magic by Dr. Wayne W. Dyer
(Harper Mass Market Paperbacks, 1993)

Relax, It's Good for You by Ed Bernd Jr.
(Original publication: Greun Madainn Foundation, 1977. Revised edition: The Institute of Psychorientology, 1982)
Available from Silva International, Avlis Publishing, or CS Marketing.

The Revealer by Jose Silva (as reported by Ed Bernd Jr.)
(The Institute of Psychorientology, 1997
Available from Silva International, Avlis Publishing, or CS Marketing.

Riches Within Your Reach by Robert Collier
(Robert Collier Publications, 1947)
Available from Robert Collier Publications.

Sales Power, the Silva Mind Method for Sales Professionals by Jose Silva with Ed Bernd Jr.
(Putnam Berkley Group, 1992)

The Secret Life of Your Cells by Robert B. Stone
(Whitford Press, 1989)
Details Cleve Backster's research into primary perceptive capability.

Jose Silva: The Man who Tapped the Secrets of the Human Mind and the Method He Used by Jose Silva with Robert B. Stone
(H.J. Kramer, 1990)

The Silva Method for Business Managers by Jose Silva with Robert B. Stone
(Prentice Hall, 1983)

The Silva Method for Getting Help from the Other Side by Jose Silva with Robert B. Stone
(Pocket Books, 1989)

The Silva Method: Think and Grow Fit by Jose Silva with Ed Bernd Jr.
(Career Press, 1996)
Contact Avlis Publishing or CS Marketing for information.

The Silva Mind Control Method by Jose Silva with Philip Miele
(Simon and Schuster, 1977)
The first major book on Jose Silva's research and course. It is still available throughout the world.

Smart Marketing by Jeff Slutsky
(Career Press, 1998)

Subjective Communication by Jose Silva with Ed Bernd Jr.
(The Institute of Psychorientology, 1984)
Available from Silva International, Avlis Publishing, or CS Marketing.

Think and Grow Rich by Napoleon Hill
(Copyright 1937. Original publication: The Ralston Society, 1945. Revised edition: Fawcett Publications, 1960)

You Can Work Your Own Miracles by Napoleon Hill
(Fawcett Books, 1971)

You the Healer by Jose Silva with Robert B. Stone
(H.J. Kramer, 1989)

INDEX